For Elisabeth

Prologue

How is it possible to miss this place before I've left?
Layla Rivers pushed open the door to the fish and chip shop, a one-time fisherman's cottage, quaint, bygone and painted pastel blue, in the pretty harbour of Porthkara. Behind her, a collection of boats bobbed at anchor, fenders tied to their hulls. The pier reached out into the calm glassy sea and the lighthouse stretched up to the sky, a vigilant seagull perched on top keeping a lookout for stray chips dropped by butterfingers. A bell jingled as she stepped inside to the welcome of a familiar face behind the counter.

'Hey, Layla. All set for your trip?'

'Yep, I'm good to go. I'll miss Porthkara.'

'Six months will fly by. You'll have a wonderful time, you lucky thing. What can I get you?'

'A portion of chips please.'

1

'Coming up.' Rosie, an old school friend, beamed and tipped a batch of freshly chipped potatoes into the sizzling fryer. A blast of familiar cooking smells filled the small shop as she took a kitchen cloth and emerged from behind the wall of brightly-lit glass and stainless steel to wipe the steamed-up window. 'Joe not with you?'

Layla tensed. Rosie was married to the man of her dreams, a gorgeous rugged trawler-man. They had two children already. And hopes for a third.

'We had planned to watch the sun go down together. A perfect beginning to our trip around the world.'

Her friend frowned. 'So where is he?'

'He cried off with excuses about sinking a pint of real ale with the lads.' She shrugged. 'He's at the pub.'

While she waited for the chips to cook she walked over to the window and gazed out across the harbour to the lighthouse and, close by it, the centuries-old seafarers' chapel built in a hollow at the base of a cliff. 'You have a great view of Saint Elisabeth's.'

'That's one of the best things about working here. It's the perfect vantage point for wedding watchers.'

Layla laughed. 'There's been a spate this summer.'

'I get to see it all. The dresses, the guests, the glitches!'

'Glitches?'

'Nothing too serious. You heard about the usher who tripped over a bollard on the pier and fell into the sea?'

'Yep.' Layla giggled. 'Poor guy! I gather somebody saved the day and found him a change of clothes.'

'Someone also videoed the shenanigans. It went viral. The chip shop was in the background.'

'Free publicity.'

Returning to her post Rosie checked the fryer and wiped the counter with her cloth. 'A couple of weeks back, there was the cutest pageboy. His mum got him an ice cream and a flipping seagull only went and dive-bombed him! He spilt ice cream all down his little outfit. She brought him in to mop up the mess and I got all the goss. The bride was pregnant! Nobody was supposed to know, but everybody did. And the bride's parents were getting a divorce right after the wedding. It was the elephant in the room.'

'Crikey.'

'No one was allowed to mention it because the bride was so touchy. Heaven knows why, pregnancy hormones maybe.'

'Or she was afraid talking about it might spoil the day?'

Rosie pulled an awkward face like she was sorry she'd brought it up. 'You know what that feels like, right?'

'I guess.'

'How long have you and Joe been together?'

'Twelve years.'

'So when will it be your turn to walk down the aisle?

3

When you get back from your travels? Or will we be hearing that you've rocked a romantic wedding for two somewhere fabulous, like Bali or Barbados?'

Layla bristled. The conversation had taken a very unwelcome turn.

'Nothing's been discussed. We've not made plans or anything.'

The door jingled and a couple more customers barged in loudly, cutting the interrogation dead, to Layla's relief. Weddings weren't Joe's favorite subject. He liked things the way they were. By the time the newcomers had made up their minds on what to have and Rosie had taken their orders, Layla's chips were ready. She shoveled out a generous portion, balanced a teeny pot of ketchup on top, and neatly wrapped them in paper. Layla paid quickly and escaped without further questioning.

'Have fun,' Rosie shouted over the jingle of the doorbell. 'Post loads of photos on your timeline, I want to know everything.'

Outside, in the long shadow of the lighthouse, Layla paused for a few seconds to take it all in; the general store, the church, the chippy. The police station had been moved and the old building sold. The new owner had transformed it into an Italian-style ice cream parlour with a cheerful striped awning. Other old buildings had been repurposed too, housing a small gallery showcasing local artists, a gift shop, and a place selling an array of vintage, with a ship in a bottle, an antiquated teapot and a starburst clock in the window. On the end of the terraced row a former cottage with a 'sold' sign outside was reported to be opening soon, reinvented as an old-fashioned sweet shop doing homemade Cornish fudge in every flavour imaginable from traditional to chocolate orange, marshmallow and banoffee. Rumours abounded about a secret recipe and a luxury specialty fudge made with locally-sourced clotted cream and laced with 'ye olde smugglers' rum'. She'd have to wait until spring to try some.

Having well and truly memorized Porthkara harbour, Layla headed to the beach. At the top of the stone steps she kicked off her flip-flops and inhaled the salty air. She loved everything about the Cornish fishing village she'd grown up in, especially its own brand of ozone. She stared out to sea watching the gentle even breakers roll in, feeling the wind on her face, the sand powder-soft beneath the soles of her feet. Overhead the gulls soared, glided and swooped. A blazing circle of red, the sun cast a beautiful light all around and turned the white clouds pink.

For a second Layla's heart wobbled and she wondered why she'd agreed to go travelling with Joe. She loved him here at home; but could she rely on him when it was just the two of them on the other side of the world?

Warmth seeped into her hands. She sat down, unwrapped

the hot, golden chips and waited for them to cool enough to eat. Cross-legged she balanced her food in her lap and opened the ketchup, trying not to get sand on her fingers and replaying the conversation from the chippy in her head.

She closed her eyes and inhaled a deep breath of sea air in an effort to shake off her apprehension. She'd spent all afternoon finalizing her packing, obsessively putting things in her rucksack, taking them out again, and then putting them back in. Mentally she went through her checklist, knowing she'd double and triple ticked off everything on the to-do list.

'Layla!'

Just as she dipped the first chip in ketchup and popped it into her mouth a deep voice she recognized startled her.

She turned her head in the direction of her name. 'Dad!'

'Hello, stranger.'

She'd been avoiding him. Things had been difficult before her parents had divorced, but since the split had been finalized a new awkwardness had settled in. 'I had a feeling I'd find you here. I just wanted to wish you and Joe well.' He looked up and down the beach, and cleared his throat, failing to disguise his surprise at finding her alone. 'Say *bon voyage* and safe travels and all that for me. First stop Paris, eh?'

He'd touched a nerve. She'd been expecting Paris to be

the first stop on the itinerary. It had been part of the original plan except Joe had contrived to veto it in favor of places he'd rather see.

'We're skipping Europe, flying to Australia first. I thought I told you.'

He shook his head. 'Shame.'

'I know. I'd have liked to visit art galleries and stroll along the Seine.' She felt a bit peculiar. When Joe's plan to travel had been suggested she'd made no secret of the fact that she'd love a romantic proposal in Paris and a bohemian beach wedding just for two on an island. With palm trees. Joe had other ideas.

'Amazing sky.' Her dad sat down beside her, stole a chip and dunked it in ketchup. 'A sky so stunning has to be a good omen.'

'What was it Granny Rivers used to say?' She offered him the chips.

'Red sky at night, sailor's delight.'

She shivered. 'That's it. Night. Delight. Morning. Warning.'

He nodded. 'I love Porthkara. Haven't ever wanted to leave.' Falling into a pattern of sharing the chips they looked at the sea, not each other. 'I regret not fulfilling your grandmother's ambitions – for her, not for me. The things she wanted weren't the same things I wanted.' Layla didn't really know what to say. Her dad filled the silence.

'Things are better between me and your mum since the divorce. It can't be easy for you – what with all of us living in the village and me getting together with Jasmine. At the end of the day I want you to know that I'm happy with my lot in life, and, well, I hope you – and your mum – will be too.'

It was hard to forgive him for the years of hurt that her mother had tolerated, for the damage it had done.

'I'm fine. Mum's fine.' The night before she set off for the airport was a funny time for a father-daughter heart to heart. They hadn't spoken about his relationship with the owner of the Porthkara gift shop before. Rumour had it they'd fallen in love during the shop's refit. Ralph Rivers was a whizz with all things building related.

'I know Joe has itchy feet, and you two have to see a bit of the world. It's natural. But I'd hate you to think I'm pushing you away.'

Did everything always have to be about him? 'Dad, I don't think that.'

'Your mum and I would be gutted if you stayed away for good.'

'I know that.'

'I don't know how we'll manage without you.'

Her chest tightened. Sometimes her love for Porthkara felt like a stranglehold. Out of the corner of her eye she spotted a couple heading for the Lobster Pot Restaurant with its whitewashed walls and blue-painted window frames. She swallowed a chip, biting back her feelings. She and Joe had worked their last shift there at lunch time. All things considered, pitching in and waitressing at the beachside restaurant, away from her parents and their troubles, and loved by Joe's family, had always been a welcome escape from playing a perpetual game of piggy-in-the-middle.

Her dream to set up a small business painting murals – the thing she liked most and did least – had been on hold while she saved for the trip. When Joe had come up with his travel plan her ambitions had been pushed aside. She'd have to save up again and resurrect them at some point.

'The season's winding down. We'll be back by the time things get busy again in the spring.'

'You'll be missed.'

'I'll miss ... home too.' She couldn't bring herself to say 'you'. After all, they managed to live in the same village and barely ever run into each other. He was respected in the community. He'd do anything to help anybody, fix things that needed mending. He was a great surfer, played guitar in a folk band on Saturday nights at the pub. She'd never spoken her mind, and it seemed like a terrible time to try to explain how she felt but she had a sense that it was now or never. The sadness, disappointment and resentment she'd been keeping in for much too long fulminated. 'You're a great dad, but you weren't a good husband, and the thing you don't get is that that was the part that hurt me the most.' Her words spilled out in a jumble and her dad looked confused and sad. She felt bad, immediately wishing she hadn't said anything.

'I didn't realize.'

She looked at her feet and dug her toes into the sand. With all the courage she could muster she said, 'It's difficult when one of you is moving forward and the other is staying still.'

'Don't I know it?'

The last blink of sun disappeared into the darkening horizon. Perhaps he didn't understand, or chose not to, but one way or another he had failed to acknowledge the impact that all his years of unfaithfulness to her mother had had on her. He had a frustrating ability to sympathize with friends, neighbours, strangers, all the while blind to her take on things so much closer to home.

They polished off the chips in complicated silence and stood up together to go. Instead of challenging his self-pitying response to her comment she back-pedalled. 'Look, it's okay. Forget I said anything.'

'Give you a lift home?'

'No thanks. I'll walk, take the cliff path.' She smiled tightly and hugged her arms across her chest. 'Brr. It's chilly now the sun's gone.' He moved a fraction towards her, his internal choreography programmed to hug his daughter, but she flinched, stepped back from him and bent to pick up her flip-flops. 'Bye Dad. See you in March.'

'You take care, love. And send me postcards.'

A nervous laugh escaped. 'Check my social media, you'll catch up with me there.'

Half an hour later, back home at the cottage she shared with Joe, Layla took the cup of tea she'd made into the sitting room and sat with her legs curled up on the sofa, still uneasy after the tense moment at the beach. Strings of words rattled in her head. Her dad didn't want to drive her away? Weirdly that's exactly what he'd done. She craved space, freedom, time out. Hopefully some distance would give her a fresh perspective, soften her attitude.

It hadn't occurred to her that something might happen while they were away, or that they might stay away longer, or not come back at all. She pushed the thought away, turned up the volume on the music in her earbuds, feeling sorry she hadn't hugged her dad and sad that no matter how many miles away she went the real distance was right here in the gulf between them.

As she put her mug to her lips the door opened and Joe lolloped in the worse for wear.

'Crikey! How many pints have you had?'

'Three or four. Or five or six. I lost count. And shots. They all bought me vodka shots.'

'You didn't have to drink them.'

'Rude not to,' he slurred, staggering into the kitchen.

Only Joe could come back this drunk on such an important night. She closed her eyes and wished she could close her ears to the sound of him throwing up into the washing up bowl. She was too disappointed to be angry. He'd have a hangover and be as cranky as hell for the next day and a half. He lay down in a sorry heap on the sofa. Resigning herself to the task in hand, and making a mental note to bin it in the morning, she went into the kitchen, rinsed the gross plastic bowl, took it into the living room and put it down next to the sofa in case it was needed again.

A firm knock at the front door made her jump. 'What now?' She opened up and found herself face to face with one of the village police officers. 'Hi Mervin. What brings you here?' New to Cornwall, her mum had invited him to join her Tuesday night pub quiz team, and he was a bit of a genius, it turned out. 'If you've come to remind me to lock the windows while I'm gone, you needn't worry, it's all taken care of.'

'I'm sorry Layla. There's no easy way to say this I'm afraid.'

His solemn tone went right through her. Outside she

glimpsed a police car with another uniformed officer in the driving seat and knew in an instant that this wasn't a friendly drop-by. Processing the grim look on his face a feeling of dread clenched her stomach and her stab at cheerfulness fell away. In absolutely no doubt that something wasn't right, she froze. 'What's happened?'

'I need you to come to the hospital straight away. It's your mum. She's been in a car accident.' He threw a glance at Joe collapsed on the sofa and let go a long desperate breath. 'I'll be upfront with you. It's serious. You'll have to cancel the trip. They've got her on life support.'

It was lunchtime the next day when she got home. Her mother was in intensive care, clinging on to life, but stable. Layla checked every room in the house, and called the restaurant. Joe had gone. Without her. She checked her mobile phone. In defiance of the patchy signal there was a text from him. Bleary-eyed, head numb, she read it.

Hi. At airport. Going ahead. No point us both missing out. Think we should be on a break until you can join. Unofficial. No point telling everyone. See you later x

Layla texted back without a second's hesitation.

Won't be joining. You and me are finished. Over! Done! Finito! OFFICIAL!

No matter how many times actor Nick Wells read and reread the email he couldn't get it to sink in. It made no sense. He was a dad? Had been for all these years? Without knowing? Detached, confused, deceived – these words barely summed up his shock.

He sat on a white leather sofa as big as a family car, in the lobby of the exclusive London apartment block where his brother Alex and his family were temporarily living in a smart penthouse until they could find a forever home of their own to move into. He'd been looking forward to meeting his new niece and nephew but since he'd seen Fran's email in the taxi on the way over from St Pancras Station, a state of emotional paralysis had taken him over. Suddenly all he wanted was to get this done and he'd be out of here. The enthusiasm of boarding the Eurostar in Paris for a flying visit during a break in his shoot had evaporated.

He'd have to speak to his girlfriend Toni. They'd hardly spent any time together the past two or three months. The chances of changing that, turning something wild into something solid, a real relationship, seemed increasingly unlikely now.

He scanned the lobby, the wall of glass at the entrance, the shiny marble walls and floor, the light-filled space – it was all very different from the ramshackle old house he and Alex had shared with a bunch of friends in North

London when he'd gone straight from school into his first acting role. During that brief time he and his twin had come close to leading normal lives. The memory tied a knot in his gut because that's when he'd met Fran, working on the television show that had turned out to be his big break.

Agitated, he shoved his phone in a pocket, got up and walked over to the reception desk. He drummed his fingers impatiently on the shiny walnut veneer. He'd brought a gift basket for the babies which was balanced on one arm. He set it down and stepped away as if it was something rather embarrassing, waiting for the militarily-efficient concierge to get the go-ahead from Alex to buzz him through to the elevator.

'Sorry for keeping you waiting.' The concierge eyed Nick curiously.

'What's taking so long?' He felt transparent as if the whole world had read Fran's email.

'They're with magazine people. Taking photos of the new arrivals. You can go up as soon as I get the okay from the other Mr Wells.'

'So they're doing a family photo shoot are they? They kept that quiet.' The reception desk phone rang and the concierge picked up. 'The okay?' Nick signaled a hopeful thumbs up.

'Yes.'

'Finally!'

He stepped into the glass elevator wishing he'd asked to use the stairs instead. His stomach churned as the ground below got further and further away. He set the beribboned gift basket on the floor, gripped the handrail with both hands and closed his eyes.

Reeling vertigo gave way to relief as he stood outside the polished oak door. When the door opened Alex locked him in a hug. 'Hey! Great timing! We just finished.'

Close behind, Nick's sister-in-law Maggie appeared holding Phoebe. 'Hi.' With her stylishly casual, blonde hair gathered up in a tufty knot, she swayed the baby and proffered one cheek. 'Welcome Uncle Nick!' He bent and gingerly air-kissed Maggie, anxious not to lean too close, scared he might crush her she was so delicate and tiny. He was awed by the baby.

He followed them into the vast living room and his stomach climbed into his throat. Through floor to ceiling glass, London lay spread out before him. He tried not to look. He couldn't live here. If he stayed well back from the windows he'd be okay-ish. He grabbed onto the nearest surface, a granite counter top in the open plan kitchen. He sucked in a deep breath and let it go slowly.

Fighting his anxiety, he flattened the palm of his hand on the cold granite surface. Avoiding looking at the windows, the London Eye, the Houses of Parliament, the river, he zeroed in on a photo stuck to the fridge with a red magnet the shape of a London bus. It was keeping in place a picture of Alex and Maggie's wedding. He picked out the figures in the wedding party. The bride and groom looking so happy. And his mother and father. They were shoulder to shoulder, smiling, in the same photo. That was previously unheard of. It was difficult to believe the picture wasn't photoshopped. Next to them was Maggie's mother, the best man, AKA himself, and the bubbly bridesmaid, the girl with the sexy curves, the vivid red hair and the green dress. She jumped right out of the photo. He'd forgotten her name but he remembered her worrying about whether or not it was bad luck to wear green at a wedding. She'd talked about nothing else in the car on the way to the church.

'Come and meet our son,' Alex prompted.

Nick forced a tight smile and let go of the kitchen counter, steeling himself to venture closer to the terrifying views.

Over by the windows little Horatio was being fussed over, cradled in the arms of the photographer while her assistant pointed out the London sights to the infant. Alex joined them and took his baby boy in his arms.

Having a lightbulb moment, the photographer waved a small camera. 'Guys, I have a brilliant idea. How would you feel about a few behind the scenes shots? Casual? The photos behind the photos?'

'Cool,' Maggie beamed. 'What do you say?' She walked over to stand next to him. 'The babies meet Uncle Nick?'

She went to hand over Phoebe. He recoiled. 'Leave me out of it.'

'But you've come specially to see them.'

'To see them, yes. I don't want to hold them.' Maggie's face clouded. She looked stricken. He felt terrible. All of a sudden he'd developed a new phobia. 'I don't know how.' He made an effort to lighten up, disguise his reaction of horror. 'I haven't done it before.'

'There's nothing to it.' Carrying Horatio, Alex joined them. 'It's amazing how quickly you get used to them.'

'Try.' Maggie held Phoebe out to him. His head pounded. He held out a finger to the baby. She took it in her little fist.

'Strong grip.'

'Take her,' she encouraged.

The tiny fingers uncurled and he reclaimed his finger. 'I can't,' he said, 'I don't want to. She'll ruin my suit.'

Maggie laughed. 'Nonsense. Take off your jacket and come over here.' He shuddered as she pushed him towards a sofa. Anchored amongst the cushions he absorbed the knee-knocking view. His reaction to heights, he'd expected. A fear of babies, he hadn't.

The photographer buzzed around, picking up a couple more cushions, and arranging them either side of him. Instead of objecting, he slicked on a professional smile.

'Crook your arms,' she instructed. 'There's a first time for everything.'

His heart lurched as he was forced to cradle not one, but two babies. In an instant the moment had been captured on camera.

Alex sat down next to him. 'Not freaking you out too much?'

'The babies? Yes, a lot actually.'

His brother laughed. 'I meant the apartment.'

'That's freaky too. But not half as scary as these.' He wished he was joking. Alex took Horatio from him. Phoebe squirmed, reached for her foot, grasped a sock and pulled it off, revealing five diminutive toes. He stared, taking in her tiny nails, her soft baby scent. When Maggie took her from him, he faked charmed reluctance, careful not to hand her back too eagerly, aware he'd offended her before. 'How's the house-hunting going?'

'Good. We've seen a place we really like, but we want to take another look round before we make an offer.'

'I bet you'll be sad to part with your place in Cornwall.'

'She won't have to,' Alex pointed out. 'We're keeping it as a holiday home.'

'You know my friend Layla?'

Layla! That was her name. 'Sure.'

'I've asked her to revamp the cottage for us, redecorate the whole place.'

'That's what she does?'

'Sort of. Amongst other things. She's very arty. Anyway, it needs an update, and she's agreed to turn it into a seaside bolt hole for us, somewhere we can escape to when we need to get out of London.'

'Great,' he said distractedly, 'Sounds awesome.'

His gaze roamed the room wondering how to tell Toni about the email. His throat dried. They'd been dating for less than a year. But he'd started to think that this could be it, he could turn his life around with the socialite.

The powdery fresh smell of the babies lingered in his nose. Seeing Alex and Maggie together, he was struck with doubt. It wasn't possible to visualize a future like this with Toni, even without Fran's game-changing news. Could a relationship with a European princess ever be halfway normal? When he was in Paris she was in Rome. She'd been in London last weekend but it hadn't fit with his schedule and this weekend she was with friends in Vienna. Unnerved, every muscle in his jaw tensed, as if he was bracing himself for a slap in the face.

As soon as the casual photos were done, Alex and Maggie took the babies into the spare bedroom-slash-nursery to settle them in their cots for a nap, while the photographer and her assistant packed up their stuff.

'Bye Nick. Lovely to meet you. Thanks so much for agreeing to be photographed with the twins.'

'You're welcome. Good to meet you too.' Nick shook her hand.

Still chatting excitedly about the babies, her new line of babywear designs, styling A-listers and the TV contract she'd landed on a popular morning show, Maggie accompanied the two women out into the corridor to wait for the elevator.

While she was away Alex grabbed a couple of cold beers from the fridge. 'How are things in Paris?'

'Not so good. The studio scenes were okay, but now we're on location I'm leaning on the stunt guys much too much. We shot a rooftop chase last week. I nearly had a heart attack. I panicked. I hate relying on stuntmen. If it gets out, I'll be the biggest joke in Hollywood.'

'What are you afraid of? That's what stunt doubles are for.'

He felt the reassuring pressure of his brother's hand on his shoulder but a shiver ran down his spine. 'I just wish I could chill about it and do my own stunt work. I'm not a natural action hero. I don't have a head for heights.'

'What does the production team say?'

'I didn't tell them. Because I wasn't the casting director's number one choice for the role in the first place. If the executive producers decide to make a sequel and word about my phobia gets around, they might rule me out, hire someone who's more cut out for the role than me.'

'That's not going to happen. There's no one better than you for the part. You'll nail it. But not if you suffer in silence. Tell somebody.'

Nick admired his twin brother. He'd looked up to him since they were kids, but Nick had never been good at taking advice. 'I can't.'

'So you'll do what? Keep quiet and hope for the best? That's not much of a plan.'

'You'll be the first to know if I think of a better one.' He slugged his beer. 'Alex?' He clenched his teeth, uncertain whether to share the news in Fran's email with his twin. He caught his brother's eyes and knew by his look that he sensed something was wrong.

'What? What's up?'

'Do you remember Francesca Matthews?'

Alex laughed. 'Of course I remember. You were crazy about her for all of about five weeks. What about her?'

'I've got a problem. Look.' He tapped at his phone and handed it to Alex so that he could read the email for himself.

'Is she for real? Why's she only telling you about this now?'

'I know, right?'

A muscle in Alex's jaw twitched. 'Have you opened the attachment?'

Nick shook his head, too deeply wounded to admit that he hadn't had the guts to look at the photo.

'Do you want me to?'

'No. Give it here.' He took back his phone and swiped the screen. 'Okay here goes.'

The picture of a girl, pretty with fair hair and almond brown eyes opened on his phone. His heart froze and he passed the phone to his brother.

'I've got to admit she's the spitting image of you.'

'What do you think I should do?'

'If I were you I'd demand a DNA test. It might sound harsh, but it's the best way forward. You've got to know for sure if she's yours. Not just for your sake. For hers!'

'What about what you just said? She looks like me.'

'Looks can be deceptive. Take us!'

'True.' Nick had to agree. They were fraternal twins, and although they were a similar height and facially their bone structure resembled each other, Alex had dark hair and blue eyes whereas he was fair with brown eyes. 'What I don't get is why she kept this from me? Why didn't she tell me eleven years ago?'

'Exactly. Just because the girl looks like you doesn't mean she didn't get those looks from someone else. Arrange a paternity test. And you should hire a good lawyer to act as an intermediary, give you some legal advice.'

'I don't like the sound of that.'

Alex shrugged. 'You might want to think it over before you do anything.'

Nick looked at the photo again. He had a feeling. He didn't reckon a DNA test would change the fact that was staring him in the face. And Fran said she needed him to make contact urgently. There wasn't time to go looking for a legal expert. He could do that later if necessary.

'Listen. Can you keep this to yourself? Just until I've had a chance to find out what it's all about? Don't say anything to Mum. There'll only be fallout and histrionics.'

Alex nodded solemnly. 'You want me to keep it a secret from Maggie?'

'I wouldn't ask you to, normally. But it's my secret, not yours, and as you pointed out I might not be the dad at all.'

'Fair enough. There's no sense in getting everyone excited about the idea of a new family member until you know if it's true.'

'Right.'

'Let me see the photo again.' Alex took the phone from his brother's hand and studied it carefully. 'I've got a feeling you're a dad though.'

'Same.'

'Let me know as soon as you get the test result. You

don't need me to tell you to be careful how you handle this. The press getting hold of it could give you a lot of grief. I can think of one or two journalists who'd have a field day with a piece on Nick Wells abandoning a baby at birth and refusing to acknowledge that she's his!'

'That's not how it is.'

'It doesn't matter. You know that.'

Nick had to physically hold back from face-palming. His reputation in the press was mud. He'd been making a real effort to change. He was tired of the love-rat image which had followed him around for the last ten years. He hadn't minded when they were acting in hit TV show *Mercy of the Vampires* in LA. In fact he'd thrived on it – part of the hype that went with heading up the cast with his brother.

'If it's true it's personal. Not for public consumption.'

'You may not have a choice. You need to tread carefully. Fran didn't want anything from you for eleven years? And suddenly now she does?'

Coming back into the apartment Maggie made a beeline for the gift basket. She untied the ribbon, and rustled the cellophane wrapping in a flurry of anticipation revealing soft toys and an array of cute presents. 'This is gorgeous Nick. Thank you.'

'I have a confession,' he said, 'I had a personal shopper pick stuff out. I don't know the first thing about babies.'

'Join the club. Funnily enough not many of us do until we have one of our own.'

Alex threw a look of love towards his wife. 'In our case two.'

Injured by Fran's email Nick bit back his emotions and buried his fear.

Chapter Two

One month later in Cornwall

What in the world have we here? It's Sleeping Beauty himself.

Layla set down her paint pots and brushes and stared at the sight of a half-naked hot man asleep on the sofa. He shouldn't be there, but she wasn't complaining. The sight of Nick Wells' broad bare chest, golden-tanned and muscle-sculpted, would brighten up anybody's morning. And if anybody's morning needed brightening, it was hers.

She was quite sure she'd never fantasized about the actor – she wasn't even a fan of vampire dramas. But if she did fantasize about him, which of course, she didn't, it wouldn't be about watching him sleep. She bit her lip, looking on dreamily. Because actually he looked beautiful – like a living, breathing statue of an ancient god in a fabulous museum of art.

Ophelia, the stray dog Maggie adopted on that day in November when Alex had come to Porthkara to propose, had trotted good-naturedly in at Layla's heels. She sat, head tipped to one side, looking disapprovingly at the sleeping male vision. One arm thrown over his head, it obscured half his face. The line of his lips drew her eyes. A shimmer of unexpected, inappropriate and highly inconvenient awareness hit Layla full force. Ophelia switched her focus from Nick to Layla as if she knew.

'Don't look at me like that,' she told her in a whisper. What with everything that was going on in her best friend's life she'd happily offered to take care of the dog, but Maggie hadn't mentioned a thing about Nick. What was he doing in Porthkara when Alex was in London anyway?

She checked her mobile phone. No new texts. Hardly surprising given the signal was so patchy.

The landline gave a shrill ring and she dived to pick up quickly before it could do it again and disturb Nick. She glanced over at him. Luckily he was dead to the world.

'Hello?' She answered in a barely-there whisper and tiptoed towards the kitchen. Still fast asleep Nick stirred and rolled over on the sofa revealing a horrendous bruise around the eye that had been hidden by his arm before.

Crikey!

Tail wagging Ophelia followed her. Ear to the phone Layla closed the door noiselessly and leant her back against it.

'Layla? Is that you?' Maggie's voice on the phone made her want to cry. 'I'm so sorry about Joe. You must be devastated. What was he thinking? He must be out of his mind. Are you okay?'

'I've been better.' Her heart sank. Maggie had seen the photos on Joe's timeline. She hadn't talked to her mum yet and the thought of facing Joe's parents made her ill. But if Maggie had seen the pictures, so had everyone else.

'Would you like me to come to Porthkara?'

She ached to tell her best friend, '*Yes, come right away, I need you*' but it wouldn't be fair and anyway it wouldn't change anything, she'd have to face Joe's big reveal on her own.

'No, it's okay. Look, there's something you don't know. Joe and me, we were finished a while ago. So technically he hasn't done anything wrong.'

'Flip Layla. I can't believe you've been keeping something like that to yourself. You two have been through a bad patch, but it's no excuse for what he's done.'

'It's more than a bad patch. It's over. I'm just sorry I didn't tell anyone.'

'I wish you'd told me. Why didn't you?'

Layla's back slid down the door and she sat on the kitchen floor feeling crumpled and unsure. 'I didn't know how to. And you had so much great stuff happening I didn't want to spoil things.' She closed her eyes fighting back tears, finally admitting, 'I was in denial. I guess maybe I thought we could fix it. I was waiting for him to come home.'

'He shouldn't have gone in the first place. I can't believe how selfish he's been. He should have come home months ago. And now this? I'd like to give him a piece of my mind. Are you sure you don't want me to come down there?'

'I'll be fine. Honest. You mustn't worry. How are the babies?' Layla changed the subject, holding back from opening up and confessing that she felt like she was living in a bad dream, multi-tasking like a crazy person, and wishing the ground would open up and swallow her whole. 'I'm making a start on their room today.'

'Beautiful. And exhausting. I'd no idea how full on twins would be.'

'On the subject of twins ... What exactly is Nick doing here?'

'He's arrived already? Oh my gosh. Is that why we're whispering? I was about to give you the heads up. He's broken up with his girlfriend. I said he could stay at the cottage. That's alright with you, isn't it? He's promised not to get under your feet.'

'Maggie, have you forgotten how small this place is? Of course he's under my feet!' With her free hand she picked at a spot of dried-on paint on the knee of her dungarees. 'Right now he's sprawled out in the living room. But more to the point, the bed's in bits, the place reeks of paint, and there's no hot water. Dad's promised to take a look when he gets a moment. But I haven't seen him for three days. It seems we get along best when we avoid each other.'

'You poor love. I'm sorry. You could use some moral support. If I'd realized you were having a tough time too I'd have put Nick off. But he's nice. Really. And anyway you two already know each other a little bit.' Silence from Layla. 'The wedding? Give him a chance. Who knows? Maybe you'll be good for each other.'

Ophelia sat next to her on the kitchen tiles, her little warm body leaning into Layla's side. She automatically stroked her head and tousled the fur behind her ears. 'The thing is with all my other commitments the decorating isn't going as fast as I'd like. The place is in a mess. What am I supposed to do with him?'

'Now there's a question.' Maggie's cheeky laugh resounded in her ears. 'You'll think of something. He won't be there long. Just until his face heals.'

She clutched the phone tightly. 'About that ...' A baby crying cut her short. 'Who's that?'

'Phoebe.' A second high-pitched cry echoed the first. 'And there goes Horatio. Listen, I'll have to hang up. Sorry.'

'It's okay. You've got your hands full.'

'Let me know how things go. And if I can help with the Joe situation in any way you just have to say. Could you get away for a few days? We could try and find a corner for you here.'

'I'll survive. But thanks. Hug the babies for me.'

'Take care of yourself.'

With that Maggie's sparkly voice was gone and Layla was left with the beaten-up brother-in-law to add to her problems. For a few seconds she remained frozen on the cold kitchen tiles uncertain what to do. She'd been planning to spend the morning setting to work on a seaside-themed mural for Phoebe and Horatio. She'd sketched out lots of ideas, looking forward to getting creative.

Putting her best foot forward, she got up and crept out of the kitchen into the living room, quietly gathered up her stuff and tiptoed over to the stairs. Like a shadow, Ophelia went too. But the second Layla set foot on the bottom step it creaked loudly and Nick blinked open his eyes. Flustered, she set everything down again and crossed her arms defensively. The bracelet on her wrist jingled and its clasp caught on a shirt button. All fingers and thumbs, she tugged at it.

'Red?' He sat up and ran a hand through his disheveled hair. A lazy, impossibly sexy smile curved his lips. She bristled.

Fabulous. He's forgotten my name.

'Good morning,' she said brightly, trying to sound like

she'd fully expected to find a celebrity on the sofa. Putting two and two together she twigged that the appallingly badly parked sports car outside was his. 'That monstrosity blocking the lane looks like an abandoned vehicle. If you don't move it sharpish you'll have the neighbourhood watch brigade after you.'

Nick stood up letting slip the throw that had loosely covered not much of him while he slept.

Not convinced that he wasn't stark naked, she clapped a hand over her eyes and held up the other one like she was directing traffic. 'Stop. On second thoughts, it can wait.' He sank back onto the sofa, and through the gaps between her fingers she saw his smile spread impossibly wider.

'That thing's a mid-life crisis waiting to happen. As soon as day-trippers start arriving there'll be a traffic jam.' Disgruntled she grumbled her words out and gingerly lowering her hand pointed out irritably, 'You're much too young for a mid-life crisis.'

He laughed. 'Okay I get it. You don't like my car Red.' His amused tone rumbled through her, spoilt by the fury that had kicked in when he called her by her hair colour. 'It's a rental.'

'Couldn't you get a bigger one?'

Ophelia barked enthusiastically and jumped up to lick his face. 'I'm glad someone's pleased to see me.'

Maggie and Alex's wedding had been the first, and last, time Layla had seen him in the flesh, so to speak. And he hadn't been in a state of undress then. As if, like Ophelia, he'd read her mind, he announced, 'I'd better put some clothes on.' The taunting glint in his eyes rattled her. 'It was raining hard last night. I got wet so I stripped and crashed.'

Her gaze darted all around the room trying to avoid staring. Who knew Maggie would end up married to Hot Vampire Guy? And here was Even Hotter Vampire Guy. Not that she was a fan. She'd wanted to believe Maggie when she'd said he was quite nice really, but she wasn't convinced. He had a dreadful reputation.

'If you'll excuse me I need to get on. I've promised to help out at the beach kiosk this afternoon. And I've got a shift at the restaurant later. The girl who usually washes up has pulled a sickie and headed off to a festival.' She gave a heartfelt sigh. 'Right this minute I'd sell my soul to just take flight like that.'

She briskly pulled the curtains and July sunshine poured into the room. 'The window's wide open.' Wearily she remembered that she'd opened it to get rid of the paint smell, and been so ready to zonk out when she'd finished work on the cottage that she'd forgotten to close it. 'Please tell me Maggie gave you a key? You didn't climb in through the window in the night?'

'She said to knock on your door and ask you to open up, but since I got here at 3 a.m. and a perfectly good window was open there didn't seem any point.'

'You broke in?'

'In theory it wasn't a break-in since somebody left the window open.' He fixed her with his gaze and shrugged his strong, smooth shoulders, everything about him golden hues, apart from the marks on his face, strong evidence of his bad boy image. 'It was late. I didn't want to wake you from your beauty sleep Red.'

In the bright daylight she took in the bruise that circled his eye more clearly. The skin was livid and dark very swollen. 'It'll take more than sleep to make that beautiful, what happened?' Her hand flew to cover her mouth, not in time to stop her adding, 'Been in a fight?'

'It's a long story.' Clearly a story he wasn't about to tell.

Uneasy and annoyed at the intrusion, she walked towards the kitchen. It was uncool not to remember her name. And on what planet did he think it was okay to call a person by their hair colour?

'Tea?' She threw the question over her shoulder. 'Don't answer, because I'm making tea whether you want me to or not. I need it, even if you don't.'

'Tea would be lovely. Thank you.' His drawl wound through her, making it hard to stay cross.

Layla's nails tapped out an impatient rhythm on the

worktop while she waited for the kettle to boil. Her nerves jangled.

He can't stay here. He's in the way. He'll have to go.

She was in enough bother without a six-foot-something actor hiding out in the cottage while she painted. All she wanted to do herself was hide and paint, and there wasn't enough room for two fugitives.

She poured hot water into a red polka dot teapot and watched a curl of steam rise from the spout. It wasn't her call. Maggie had said it was fine – so she'd lump it.

Turning to grab a couple of flowery mugs, her skin prickled as she realized she was being watched. Dressed in jeans and a grey tee, Nick filled the doorframe. Her eyes about level with his broad chest, she tipped her head to meet his distracting face.

'I've moved the car.'

'Hopefully, none of the neighbours have called in the constabulary quite yet.'

Despite the shiner, his amazing almond-brown eyes triggered fantasies of places she'd like to go – Spain, California. She gritted her teeth, fighting his intensity.

He had the reputation of a scumbag. He was famous for it. The gossip mags claimed he'd treated his co-star girlfriend abominably, although if Maggie was to be believed that stuff was all rumour and nothing to do with reality. He hadn't behaved badly at the wedding. She'd used the excuse that she'd been having physio for an ankle sprain to try to avoid dancing with him at the party. But he'd convinced her that it would be bad luck for the bridesmaid not to dance with the best man, and made himself impossible to resist. But still. Nice or not, Nick in Porthkara was the final straw.

Turning her back on him she took a bottle of milk from the fridge and poured the tea. Her grandmother's lucky charm bracelet shifted slightly on her wrist. Somewhere down the line she reckoned the luck must have run out. As she passed him the hot mug their fingers clashed. Heat climbed up her neck and spread to her face no doubt turning it a colour that rivaled her hair dye. Zapped by awkward sparks, her hand fluttered up into her hair and landed on the pink silk scarf she'd tied it up with.

Crikey! What must I look like? Something the cat dragged in!

'So why do you want to take flight?'

'I didn't mean that. I don't really want to leave, not permanently at any rate.'

'But?' His gaze suddenly soft and serious trapped hers searchingly.

'I was supposed to go travelling with my boyfriend. And I didn't. I couldn't. My mum was in an accident. Car crash. Head-on collision. She's lucky to be alive. She was in intensive care for a week.'

'She pulled through?'

'She's okay.' She nodded earnestly. 'No lasting damage, thank goodness. But that week was the longest of my life. It felt like the world had ended. The waiting was horrible.' She shrugged it off, not relishing dredging up the memories. 'It happened the night before we were due to go away. So I couldn't leave. Joe went without me.'

'Nice.'

'Well, he said I could join him in Australia when I was ready.' There was no point telling him all the little details. 'With one thing and another it never happened.'

'Why not go meet up with him now?'

'It's too late.'

'It might not be.'

It was polite of him to show an interest, but she wished he wouldn't. He wasn't in full possession of the facts. 'I finished with him, and I didn't tell people and neither did he, and now I'm in a bind because it seems he got over me quicker than I got over him. He's announced on social media that he's gone and got married in Mexico.'

'Ouch.'

'So it's not so much that I want to go far away or stay away a long time or anything, but just at the minute I'd love to escape.'

A gust of fresh sea air blew in fluttering the curtains. She inhaled deeply, welcoming the familiar smell of salt and home. Nick watched her sip her tea. At least being scrutinized by him was a distraction from the prospect of half the eyes in the village analyzing her. The idea of being an object of pity smarted terribly.

She looked at the kitchen clock. 'Joe's post went up on his timeline roughly twelve hours ago and that's exactly how long I've been feeling like I want to run away.'

'Am I getting this right? You'd like to scurry off somewhere and hide and instead you're stuck with me. The unexpected guest.' Nick gulped his tea. 'I can only apologize.'

Ridiculously self-conscious, she fumbled in a cupboard for the emergency stash of chocolate biscuits. She popped off the tin's lid and held it out to Nick, tightening her fingers to control the shake.

'I'm being terribly rude. You've caught me on a bad day. Biscuit?' She smiled, dredging up some cheerfulness she didn't feel.

'I've got a photo shoot coming up soon. I'm on a strict nutritional programme. I daren't risk it.'

'You wouldn't risk it for a chocolate biscuit?'

He shook his head slowly, the line of his lips hard and tight.

'I'd say "bad day" is one hell of an understatement. I have a suggestion. I'll lie low here for as long it takes to sort my face out, keep out of your way, help you out in any way I can. And when it's time for me to go you can tag along for a couple of days, keep me company on my photo shoot.'

'That's sweet, but really I couldn't.'

'Of course you could.' The coaxing drawl fuddled her head. 'It'll be fun. The shoot's in Paris.'

Chapter Three

'You're inviting me to Paris with you? Seriously?' To make things more stupefying she had a flashback to the delicious hold his body had had over hers when they'd danced together at the wedding on Christmas Eve. It was some sort of caught-on-the-rebound related delirium evidently. Either that, or overwork.

'Think it over. No need to decide right away. Sounds like you could use some fun.'

Discombobulated she walked away from him carrying her mug of tea and the biscuit tin into the living room.

'We don't know each other.' Balancing on the arm of the sofa she bit into the crumbly digestive and tasted the smooth milk chocolate on her tongue. 'I feel a smidge bad. You sure you don't want one?'

He shook his head and opened a smart holdall with a posh label on it and took out a selection of vitamins and potions. He unscrewed the top of what looked like a toothpaste tube and squirted green goo onto his tongue, chasing it with a swig of tea. 'What I want to do and what I can do are two different things.'

'What the heck was that?'

'A food supplement.' He made a face. 'Part of my energizing diet.' Nonchalantly, he opened each of the multiple pots in turn and popped a single pill from each.

Layla pulled a face. 'Crikey. Give me a chocolate biscuit over that lot, any day of the week.'

He put all the little tubs, packs and tubes bag into the holdall and stared at them for a second or two before zipping it up, a thoughtful look on his superlatively handsome face. 'You know what, Red? You're probably right. I think I will have a biscuit.'

That contagious smile twisted his lips and she handed over the packet.

'Hello? Anybody in?' Mervin wiped his boots on the doormat and stepped into the cottage. 'You left the door ajar. You want to be careful about that. You don't want just anybody letting themselves in.' He gave Layla a quick once over. 'By jingo, Layla love. What have you come as?'

'I'm here to paint.'

He nodded wisely, and turned his attention to Nick. 'What's all this then?' He bobbed his head in the direction of the doorway and gestured outside with his thumb. 'I've had a report of an abandoned vehicle and lights on in a property that's known to be unoccupied.'

'Told you,' Layla muttered at Nick in a whispered aside. 'He's here to arrest you.'

'I take it that's your car outside sir?'

'It is. It's a hire car.'

'And the lights in the night?'

'Guilty.'

Layla cringed. 'You probably don't want to be saying things like that.'

The puzzled policeman, eyebrows knitted, stood his ground, taking in the battered state of Nick's face.

'Cup of tea, Mervin?' Since his arrival in the village he'd fast become the protector of his adopted community. He'd transformed her mum's pub quiz group into the crack team to beat. To regain fitness after the accident Shelly had taken to hiking the coastal path, and Mervin often went too, the pair of them chaperoned by Ophelia.

'No thanks, love. Things to do. I wouldn't say no to a misfit though.' His face turned red. 'Sorry,' he corrected, 'I don't know where that came from. I meant biscuit.'

Nick offered him the packet. 'Help yourself.'

Layla knew exactly where the slip of the tongue had come from. He didn't like the look of Nick.

'Well, if everything's alright here,' he said through a mouthful of crumbs and not sounding entirely convinced, 'I'll leave you two to it.' He beckoned Layla over to one side lowered his voice. 'Looks like he's seen better days. Are you sure he's not bothering you? We had three complaints down at the station. I thought I'd better look in.'

'He's Maggie's brother-in-law. He's come to stay.' She hesitated. 'For a while.'

Mervin harrumphed, and Ophelia yelped, hinting that she'd like a biscuit. Nick took one, snapped a bit off which didn't have chocolate on it, fed it to her and polished off the remainder himself.

'I'm sorry I wasted your time,' he told the policeman. He pointed to his eye apologetically. 'I got into a scuffle with the press. Someone hit me with a camera.' Silence. 'By accident,' he added. 'Maggie kindly offered me the use of her place.'

Mervin stepped out into the sunny lane followed by Layla and the dog. He squatted and ruffled the dog's fur. 'I was sorry to hear about ...' He stumbled to find the right word and failed. '... You know!'

'Yep. Thanks. Bye now.' Layla avoided meeting the concern in his eyes.

The policeman stood his ground, not quite ready to leave. 'You deserve better.' He shook his head in disbelief. 'As for Mr Pathetically-Poor-Parker in there.' He gestured towards the house with his thumb. 'The slightest whiff of trouble with him, and you know where to find me.'

'Everthing's okay, honest.' She drew an X in the air with her finger. 'Cross my heart.' Since her mum's accident and Joe's departure everyone in Porthkara had been wrapping her in cotton wool so tightly, that it felt like she was in a straitjacket. She called Ophelia, walked briskly back inside and closed the door quickly. In a weird way, although she'd been shattered by the news that Joe was married, she felt calm – free to get on with living her own life.

There was a glimmer of curiosity on Nick's compelling face.

'Eavesdropping?' She shut the door, closing everything out except him.

A muscle twitched in his cheek. 'Not on purpose.'

The object of Nick's mesmeric stare, she balled her fingers into fists, fighting off the chemical craziness of the smouldering attraction that had been distracting her since she'd walked in and found him asleep like Goldilocks. He was ridiculously fanciable, despite a black eye. Somehow it added to the loveable rogue thing he had going on. Even supposing the scandals written about him weren't true, he had an undeniable air of mystique.

'Since you're here, I wonder if you'd mind helping me lug this lot upstairs?' His cool vibe attracted and unsettled her simultaneously. She made a lunge for a bunch of paintbrushes and a colour chart, feeling like a klutz.

'Sure thing.'

As he followed her up the narrow staircase, laden with paint pots and dust sheets, he marveled at his not entirely perfect view of her dungaree clad behind. At the top of the stairs she elbowed open the door to a small bedroom and dumped everything on the floor.

'This is the nursery. There's some furniture that needs shifting. It would be great if you could help.'

'Okay, Red.'

'The name's Layla.'

'I know that.'

'Oh really?' Her eyebrows shot up. 'I thought you'd forgotten my name.'

'No, I didn't forget. I guess I kinda like your hair.'

'Well don't.'

'Don't like your hair?'

'Yes, well, no.'

'It's super high impact.' He stifled a laugh while she thought about it.

'I know that. But there's more to me than my redness in case you hadn't noticed.'

'Oh, I noticed!'

Either she didn't hear his half-whispered reply or ignored it. She was insanely attractive. Her perfect curves grabbed his attention. When he'd met her on Christmas Eve at Alex's wedding he'd been dating Toni, otherwise he'd have been tempted to …

But now the thing with Toni was as dead as a dodo. It had imploded the moment he broke the news he'd received in Fran's email. She'd been categorical. She couldn't see a future with him. Which was just as well because he'd realized that he didn't want that either. He wasn't a long-haul type.

'You must be wondering if it's pantomime season already.'

'I wasn't thinking anything of the sort.' He swept her with a slow, appreciative glance amused by her paint-spattered clothes, and the baggy purple shirt covered in what appeared to be a cats-and-dogs-holding-umbrellas print and concluding that it wouldn't go down well if he admitted that, in fact, he thought she looked hot. Waking up staring into her pretty eyes had been quite something. 'Anyway, it's the middle of July.'

'Come to think of it, you and Alex would make awesome Ugly Sisters. You should mention it to your agent.'

'I'll keep it in mind. If I'm ever offered Widow Twanky, I'll know exactly where to come for a hot pink headscarf.'

Layla laughed, relaxing. For no apparent reason she untied and retied her hair. It was good that she'd lightened up. 'I expect the costume supervisor will have something much zanier in mind.'

Acting on his attraction would be a major detour off plan. All he wanted was somewhere to stay – well away from cameras. He needed to clear his head. It was lucky that the policeman had turned up when he did and his impetuous suggestion about Paris had been forgotten. He needed to pull himself together.

It pained him to admit it, but he was out of control. He'd gone to see Fran but there was so much distance between them. Still, he'd agreed to everything she'd asked of him; promised to be her back-up in the event of a bad outcome given what she was facing. He owed her that. The word mess didn't come close to covering it.

He shut everything out. Except for Layla. Apparently, she came with the accommodation. She went to pick up a flat packed baby crib.

'Here, give it to me.' He reached out and took it from her. He'd been crass, calling her Red. He'd treated her like there was nothing more to her than her appearance. 'I'm sorry if I offended you. I didn't mean to.'

'That's okay. I don't know why I got so touchy about it.'

'Because I was being an asshole?'

'You're forgiven. I'm glad you're here. You make lifting that thing look like it's a box of matches.'

'Careful, there's more to me than a bunch of useful muscles, you know. Where do want it?' He fired her a look. He couldn't help it. Her eyes sparkled right back at him. Her smile was sunnier than the summer day outside.

'In the other room. Please.' He felt the way she averted her gaze, trying not to look as he hefted the first flat pack into the other bedroom. She was staring out the window at the far horizon when he came back for the second. There was something potent about that avoidance. She magnetized him. He watched, feeling like an obstacle cramping her space, as she snapped the lids off pots of paint and set to work focusing on her drawings and her paints.

'Is it alright if I take a shower?'

'Uh-huh.'

'And then I'll go for a walk. I've got some things to figure out. I'll do my best to keep out of your way.'

'Yep. Okay.' Not turning away from the wall where she was painting dabs of colours from different test pots she chewed her lip thoughtfully. 'See you later.'

'Towels?'

Concentrating on the wall she asked, 'Which blue do you like best?'

It wasn't the answer he'd hoped for. He stared at the colours seeing virtually no difference between the two blues. 'Both.'

'I prefer the lighter one, it says summer to me and it will make the room feel bigger, I think.'

'Absolutely.'

Leaving Layla absorbed in her work he went into the bathroom figuring he'd air dry. A minute later blasted by an icy jet of water he let out a yelp several decibels louder than Ophelia's.

Just desserts?

Layla's arm appeared around the door, her hand offering a large fluffy towel. The rest of her stayed strategically outside the door, but he could hear her muffled giggles. 'I forgot to say. There's no hot water. The immersion heater is on the blink.' She paused, and added charmingly, 'Oops!'

His wet fingers grazed hers as he clutched for the towel. She pulled her arm away quickly, as if she'd had an electric shock.

'I guess you could go next door and use mine. In fact, look, given the state of this place, perhaps you'd better stay with me.'

Still hidden behind the door, he didn't need to see her face to know from the tone of her voice that she wasn't exactly thrilled at the prospect. 'I've had more enthusiastic propositions,' he joked.

'I don't doubt it,' she challenged, mockingly sweet. 'My spare room's not exactly the Ritz. You might be more comfortable at the Manor House Hotel. In fact, you definitely would be.' Suddenly as jumpy as a box of frogs she babbled her words in a rush. She made him smile from the inside out. 'If you like, I can call and see if they have availability.'

'Your spare room sounds good to me.'

'I'd better warn you I don't cook. I don't have time.'

'That's not a problem. I do. I'm a domestic god in the kitchen.'

'Even if you do say so yourself.'

'When I'm not bingeing on vegetable soup, vitamin supplements and egg white omelettes, that is! To tell you the truth, when I'm prepping a role or a photo shoot I need to be careful.'

'Super. That's settled then.' The forced breeziness of her reply betrayed an undercurrent of second thoughts.

'Layla?' He emerged from the bathroom, tucking the towel around his waist, and forking fingers through wet strands of hair. Back in the nursery, he found her intently painting, a sketching pencil tucked behind one ear. He walked across the room, reached out and gently touched her arm. 'Listen.' Forced to turn her face, her eyes met his with an intense focus. 'Thanks.'

An icy shower hadn't taken the edge off the raw attraction.

Chapter Four

A cloudburst, accompanied by a rainbow arching out from the headland into the sea, cleared the beach, scattering the holiday people and cutting dead the run on ice cream at the Kandy Shack. Finishing a run-off-her-feet shift, Layla locked up the shop and headed home, wending her way uphill. The winding lane took her past the pastel-painted jumble of higgledy-piggledy houses with their colourful window boxes and pots crammed with summer flowers. At her side Ophelia trotted obediently.

When she reached the bridge over the brook that ran down through the village into the sea she stopped. A small padlock dangled from a curlicue of ironwork on one of the rusty railings. The sight of it made her sad and disappointed, totally humiliated. It was a horrible feeling. She glued her eyes to the padlock. She and Joe had been wearing school uniforms when they'd put it there and thrown away the key. The memory had been eating away at her all afternoon. He'd bought the padlock in the village general store and she'd painted the heart on it in red nail polish. She remembered the name of the colour on the bottle wistfully.

Forever Yours! So much for that.

A year ago, on the anniversary of the day they'd put their lovelock on the bridge she and Joe had stopped there and he'd given her a gummy sweet ring and a promise that when he got the money together he'd buy her a real one. She'd eaten the ring. That was probably a bad omen. At any rate, everyone considered them to be practically engaged, and she'd been dreaming of him giving her an engagement ring in Paris. Her hope had been to put a lovelock on the Pont des Beaux Arts to mark their commitment to a shared future.

Joe hadn't shared her vision. And now she was stuck. She wanted to get rid of the padlock so badly, the sight of it made her physically sick. It conjured up the image of Joe down on one knee in the most romantic city in the world. Utterly, irritatingly wrong. She couldn't bear to see it dangling from the bridge a single day more.

She pulled a hairgrip out of her unruly mop. Unpicking locks with a hairpin struck her as something she'd seen at a village vintage cinema night. It was the kind of thing which only ever really worked in films, but it had to be worth a go. With a theatrically furtive glance left and right to check that nobody was watching, she crouched down, took the padlock between her fingers, inserted the wire hairgrip, and twisted. Nothing happened. She straightened the wire, and tried again.

Ophelia sat looking on dolefully. 'It's got to go, O!'

In that precise moment Nick came walking round the corner. He was in such unbelievably great shape that trotting up the steep hill from the harbour didn't appear to fizz on him. A big smile broke out across his face when he heard her chatting to the dog.

'Is this a private conversation or can anyone join?'

'Are you making fun of me Nick?'

'I wouldn't dream of it.'

'For your information Ophelia's a very intuitive dog. She understands me.'

The dog gave a well-timed yelp of agreement and Nick laughed. 'I can tell.'

'You've been in the village barely a day and somehow you've developed the uncanny knack of being exactly where I don't need you, exactly when I don't want you.'

'Harsh! I didn't hear any complaints when I helped you move the heavy boxes.' He studied her with a puzzled look. 'In fact, you said you were glad I was there.'

'To be fair, you are a useful pair of hands.'

His lips twisted into that much-too-sexy smile.

Sheepish, she positioned herself in front of the lovelock.

'How was your walk? Porthkara beach is amazing, don't you think?' She gave an impatient wave of her fingers. 'Don't let me keep you. Why don't you jog on? Find a bit more of Cornwall to explore?'

'What's up?' He crossed his arms over his broad chest and fixed his eyes on her. An unnerving combination of darkness and honey in his eyes, he waited, getting under her skin. When she didn't reply he stooped to greet Ophelia, ruffling her soggy fur. 'Hey, how're you doing?' The dog jumped up and placed two paws on his thigh leaving wet prints on his leg.

It was on the tip of her tongue to tell him to butt out. Instead she held the less-than-useless piece of wire out to him on the flat of her palm and cringed. 'I'm just standing here in the rain making a complete fool of myself. If I tell you why you'll probably think I'm the village idiot.'

'That's a thing?' The downpour that had cleared the beach had turned into gentle, steadily falling rain. Sheltered beneath the branches of the trees that spread out over the bridge like a big natural umbrella Nick didn't budge. 'I'm no Sherlock Holmes but something tells me you're not waiting for the rain to stop.'

She managed a weak smile. 'I'm picking a lock.' She met his eyes. 'Only breaking and entering isn't my field of expertise, so I'm not having much luck.'

His gorgeous masculine features melted her like ice

cream and at the same time she felt ridiculous and conspic-uous and as weirdly hilarious as a Punch and Judy show. The Nick effect spiralled through her. She struggled to get a hold of herself, to stamp out the badly-timed attraction.

'I'm not an alien. Contrary to appearances I wasn't beamed in from a celebrity-holding planet in outer space. If there's something I can help with, please just tell me.'

She stepped aside and pointed. 'I have to find a way to remove this padlock. It's outstayed its welcome. Any sugges-tions?'

He shook his head. 'I don't see it's much of a problem where it is.'

'That isn't helping.' The padlock encapsulated things she couldn't define – emotions, memories, elapsed time. Things she couldn't begin to explain. Not wanting to appear unreasonable she attempted an explanation all the same. 'Joe and I put it here, a long time ago, so you see its pres-ence is no longer required. I don't want to have to see it every day.' She peered over the side of the bridge. A long way below in the gully the clear water flowed over moss covered stones. 'The key might still be in there, hidden.'

'Unlikely. Precisely how long ago did you throw it in?'

'About twelve years.'

Without looking down, she swung first one leg, and then the other, over the railings at the side of the bridge. Holding on tight she shimmied along until she reached a sturdy overhanging tree branch, grasped onto it and clambered onto the big rocks beyond.

'What the hell are you doing? Stop.' Nick's voice crackled electrically.

'It's okay.' She laughed nervously. 'It sounds crazy but it's worth a quick look.'

'Crazy. You're a lunatic.' His words sounded like something trapped in his throat.

She scrambled carefully down the steep bank, jumped off the lowest mossy rock, landed safely and looked up at him triumphantly.

Standing at the railings he glared down into the gully, his face granite-like and ashen. 'At the risk of sounding pessimistic,' he shouted, 'won't it be all rusted up by now?'

Ignoring him, she kicked off her flip-flops and paddled into the stream. Crystal clear, cool water flowed gently over her feet. All around her raindrops made circles in the stream. In defiance of Nick, and good sense, she lifted pebbles and looked under rocks.

She picked up a slippery stone, dropped it with a splash and dug around hopefully in the empty hole it had left behind.

'Any luck?'

'Nope. But I'm not giving up.'

She doggedly shifted another large stone and the water beneath it clouded with disturbed silt, obscuring her bright pink toenails. *Hot Day*, it said on the nail polish bottle. Not counting Nick, that particular nail polish related prediction had been wrong too. The day that had begun so promisingly sunny had turned cloudy and grey and wet.

'Face it. It's not in there.' Nick's deep voice rumbled down into the gully like thunder. 'You're wasting your time. Twelve years is much too long, it'll have been washed away in a storm years ago.'

She was ankle-deep in water looking for something that she wasn't going to find. 'That's positive. Thanks for nothing,' she yelled, a sour taste at the back of her throat. 'I thought you said you wanted to help.'

A darkening sky and a deafening thunderclap got her to face the futility of what she was doing. Ophelia whined pitifully, so Nick picked her up.

'I do. But I think it's time to call it quits. You're shivering like you've seen a ghost and there's going to be another heavy downpour any second.' He took hold of the padlock between his thumb and forefinger and gave it a tug. 'We'll think of another way to shift this thing.'

'That thing, as you call it, is a symbol of my broken heart,' she yelled. 'In case it's escaped your notice, I'm falling apart. My ex got married. And the pictures are everywhere on social media. All one hundred and fifty-three of them.'

Admitting defeat and that she now qualified for fully certified village idiot status, she began to clamber back up over the rocks, searching out footholds with her bare feet, carrying her flip-flops in her teeth, and avoiding looking down.

When she reached the top, grim-faced Nick grabbed ahold of her and clung on like a rather lovely limpet while she climbed back over the railings to safety. Since he was still steadying her with his arms even though she was out of danger, she hinted, 'You can let go now.'

'On one condition. Promise me you'll not do that or anything like it again. He's not worth breaking your neck over. Hearts heal.'

She glared at the padlock taking in how insignificant and tiny it looked, hardly noticeable to anyone but herself. 'True.' She met his eyes and realized he'd gone a funny colour. 'Are you okay?'

'I'm scared of heights. You have the agility of a primate and I wish I had your head for heights. Just watching you made me panic.'

'But you're the new Mr Hollywood-Action-Hero. You can't be afraid of heights.'

He nodded slowly. 'Yep. So I'll have to swear you to secrecy – either that or shoot you.'

'Crikey! That must be awkward.'

He nodded and abruptly fired a non sequitur at her.

'So, about these photos. Why not ignore them?'

'I couldn't help it. I can't stop looking at them.'

'Because you enjoy self-torture?'

She managed to conjure up a hint of a responsive smile, but wrapped her arms across her body miserably. 'Because I keep looking at her and asking myself, why her and not me?'

'Let me guess. She looks a lot like you?'

She stared at him long and hard. 'That's spooky.' Had he been stalking her friends on the internet? 'Joe's wife ...' Saying the word out loud practically made her gag '... and I do look alike. How did you know?'

He held his breath and then let it all go at once in exasperation. 'A hunch. Most of the women my father was photographed with after my parents' split resembled my mother. I remember asking myself why he'd destroyed a family to be with women who seemed like brand new versions of the one he'd left?'

'I suppose there was more to it than that.'

'Right.'

Ophelia had skedaddled ahead of them and was lying down in a muddy puddle.

Layla groaned. 'This day really isn't getting any better. And she's having way too much fun.'

As if on cue Ophelia rolled onto her back completely

coating herself in mud. He couldn't help but laugh at the sight of the mischievous little dog covered from head to paws. 'She looks like she's been dipped in chocolate. We're going to need a pint of dog shampoo.'

'At least.' Convulsed by a sudden fit of giggles the warmth of Layla's laughter broke over him like a wave.

Oddly reluctant to tear himself away he started to walk back in the direction of the little store he'd spotted down by the harbour. The rain had stopped as suddenly as it had started. The clouds parted and the sun warmed the cobbles in the lane. 'I've never been anywhere with such whimsical weather.'

'That's the Porthkara microclimate for you. It's one of those if-you-don't-like-the-weather-wait-fifteen-minutes days.' She gazed at him wide-eyed. 'Where are you going?'

'To the store. I've had an idea. I'm going to see if they have pliers.'

'This very minute?'

'Right now.'

Fran had cut him to the core. The news about Beth hadn't gotten out there – yet – but it was in his shattered heart. He couldn't stop himself looking back into the past without the foggiest idea what to do about it. But if pliers to cut the padlock would free Layla from the memory of a relationship gone bad, then at least he could fix that.

'I said I'd make myself useful, didn't I?'

'It can wait. Honestly.'

Nick pointed at the padlock. 'Your past stops there. Exes! Who needs them?' He wanted her to feel better but he was at a loss when it came to a broken heart.

'For someone who doesn't need exes, you've got enough of them. Allegedly!'

Despite the obvious humour in her tone, the remark stung. It hit a nerve. He didn't usually care about the truth. But lately the blurriness of ten years' worth of indeterminate relationship status had swum into sharp focus. He snorted. 'So I should know, right? You go on home. I'll see you back there.'

Intensely wound up, he marched down the lane like he was going into battle.

Chapter Five

Layla arrived back at the cottages to discover that her dad had at last turned up to take a look at the broken immersion heater that supplied Maggie's shower with hot water. He'd squeezed his white van into the parking space next to Nick's flash sports car. Sporting a hi-vis orange vest over his white overalls, he leant against the van, arms folded across his chest.

'Hi Dad.'

He threw a not unimpressed look at Nick's hire car. 'I gather you've got company. Don't take any nonsense from him. Maggie got the nice brother, or so I hear. That one's nothing but trouble. I'm telling you. Caps lock style, TROUBLE. You watch yourself there.'

Ignoring the embarrassing dad warning she looked him up and down. 'Interesting look you've got going. Not unlike a giant traffic cone.'

'Hey, less of the cheek, you.' He performed a mock bow. 'Mr Fix-It at your service. What kept you?'

An irritated shiver ran down her spine. Concerned father patter and stabs at humour apart, they both knew they were on eggshells still. 'What kept me? Where in the name of Cornish pixies have *you* been dressed like that?'

'I've been up a ladder.' He opened the van and took out his toolbox. 'Clearing some blocked guttering at one of the holiday lets. I wanted to make sure everybody could see me. Didn't want some plonker walking under the ladder and sending me flying.'

'Nobody walks under ladders Dad. It's bad luck.'

'Bad luck for the poor so-and-so on the ladder.'

'I haven't seen you for days.' A wince of embarrassment lanced her realizing that she could have asked her dad for help with the padlock instead of getting Nick involved. 'You're like the invisible man.'

He pulled a face and she had to laugh at the ridiculousness of that statement given his hi-vis get-up. 'Well I'm here now.' He threw a look at the bedraggled dog. 'What's she been playing at?'

'Rolled in a puddle.' She closed the gate to stop Ophelia from escaping and running off, and pulled a bunch of keys out of her pocket. Fidgeting more than necessary over fitting the right key in the lock she opened up. As she burst through the door, avoiding her father's concerned look, she bent down and scooped up the handful of junk mail from the doormat.

'I popped by earlier and things were rather quiet.'

'I was at the kiosk,' she said, finally meeting his eyes, 'keeping things ticking over for Mum.'

'It's high time the three of us sit down and take a look at all this. You're working too many hours. It can't be good for you.'

Her parents had split their assets in the village fifty-fifty. They'd built up a portfolio of properties in the area running them as holiday lets. When her grandmother died they'd converted her lovely rambling old house into a boutique B&B. In the divorce settlement her dad got the cottages and her mum the house.

That left the Kandy Shack. The beachside kiosk was a popular landmark and her dad was excessively proud of it. He'd bought land from an elderly fisherman, demolished the run-down boathouse on the plot and built the Shack. Her mum was attached to it too and they hadn't been able to agree on who should keep it. Although it had started life as his idea, her mum had taken charge of the business, made a success of it.

She suppressed a flicker of reaction sensing that what was really bothering him was not knowing how to broach the topic of Joe. Swiftly she changed the subject. 'Come see.' She closed the door to keep Ophelia in the tiny front garden. 'I'm ready to start the mural. I'd appreciate your advice on which colour blue to go with.'

Upstairs she opened a window and bobbed her head out to check on Ophelia while Ralph stared at the paint tester colours on the wall. 'The lighter of the two,' he said, 'but you don't need me to tell you that.'

She smiled.

'Listen. This business with Joe. It should have been you, Layla love. I don't know what to say.'

'There's nothing to say. We're finished. He's with someone new.'

'Still. You're bound to be upset.'

'Nope.' She crossed her arms tightly. 'I'm fine.'

'Right.' He nodded and opened his toolbox to take out a screwdriver. 'I'll see to that shower then.'

A bundle of awkwardness and avoidance, she made to scuttle off. 'I'll be next door. Bathing the dog.'

'Hang on a second. I need you to turn the power off at the mains.'

Feeling fragile and determined not to let it show she went down to the cupboard under the stairs and flicked up the switch in the box in the cupboard under the stairs.'

'Done,' she called out. 'See you later.'

'Don't go yet.' Her dad's head leaned over the bannisters and he shouted into the stairwell. 'This won't take a minute and there's something I need to speak to you about.'

'There's really no point Dad. I told you. As far as me and Joe go the subject is closed.' She groaned and plodded unwillingly back upstairs.

'It's not about that.' He stuck his head in the airing cupboard and got busy unscrewing something. 'The timing's terrible. And Jasmine says we should leave it a few days. But I don't want you hearing from someone else, so ...'

'Leave what?'

He shuffled backwards out of the airing cupboard and stood up. 'That thing's as old as the hills. It's completely knackered. I'm amazed it's lasted this long to be honest. I'll price up a new hot water tank for Maggie and you can run it by her. I won't charge for labor, obviously.'

'Hear what Dad?'

All her life her dad had been busy with this and that. 'Where's Dad?' she'd ask her mum when she was too little to understand much of anything. 'He's off gallivanting,' she'd say, a euphemism for his womanizing. At some point, she wasn't sure exactly when, she'd learned not to ask. Now he was here, talking about Joe when she didn't want to, and he looked hassled and it felt like it would be best if he would just leave.

'You haven't heard already, have you?'

'Blast it, no. What haven't I heard?' she demanded.

He looked down at his feet. He dug his hands in his

pockets and pulled them out again not knowing quite what to do with himself. He looked at his watch, although he patently didn't need to check what time it was. 'Here goes. It's like this ...' He sucked in a gulp of air. 'Jasmine made an announcement last night.'

'That sounds ominous.' Layla almost laughed.

'She proposed,' Ralph blurted.

'Why? It's not a leap year! Anyway, February was months ago.'

Her dismissiveness masked the fact that she didn't want to deal with this news, let alone predict the fallout. Since the accident her parents had put any decision-making about the Kandy Shack on hold. She had a gut feeling that a new round of wrangling over the shared ownership was on the horizon. Her dad shuffled from one foot to the other. His blank expression gave the impression that the proposal hadn't sunk in yet. 'Jasmine's pregnant. We're getting married.'

'Ohhhh!' Her exclamation drifted out through the open window into the garden and Ophelia gave a yelp at the sound she'd learnt to recognize as her name. 'That's – terrific. Congratulations.'

* * *

Nick had come to Cornwall to hide, not from the paps and the journalists, not from anyone but himself. Porthkara was just as he'd remembered it – tranquil and beautiful. Even now at the height of summer when the place was a hive of activity, the pub and restaurant buzzing and the beach alive with people and surfers galore, there was a sense of calm about the place that he loved. And the weird weather was really something else. He'd just walked past a house that looked like something straight out of *Poldark*, only it had a palm tree growing in the front yard.

Heading back up the hill towards the bridge he smiled and tried to look nonchalant as a family of holidaymakers rounded the hairpin bend. They were the whole enchilada, mum, dad, and three kids of varying sizes, topped off with a baby in a buggy. The sight of them spooked him.

'Hey!' Nick said, waving and trying to look like he belonged. It was difficult to blend with the scenery sporting a hessian eco shopper bearing the message 'I Heart My Old Bag' in big green letters.

The couple gave him a funny look. It was one he recognized. Such looks often came accompanied with words along the lines of 'I know who are, but I can't quite place you. Have you been on TV? It'll come to me in a moment.'

His heart twisted wondering if he should bring Layla up to speed with the reasons he'd decided to spend some time in Porthkara, or whether to keep her at arm's length. She was nice and she had the problem ex on her mind. Best keep his baggage to himself and spare her the details.

He and Fran hadn't lasted long. That didn't mean she hadn't mattered. He couldn't pinpoint an exact moment when the hurt had gone. Her email all these years later had hit him like a lightning bolt. Meeting her had turned him upside down.

He'd fathered a baby. It hadn't sunk in at first. He'd wanted to believe it was a mistake but reality had hit him square on the jaw when they'd talked. She wasn't lying. Why would she? The dates, the timing, the photos of a child who tangled up his heartstrings, it all added up. Fran had seen no point in telling him about the pregnancy. He was in LA, and she was in the UK, focused on her career, determined to make a success of being a single mother. He had to hand it to her. Her career was on fire, her daughter was amazing, and he felt like a third wheel. The emptiness was terrible. He'd been a dad without knowing it and no amount of regret would bring the lost years back.

For years, pretending to be his co-star Ella Swift's lover for the cameras and for the publicity had given him carte blanche to do what he wanted, with whoever, whenever. It was PR perfection, got lots of attention for the show, and kept the team in the press office happy. In the world-according-to-Nick his thing with Ella Swift was fake, the women he hooked up with were on the same strictly-no-strings page as him, and he wasn't harming anyone.

Or so he'd thought. The notion of his cheating-player-love-rat image affecting his tween daughter's view of him was nowhere on his radar. Until now. It was one thing acting for a living. He couldn't imagine doing anything else. It was who he was. But he'd carried it over into his personal life, and a publicity stunt that had started as harmless fun had gone way past its best before date.

Back at the bridge, tugging on the unwanted lovelock, he had a sense of déjà vu. He'd give anything for his life to be like one of those movies where time keeps repeating over and over. They'd done an episode like that on *Vampires*. He looked about almost expecting to see a crew ready to shoot.

He peered over the edge of the bridge through the railings and his head swam. He felt fearful and nauseated at the thought of how the sides dropped away into the deeply carved gully. He'd pay good money for a head for heights like Layla's. As he grabbed onto the railing to steady himself he caught sight of something hurtling through the air in his peripheral vision. He groaned sensing that a form of distinctly undesirable goo had landed in his hair. He touched his head and a wet, chalky sensation confirmed his suspicion.

'Yuck!' Looking up he spotted a magpie watching him beadily. 'Thanks a lot! Dammit!'

Regretting that he'd pitched in with his offer to help he got out the pliers that he'd bought from the DIY section at the village store and set to work. They snapped easily through the metal, so he quickly dropped the tiny lovelock in to his environment friendly bag and set off up the hill.

Striding up the lane his heart sank at the sight of the police officer from earlier approaching on his bike. He didn't look any more pleased to see Nick than he had the first time, making him feel like he actually had slipped into a life-on-a-loop time warp. Mervin braked to a halt eyes glued on Nick like he was the prime suspect in a crime drama.

'What have we here then?'

'Provisions. Champagne and dog shampoo – and a few other things.'

'Ophelia up to her old tricks?'

'She got quite muddy. After it rained.'

The policeman coughed. 'Is that ... er?'

'Bird crap on my head. Yep.'

'Lucky you got that shampoo!'

The policeman chuckled at his own joke and Nick couldn't help but warm to him ever so slightly. 'So if you'll excuse me?' he said, smiling.

Wait.' Mervin evidently had something important on his mind. 'So. Layla. She's had a setback.'

'I know that.'

Mervin shot him a steely look. 'It's nobody's business but hers.'

Nick nodded solemnly. 'I totally agree.'

'Keep it in mind,' he warned. 'There are only so many let-downs that girl can take. She hides it well and things might look fine on the surface, but underneath Layla's been hurt.' He stopped, then added. 'Look I don't want to be rude but I'm going to come right out and say it. It's well known that you're not a reliable type.'

'Okay. Right.' He straightened his shoulders in an effort to look less dodgy than he felt. He felt like an idiot schoolboy caught red-handed about to prank the teacher. 'I'll keep that in mind.'

'Make sure you do.' He eyed the shopping bag suspiciously. Nick shouldn't have mentioned the champagne. He'd bought it to leave in the fridge as a thank you for putting him up, but it probably sounded to Mervin like he planned to take advantage of her. 'She's well-liked. People round here are gutted seeing her upset. And I don't want some fly-by-night making things worse.'

'You don't trust me. I get that, but ...'

'No offence. You seem nice enough. But you don't need to be a psychic to work out why I'm sceptical.' With that he pedalled off down the lane on his bicycle.

Nick attempted a friendly wave and called after him. 'There's no need to worry. I promise. I'm not here to cause trouble.'

Chapter Six

Nick knocked on Layla's door, hoping she'd open up quickly before he met any more knights-in-shining-armour types.

'I picked up some shampoo for your canine friend,' he said as the door swung open. He ducked so as not to bang his head on the lintel, and stepped straight into the cottage's living room. A soaking wet Ophelia ran in from the kitchen and shook herself, showering his legs with cold water. 'I guess you've got it covered.'

'I gave her a hose down outside. Thanks, anyway.' Layla's smiling eyes were a sparkling contrast to the dog's uncer-emonious welcome. She was wearing a promotional top with Kandy Shack emblazoned on it. Its bright, psychedelic colours had a distinctly retro vibe, and, heaven help him, thanks to having bathed Ophelia it looked like she'd entered a wet tee shirt competition. From this angle, and if he was the judge, she'd definitely take first prize. No contest.

'On what planet did I think keeping my head down in Porthkara would be a great plan?'

'On that holding planet you mentioned?' Layla smirked. He put his hand to his head and pulled a face. 'Crikey! What happened?'

'I've practically been run out of town by that over-protective policeman. He told me in no uncertain terms that he thinks I'm bad news.'

Settling in her basket in the corner, Ophelia hid her muzzle under both paws.

'Don't pay any attention to Mervin. He means well. He's dedicated. And quite friendly really.'

'I can't say I've noticed.'

'He's not had an easy time of it. He transferred here after his wife passed away. Made a new start.'

Nick winced. 'I think it's safe to say he's not my biggest fan. As if being told I'm an undesirable isn't bad enough, I've also been crapped on by a stupid bird.'

She giggled. 'Do you think it was in cahoots with Mervin?'

'The way that magpie was watching me I wouldn't be surprised. I bet he's trained it to target undesirables.'

'You're many things Nick but undesirable isn't one of them.' She flashed a flirtatious glance his way. 'A magpie? That's bad luck.'

'You're telling me.'

Feeling oddly self-conscious, he touched his head and felt a twig tangled in his hair. Layla reached up and untangled it.

'No. I mean that's really bad luck!' She sounded pessimistic. She rummaged under the sink and pulled out a yellow pack of lemon scented kitchen wipes. 'Was there only one?'

'I think so. Why?'

'One for sorrow, two for joy, three for a girl, four for a boy, five for silver, six for gold, seven for a secret never to be told.'

'I have no clue what you're talking about, but I think I wish I'd seen seven.'

'Then again, maybe not,' Layla couldn't control her giggles. Again. 'Imagine the mess seven would have made.' She dabbed at his hair. He lowered his head so she could reach. 'Two would have been better, though. Think, Nick. Are you sure it was only one?'

He wanted to tell her two because clearly it mattered to her, a lot. He shook his head. 'I can't lie. There was only one magpie.'

She gave a heartfelt sigh. 'Hold still, I think I've got most of it out. But you might want to take another shower just in case.' She put her foot on the pedal bin and the lid popped open so she could chuck the wipe in. Turning her back to him she walked to the sink and turned on the tap to wash her hands.

Nick opened the bag and set a bright orange flower in a little black plastic pot on the kitchen counter. He opened the fridge and stowed the champagne and the rest of his shopping.

'There's something we – you – need to do.' He set the lovelock on the draining board.

Layla turned off the tap and glared at it, poker-faced, as if he'd brought something unbelievably unpleasant into her kitchen. 'Magpies like shiny things.' She pointed at the lock. 'Maybe it liked that. Well, it's welcome to it. I don't want it.' She glanced away as if it was hurting her eyes and spotted the plant. 'Why did you buy a marigold?'

'It's a moving-on flower.'

'There's no such thing.' There was something about her that sparked off him. Her eyes flashed.

'There is now. I invented it.'

'What the heck use is a moving-on flower?' she scoffed. 'What am I supposed to do with it? Make the petals into tea and drink it for my wounded heart?'

'Just plant it is all.'

Ophelia pottered into the kitchen, lapped at her water bowl, and returned to settle herself in her basket in the living room.

Nick was a breath of fresh air. He'd blown into the village

on the wind, like he'd been sent to rescue them. And he was funny.

From Layla's kitchen, French doors led onto a small back yard. A tree and a low wall separated her yard from next door's. She'd whitewashed the walls and filled the yard with flowers in pots and a bistro table with a couple of chairs.

Avoiding the issue of what to do about the padlock now she had it, Layla wandered outside into the warm evening sun. Nick followed her holding the marigold in one hand and the embarrassing lovelock in the other.

'I was counting on a flower bed.'

'I haven't got one of those.' She made a sad face.

'Have you by any chance got an empty flowerpot?'

Nick's eagerness to plant flowers seemed bizarre but sort of sweet. The best bit about him right now was that he didn't belong in Porthkara. She pointed to a cluster of unused terracotta pots in a corner next to a half-empty bag of compost.

'Perfect.' He selected one. 'There you go.' He set his chosen pot on the ground and gave her the lock and the marigold.

'I don't think I know this game.'

'It's called "plant a flower and move on."'

'Really? Or I could just pop it in the bin.'

He shrugged. 'Work with me. It's the best solution I could

think of. I figured that since you didn't like looking at the padlock, I'd get you something you will like looking at.'

'Oh ... kay.'

'This marigold. So.' He picked up the compost bag. 'You put the lock in the bottom of the pot, you add compost, and you plant the flower. Go!' When she pouted and didn't do it, he dropped the padlock into the flowerpot. 'By next summer this flower will have made seeds and new flowers and that thing will be a rusty-but-useful piece of scrap. It's going to stop the water running straight out the bottom when you water it.'

'You know a lot about these things?'

'I spent a lot of time kicking about with gardeners and housekeepers when I was a kid. I have tips. Believe me. This big orange marigold will make you feel better.'

She wondered if all the associations she felt for the lovelock would ever go. 'It's alright for you to say. You don't have half of Porthkara giving you pitying glances, and the other half refusing to look you in the eye. Joe's gone but he's not forgotten.'

'Funnily enough, I do know how it feels to be in the spotlight when you'd really like not to be.'

'It's different. You get loads of strangers staring at you like they think they know you. The difference with me is – they do know me. And they know Joe. And everything about us, going way back.'

'Think of this as the beginning of new things.'

'That's easier said than done.'

'Trust me. Out of sight, out of mind. Burying the lock and putting something cheerful in its place is the first step to new horizons.'

She couldn't help rolling her eyes at him. 'Trust an actor to come up with something so dramatic.' She batted away her doubts like she would an annoying fly, realizing that he was right, she needed to feel like she was doing something. And hiding the lovelock in a plant pot was better than anything she could think of, so she set to work.

When she'd finished Nick hid it in amongst some other pots of flowers where Layla had to admit she'd hardly notice it. She brushed the dark crumbs of soil off her hands and sat down, closed her eyes and turned her face into the sunshine. After a few seconds of luxuriating in the sunrays she turned to Nick and opened her eyes.

'Dad swung by Maggie's earlier. The water heater's kaput. He reckons the whole thing'll need replacing.'

Nick sat down opposite her and she looked away, picking nervously at the compost under her nails, but not before a whisper of awareness hit her. She couldn't help taking in the sexy shadow of fresh stubble on his jaw and chin. She desperately didn't want to go and wash dishes at the restaurant, but they were in a bind and she didn't want to let them down. At least she wouldn't be waiting tables. She could hide in the kitchen.

Like they were on a see-saw, Layla bobbed up, though she was reluctant to drag herself away.

'He also had a bit of news. Quite the surprise really. He and his partner are expecting. They've decided to get married.'

'That's good news.' Nick hesitated. 'Right?'

'I can't quite believe it.' She snapped her lips into a jolly smile. 'Yes. Of course. Lovely. I'm going to have a sibling. Imagine that. After all these years.' She felt like she had two left feet and was trying to remember the steps to an elaborate dance. 'It's a bonanza day for wedding news. Listen. Thanks, for this. I love my moving-on flower. And you're absolutely right. By this time next year things around here are going to be all kinds of different.' She backed away from him towards the doors into the kitchen her gaze riveted to his gorgeous, curious face. 'I have to go. I've got a job to go to.'

'Another one? How many jobs have you got?'

'Too many.'

'I was going to ask you to dinner at the Lobster Pot.'

'That's sweet. But I work there, actually.' She laughed awkwardly. 'That's where I'm going now. I'm doing the washing-up shift tonight.' She wrinkled her nose apologetically. *Crikey! He wanted to ask her to dinner?* She wished

Porthkara wasn't so complicated. She placed her palms together. 'Make yourself at home.' He already had. Still, it was only polite to say so. 'Help yourself to whatever you need. We can make the bed in the spare room up for you when I get back.'

'Cool.' His wicked grin put her in a spin and her heart did an uncalled-for somersault.

Practically falling over her feet she hurried off to change, only turning to call back to him through the French windows. 'Would you mind feeding Ophelia? Her food's in the cupboard next to the washing machine. There's a scoop in the bag. She gets one. Don't let her con you into more.'

* * *

At a loose end Nick fed the dog, filled an empty wine bottle at the sink and watered the marigold before spending a while working out how to use Layla's channel changer and spending another while flicking through channels. Nothing held his attention. He watched the beginning of a movie, but quit when his mother appeared on screen in a cameo appearance he hadn't known she'd made.

Leaving Ophelia snoozing contentedly in her basket he set off to explore the path that ran up a hill behind the cottages. Having followed the path through a field carpeted with purple heather and clumps of spiny yellow gorse he climbed over a stile and found himself within feet of a wall of sheer cliffs that stretched around the bay and off into the distance. His fear of heights kicked in big time. The thought of walking any further made him ill. A weathered wooden bench sat well back from the edge so he perched on it and felt better, safely anchored.

The sun, which had been high over the sea, was slipping towards the horizon. He sat and absorbed the magnificent sundown colours, awed by the mysterious beauty of the cliffs and the sea. Across a couple of fields there was a quaint old farmhouse, and way in the distance on the far-off headland he could just see the ghostly shape of a long abandoned tin mine. It was hard to imagine anywhere more special and so far removed from his ordinary life. All he'd ever cared about was making *Mercy of the Vampires*. He'd spent large portions of the last ten years hanging out in nightclubs, often with eyebrows tweezed at a jaunty angle to suit the part of Jarvis. He'd like to blame his disastrous personal life on all that stuff, but it ran much deeper than strange-looking eyebrows and scandalous headlines.

He looked at his phone. The signal on the cliff bench was a hundred percent better than at the cottages. He took a photo of the view and texted it to Alex. Then he called him.

'How are you doing?'

'Apart from the lack of sleep I'm good. Did you speak to a lawyer? I can get you a name.'

He bristled. 'I don't want to go down that route.'

'This is hot water Nick. At least tell me you've done a paternity test.'

'It's pretty clear she's my kid.'

'So what next?'

'I talked to Fran. It's a bad situation. I'm taking it one step at a time. I don't want to go into it just at the minute. I'll let you know when I have more information.'

'How's the black eye?'

'Horrible.'

'Toni?'

'Over.'

'Porthkara?'

'Beautiful. Like an out of body experience.'

The sound of Alex's laughter on the phone lifted his mood.

'Give Layla our love. And hug Ophelia for us.'

'Sure. Are you guys coming down here anytime soon?'

'We'd love to. But we're tied up.'

The line distorted Alex's voice into a jumble of noise and cut out before Nick had time to mention that the cottage was so far off being ready that apart from the super comfy sofa it wasn't habitable.

Brimming with restless energy and sick of haranguing himself he wondered how Layla was doing. With her he'd almost forgotten that his life was falling apart. Why was someone with so much artistic talent wasting so many hours doing other things? Her schedule was as crazy as an actor's.

He checked the restaurant closing time on his phone, and set off to find her.

Outside the Lobster Pot he sat on a low wall to wait, watching the customers straggle out. Darkness had fallen, but a line of old-fashioned lamp posts dotted the seafront with pools of light. Behind him he heard the steady shushing break of waves, advancing and retreating. The tide was turning. He checked his watch hoping he hadn't missed her.

A group of chattering girls emerged. High heels. Pretty dresses. Their high style reminded him of his mother, the way she flicked through piles of fashion magazines, excited about her next new look. That was during the ups. Other times, being with her had been a chaotic nightmare. The current Cassandra Wells was unrecognizable compared to the fragile, broken woman he'd grown up with. He put it down to having a man in her life she could trust.

One of the girls sat down on the wall along from Nick. 'The taxi's late.'

'Give it five minutes.' Another of the girls sat next to her friend.

'Did you see Layla Rivers? I hate to see her looking so sad. Joe treated her like a doormat.'

A flicker of tension rolled through Nick's shoulders.

'No one deserves that. Especially not Layla.'

The rest gathered round.

'She's sweet.'

'And cool.'

'And so talented.'

Nick glanced up and down the seafront hoping for a sign of the taxi.

'Do you think she knew about Joe getting married?'

'No one did. Not even his parents.'

'Poor thing. How embarrassing!'

Nick tried to block out the snippets of conversation. And failed.

'She was as white as a sheet tonight. You'd think the last thing she'd want to do is wait tables in his mum and dad's restaurant.'

Nick's jaw clenched and his fists balled up tightly. This was Joe's parents' restaurant?

'She'd do anything for anyone. But it must be horrible for them all.'

'I heard that instead of an engagement ring he gave her one those gummy sweets. You know? The ones that come in a mix with fried eggs and little hearts! He never did get her a real one.'

'One gummy ring does not a fiancé make.' The group of girls sighed in unison.

'Apparently he promised to get down on one knee and propose for real in Paris.'

'He proposed alright. To someone else.'

'The two-faced toad!'

'I heard he was never going to take her to Paris. Even before her mum had the accident and their travel plans went wrong.'

To avoid overhearing details that made him uncomfortable Nick stood up, tense, anxious to put some extra distance between himself and the gossip.

The taxi with its neon light swung into view, and the girls on the wall got to their feet. At the same moment Layla exited the restaurant. Far from appearing frazzled she looked phenomenally attractive.

He strode out of the shadows, heading straight for his target – Layla. Before he could reach her, she was surrounded. One by one, teetering in heels, the girls wrapped her in hugs.

'You'll bounce back.'

'Onwards and upwards.'

'We're going to a club in town if you'd like to come too.'

Layla shook her head and whispered an excuse.

'Gotta get back out there.'

'Absolutely,' Layla agreed with a fixed smile. 'It's time to start looking for the man of my dreams. Just not tonight.'

Desire to see genuine happiness on her face filled some deep void in Nick. He knew his limitations, but a sensational one-off performance he could do.

'Hey!' Sudden surprise turned all the girls' heads. He stepped into the middle of the group.

'Nick?' Layla looked puzzled, but pleased. Result.

'Go with this,' he mouthed in a barely-there whisper. Seizing the moment, he pushed away the growing list of things he'd like to do better if only he could. Playing a part, he slung a casual arm across her shoulders. 'I'm the first in line to audition for dream man,' he announced.

The girls' eyes lit up.

'What the ...?' Layla uttered a faint muffled sound as she attempted to speak and Nick's lips collided with hers.

The taxi window slid open and the voice of the driver cut through the stunned silence. 'Do you people want to go into town tonight? Or will sometime in the next decade do?'

Eyes on stalks the group of girls piled into the taxi. As it moved off Nick broke the kiss. In the electrified stillness he held her gaze, his arms still tightly wrapped around her. 'I came to meet you,' he volunteered.

An irresistible smile spread to her lips. 'I'm so glad you did.'

Chapter Seven

Layla fizzed from his kiss. He'd taken her breath away. Half the village had been wrapping around her like a security blanket. Now she had Nick Wells wrapped around her and ... he felt great.

Suddenly he was kissing her again, this time for real, and she was kissing him back. Buttoned down emotions bubbled inside her. Eclipsed by Nick, for a few fabulous moments Porthkara vanished. The delicious oblivion of physical heat blotted everything out. Her curves molded against his chest as he held her tight in his arms, strong and gorgeous. Beautiful sensations danced in her veins. His kiss had sent her into free fall. It felt unbelievably good – and kind of unsafe. Nothing like Nick had happened to her before. He pulled her closer. Heat and desire crashed together like two waves approaching the shore from opposing angles, a world of temptation condensed in his kiss.

She didn't know how he'd got it so right. He just had. In a single moment he'd taken her pain away, and given her hope that her pitiful humiliation would heal.

'Friends?' Nick's question cut through the electric current.

'We went to the same school. One of them's Rosie, the owner of the chip shop. I know her quite well. We don't hang out much. Mostly I'm too busy.' She paused pulling back from the edge of danger, realizing that something must have been said to instigate Nick's award worthy performance. 'Why?'

Nick shrugged. 'They reckoned working at Joe's family restaurant must be hard on you. You kept that quiet!'

'News spreads like a rash in a little place like this.' She bit her lip. It had been the most excruciating evening of her life. She'd been all too aware of the tipsy group and the whisperings at their table.

'Why put yourself through that?'

She sighed. 'I can't just resign. And they won't give me the sack – even if they'd like to. One of the waitresses was a no-show because her child was sick, so I doubled up and waited tables as well as washing dishes.' When Nick didn't speak, she added, 'What else was I supposed to do? They're practically family.' Her voice trailed off. 'At any rate, they nearly were ...'

He took hold of her hand, his smooth palm and his

fingers interlaced with hers. She felt small next to his tall masculine height, in a good way, not weak and pathetic – turning up when he did, he'd given her strength.

'You and I need to get our priorities straight. For starters quit working at the Lobster Pot. That way you can focus more on what you're good at. Your artwork in the nursery is awesome.'

'I've barely started.'

'I know. That's because you've hardly any time to focus.'

'Point taken. Every one of those girls is either married, or getting married, shacked up, knocked up, or both. There isn't a single one who hasn't got her life on track. Careers. Businesses. Kids. I feel like I got stuck in time and I can't move forward.'

'That makes two of us.'

The rumble of Nick's voice did things to her. Things that made her feel like nothing mattered as much as being held tight in his arms and kissed into a frenzy of deliciousness. Heading towards home, chemistry brewed intensely between them. Instead of being dead on her feet she felt like she'd grown wings. With very little effort she'd probably fly up the hill.

At the bridge over the silvery stream he stopped and pulled her into his arms again. There was a sky full of stars and spatters of moonlight danced around their feet, the pattern of light and shade shifting with the movement of the leaves and the branches of the trees rustling above them in the gentle summer breeze. His lips brushed hers and she kissed him back with a longing so fiery, deep, and urgent that her feelings completely overwhelmed her. Their mouths moved in synchronicity as they lost themselves in each other, wordlessly spelling out desire. Finally she broke away from the spell of his incredible charisma. Fingers tightly laced with his he drew her with him into the deepening darkness hurrying silently past all the village houses with their lit windows.

A black cat shot out from beneath the gate of a cottage garden. The moment the cat saw them, hackles raised and green eyes wide, it arched its back, legs stretched tall like built-in stilts. Layla jumped, almost as startled as the cat.

'That's good luck.'

He fired her a disarming sideways glance. 'I don't see how. We gave it a fright and it made you jump.'

'Well, in some places a black cat crossing your path is bad luck. But not here.'

'You learned the superstition handbook off by heart?'

His mid-Atlantic accent triggered tingles in her spine. She shook her head as the cat slunk between two parked cars. 'I like lucky things,' she said brightly, 'But if you believe in good luck you can't ignore the bad luck stuff. I mean I'd hate to break a mirror, wouldn't you?'

'It's not something I really think about.'

'A broken mirror is seven years bad luck.'

'You can take a thing too far.' His eyes shone, full of intrigue, compelling, drawing her right in.

They were still holding hands and there was no one here, no one to convince that she was over Joe. It was clear that it wasn't about that any more, the energy from Nick's touch crackled in her veins.

'I want to set up a business, buy a van, design a logo, get a website. I've got lots of ideas. It won't just be nursery murals. I want to decorate all kinds of play spaces. And run workshops.' She stopped talking abruptly, finally adding, 'That's the plan. It might even happen – some day. I've been saving for a long time. I'm pretty much there, to be honest.'

'So what's stopping you?'

'I'm waiting for the time to be right.'

'You can't wait forever.'

'When you put it like that ...' She paused and pushed a strand of unruly hair behind one ear with her free hand. '... Things have been a bit unsettled.'

'Go for it. Do what you really love. Start by quitting the restaurant. It's making you unhappy.'

She could while away hours painting and it didn't feel like work. Her other jobs were getting in the way. Since Joe went away without her she'd had the perfect chance to make her own plans happen. Instead she felt tied to helping out the people who loved her, doing jobs she'd outgrown.

'You know what? You're right. Starting tomorrow, I'm getting my life straight.'

'This is starting to sound a lot like something to celebrate.' Nick drawled his words with a charm that sent tingles fizzing through her system all over again.

At the cottage he went to the fridge and took out a bottle of champagne.

'How did that get in there?'

'Guilty.' He ripped off the gold foil. 'I snuck it in to leave as a thank you for letting me stay. But since we're celebrating ...'

'We are?'

'Certainly.' He twisted the bottle with the skill of a sommelier and popped the cork without a single drop bubbling over.

She wrinkled her nose and rummaged at the back of a kitchen cupboard to produce two vintage champagne glasses she'd found at a car boot sale. Intrigued by the unfamiliarity of Nick she watched him pour the champagne, his electric energy far outside her comfort zone. She clutched the glass he handed her and sipped the champagne, unnerved by this too-good-to-be-true invasion of her space but certain that she'd been in denial for months and she was ready to reboot her life.

She clinked her glass to his. 'A toast,' she breathed in a whispery voice she hardly recognized. 'To flowers, and new beginnings.' She flashed him a brazen look. 'And things.'

'And things?' His eyes twinkled. 'To "And things!"'

He opened the door and she followed him to the seats outside. She struck a match to light a candle in an empty wine bottle on the table. In the flickering shadows his distracting face looked even more attractive than it had before he'd kissed her. Clouds drifted across the sky playing hide and seek with the smattering of stars and the pale moon. A single streak of wax dripped from the candle and spilled down the side of the bottle solidifying against the cool green glass.

'Thanks for tonight,' she whispered, hardly believing that she was sipping expensive champagne under a moonlit sky with this fabulous guy, and that she was thanking him for kissing her.

His delectable lips quirked into that smile. 'You're welcome.'

Layla knocked back a slug of the bubbles, drinking like it like lemonade. 'Last night, before you arrived, after Joe's explosion of happiness on the internet I felt as if I'd taken a bucket and spade down to the beach, dug up my buried emotions and put them on display for everybody to examine. I was suffocating.'

'What happened with you guys?'

'I don't really know.' She didn't feel like explaining. 'Let's not spoil things. I'd rather not rake it up.'

'Maybe Mexico's like Las Vegas. Perhaps he got very drunk, and woke up the next morning to find he'd said "I do" by mistake.'

Layla swallowed some more champagne. She pushed a hand into her hair and ran it through to the ends. 'And he doesn't remember a thing about it? It would serve him right!' She appreciated the comic take but gut instinct told her it hadn't happened that way. The photographs depicted a different story. The dress. The cake. Joe's wedding might have been spontaneous, but not falling-down-drunk-don't-know-how-it-happened spontaneous.

She smiled. Something had changed. Joe was in a place labeled 'The Past'. Staying stuck in a stale relationship because it felt easier than striking out on her own had been her default setting. Joe had done the right thing the wrong way. He'd made the break for both of them.

Totally in the moment she looked at Nick, transfixed, craving more of his heat, his touch, his body close to hers. She tore her eyes away and fixed on a line of bubbles in her glass rising and vanishing.

'I hope he's happy,' she said, picking up the bottle of fizz and topping up their glasses.

'You'll be happy too. You just aren't meant to be happy together.'

Nick's statement was blunt, but accurate.

'Right.'

'I shouldn't have worn green to Maggie's wedding. I very nearly refused. I had serious doubts. I didn't want to bring any bad luck on Maggie and Alex. At the end of the day I'm the one that got unlucky. Maggie laughed it off. She chose green because it was Christmas Eve. And it's top of my colour chart. The problem is she doesn't take my superstitious tendencies terribly seriously. At least not the bad luck stuff.'

'Green at weddings? Magpies?' He held up a hand like he was begging her to stop. 'I like you a lot Layla, but do you think it's possible that you take this superstition thing of yours to an unhealthy level?'

'It's easier to blame bad luck than face facts. We were in a rut. A trip around the world wouldn't have fixed it.' She jingled her bracelet. The antique gold gleamed in the candlelight. 'These are my lucky charms. From now on I'm only into the good stuff.'

'No more counting magpies?'

'That might be a stretch.' She gave a little shrug. 'I'm not making any promises, but I'll try.'

He reached across the table, took her wrist in his hand and ran his finger over the pulse point. The way he made her feel felt like some sort of wizardry. 'If you ask me, which I know you didn't,' he said. 'We make our own luck.'

'Nick?' Newly spontaneous, she breathed his name.

'Yes?' He hit her with the full dazzling force of his eyes. His lips twisted into a seductive half-smile and she buzzed with the urge to take a risk. His smile and his smouldering gaze were full of possibility. She dived head-long into the fizz-popping chemistry between them.

'Do you get propositioned much? You know, by women wanting mind-blowing sex?'

He leaned back in his chair, 'I'd say that's the champagne talking.'

'No, it isn't.' She paused, assessing his comment, her neglected inner flirt unleashed. 'Well, it is. But I'm not legless. Or anything. Answer me.'

He forked a hand through his hair, sexy as hell and pulled a mock sorry-for-himself face. 'Tough gig, right?

His eyes played with hers in the shadowy light and sweet heat spiralled through her. She couldn't throw herself at him. Could she? She blew out the candle and stood up, ready to go look for fresh sheets to make up his bed. Picking up the bottle he followed her into the kitchen.

'We're not so very different, you and me. We've both got pasts to bury.' His drawl murmured against her ear. Her heart banged against her ribs as his arms closed around her pulling her against him, her curves molded to his muscles. His heightening desire was unmistakable, his erection pressed against her tightly. Desire bubbled through her, his breath hot on her neck.

'I'm learning to live in the moment,' she whispered.

'That's what I do best.'

Locked in the circle of his arms, her breasts jutted, taut and aching to feel the blaze of his skin on hers. 'What do you want?'

'One night of amazing ... hot ... you.' His hands slipped beneath her top, smoothing over her back, drawing her impossibly closer. 'You?'

She moaned. 'Same.' She tipped her head to meet his and his mouth crashed with hers, soft and strong, possessing her with his demanding kiss. She'd stopped looking back, and she wanted him, so raw she'd topple with him into a sea of dangerous.

Chapter Eight

Nick could set off fireworks with just his smile. The full onslaught of his hot, heavenly body left her both powerless, and empowered. Her bones melted, the fuses of her mind blown, the future lay ahead full of possibility. Nick had done that. He'd turned everything on its head contorting her emotions into something resembling plastic that had been heated too long in the microwave.

She swayed against him with can't-wait-a-second urgency as if at any moment her knees might stop working and the only thing stopping gravity from dropping her onto the kitchen tiles in a crumpled heap was his strong arms, locked around her. She reeled, realizing that everything she felt was mirrored in his eyes, his lips, his urgent hunger. He wanted her as badly as she needed him. It was a powerful feeling, and it filled her with a surge of sexual confidence.

She kissed him back, wild with desire. He picked her

up and somehow she wrapped her out-of-control limbs around his body of rock. He carried her from the kitchen to the foot of the stairs and set her on her unsteady feet. In a raging fire of kisses they brushed and bumped the wall on the narrow staircase as she led him upstairs. The door to the bedroom banged against the wall as she pushed it open in a hurry.

Her eyes adjusted to the dark and she touched his face, smoothing over the hard contour of his jaw, feeling the prickle of stubble under her hands. In one impressive move, his hand slid up her back and he unclasped her bra and peeled it from her along with her top. His t-shirt went next, discarded on the floor. Breasts pressed to his chest, the contact of skin on skin gave her a pleasure rush. His fingers skimmed over her curves, smooth and feather-light one moment, deeply firm the next. Her nipples jutted, wanton with desire to be taken in his mouth.

She gave a high-pitched squeal as he scooped her into his arms and laid her down on the bed beneath him, straddling her with strong legs and cupping her breasts in his hands.

His lips touched her breast and swirls of dreamy Nick-induced sensation rippled through her, giving way to smouldering ecstasy, intensifying at her core. She responded instinctively when his mouth on her nipple triggered wild pleasure that spun through every atom of her body. His hand moved slowly down over her stomach, lower and lower until he was unbuttoning her jeans, undoing the zip, sliding beneath her underwear, gently caressing and teasing, slipping inside her, tormenting her body with white heat. She writhed and pressed her hand to his to stop his taunting fingers.

'I need to see you.' He reached to switch on the bedside lamp and soft light glowed in the room. He pulled her tight black skinny jeans down her legs turning them inside out as they went, throwing them across the room in his hurry to have her naked.

'You too,' she urged, unbuckling his belt and feeling the push of his erection encased in tight denim beneath her hand. He helped, stripping with ease. The irresistibility factor of totally naked Nick was off the charts. She pressed the palm of one hand to his thigh, crazed with desire for his hardness inside her.

Pupils hotly dilated, his eyes gleamed. Light golden brown at the centre with dark rims, they burned into her heart.

He kissed her mouth softly and emotion grew inside her, fragile like a shimmering, wobbly soap bubble. He'd got inside her head, and she'd revealed her feelings to him with unfamiliar openness. It was hard to think cool when he was so smoking hot. She'd rushed headlong towards a place that was purely physical fantasy, and he'd read her with an intuition that made her head spin and her heart soar.

Breaking the kiss, Nick pulled away. 'Wait,' he rasped, fighting their impatience. 'We need a condom.'

'I haven't got any.'

'Me neither.'

'How come? Don't international playboys come equipped with protection?' Her trepidation fluttered from her lips in a volley of snarky words that she couldn't take back.

'I thought you'd realized I'm not so much the playboy.' His mouth twisted up in that signature smile. 'And, no, I don't carry condoms at all times.' Her heart dipped like she was riding a roller coaster heading perpetually into a fall, and they untangled in a difficult pause. 'Note to self, I need to fix that.'

'Hang on a minute.' Hope dawned. 'I just remembered. I think I might have one.'

'Yay.' He rolled onto his side, head propped up with one elbow, a full-blown mockingly lazy smile on his face. 'Where is it?'

She rolled off the bed and scurried into the bathroom. Her kiss-stung lips and smudged eyeliner struck her as she opened the mirrored door of the bathroom cabinet.

She realized that it wasn't too late to stop, that something so physically and emotionally potent could have a potential downside – more hurt. But she was in an exhilarating danger zone, over-powered by her own desire to spend the night with him, and it was much too good to back out now.

She rummaged in a fluster, lighting on the long-forgotten condom, a goody bag gift at Rosie's hen night five years ago. She picked up the foil pack and returned to the bedroom.

She slid her knickers down her thighs as she went, kicking them into a corner and crossing her fingers that in the dim light Nick hadn't noticed that they were turquoise with little purple wide-eyed owls all over them. The day she bought them the checkout lady's eyebrows had been judgmentally raised, the unspoken inference clearly that a woman of Layla's advanced twenty-nine years should think twice about purchasing cute motif undies. Back then she hadn't expected to be requiring sexy lingerie anytime soon. She winced. They'd been on a 'buy one get one free' deal, so she had two pairs of owl print undies in different colours.

Who cared about the state of her underwear? Going by his erection, not Nick. Back in the bedroom, astonishingly, it hadn't died. He lay on his back, and she straddled him, kissing him hotly. She took him in her hand and ran her fingers over him, tightening around his silkiness, marveling at the perfect contradiction of soft skin and hard man. Super-aroused, he groaned from deep in his throat. With the fumbling fingers of one hand she attempted to open the condom. He took it from her, opened it with ease, and unrolled it over his length turning his erection green.

'What the blazes? That's got to be the worst condom ever.'

'It's all we've got.' She bit down on her lip. 'I didn't buy it, or anything. I ...'

'Another long story?'

'Sort of. There was a hen party. And goody bags. And an assorted pack of rainbow condoms. We got one each.'

'And you got green?'

'Unlucky.' Still biting her lip, she worked hard to contain her laughter. 'I guess that's why it never got used. I mean resembling an unripe banana has got to be the worst turn-off ever.' She pulled a face, and stifled the burgeoning fit of the giggles. 'It's not exactly a good look.'

Nick let out a rapturous groan and in one swift move rolled her under him so that he'd flipped her onto her back, and pinned her softly to the bed with his beautiful body. 'Let's put that to the test, shall we?'

She inhaled the scent of his skin. He was breathtakingly intense. He'd tapped into her feelings and amazingly she trusted him. She twined her fingers into the hair at the back of his neck, drawing him close, and then relaxed her hold to smooth her hands over his perfectly-honed pecs. His tip pressed erotically, tantalizingly just outside of her, sending her crazy with need. The intoxicating heat of the moment whirled her emotions into a confusion of desire and delight. She was utterly, deeply, madly in lust. In Nick's hands, every inch of her body was an erogenous zone, every second pleasure-filled.

The temptation to do this crazy fast was immense. But she felt so real, he ached to take it slow and make it last, lock her in his hold, and just be. He tangled his fingers in her hair, which was cherry red in the low light.

'Layla, you're gorgeous.' He rasped out the words. 'But I'm not looking for a relationship. I'm not a forever guy.'

He hesitated, struck by the need to know he couldn't hurt her.

'I don't care about forever. I want now. I want a fling.' Sexy mouth, voluptuous breasts, soft curves, silky skin, enticingly, guilelessly provocative, her breathless gasps drew him in. 'Don't overthink this,' she whispered. Deep want burned in her dark eyes. 'It's a heat of the moment thing.'

She couldn't have made things any clearer. 'Heat of the moment, I can deliver.' Taking it slow, he trailed a hand the length of her thigh. She captivated him. When she wrapped herself around him, he closed out everything he didn't know how to deal with, and focused on making her happy.

Long and slow, he controlled his urge to thrust deep

inside her. His eyes on hers, his hands cupped her face, and he kissed her, lingering, incapable of breaking apart for a single second. She let out a soft moan turning him on so much that finally, unable to hold back a micro-second longer, he entered her, moving with rhythmic strokes, decoding her responses by instinct like it was in his DNA to be deeply joined with her, body and mind, innately in tune. All his intended subtlety fell away in a fusion of passion.

Deep in ecstatic oblivion he moved inside her, feeling her tight around him, wet, hot. Their bodies seared together like a work of art, living breathing melded metal, an insane moment of oneness. He took her higher and higher, and she moaned again, louder this time, more demanding, her responses echoing his, his body following hers. He rocked into her and she matched the rhythm, the motion intensifying everything he wanted her to feel. She shattered around him and his pleasure couldn't have been any more intense. In virtually the same split second she took him with her, his climax awesome.

His red hot energy far from extinguished, for a moment he lay, spine sinking into the soft bed, neck stretched against the pillows. Head turned away from her, he stared fixedly at a painting on the wall. A white house, on a cliff, under a mackerel sky, its combination of vibrant colours and subtler tones intrigued him. Overwhelming emotion strangled him. The only happiness he could bring a woman was physical, fleeting and shallow. That didn't feel good any more. It felt so awful, it hurt.

The memory of the lurid green condom jolted him out of his pain and he reacted speedily to dispose of the vile thing, swinging his legs off the bed and heading for the bathroom. When he returned Layla had slipped beneath the covers and drifted off to sleep. Uncertainty swamped him, tensing every limb. What now? Did he go in search of bed linen and make up the bed in the spare room? Would that be rude? Did it matter?

It had been so long since he'd experienced anything close to Layla's brand of blow-your-mind sex he didn't know quite what to do. She was a first. Nothing – no one – like her had snuck past his barriers before. There was no precedent, so he switched out the light and slipped into bed beside her, his body sinking willingly into the softness. She gently moaned and hesitantly he reached out and gathered her in close, his chin resting on top of her silken hair. The warmth of her body next to his radiated through him. Stirring, she shifted slightly as she slept.

'Sleep, Layla, sleep.' Soft against his chest, her scent of sweetness, summer and sex filtered into his senses. Fighting sleep, holding her in his arms, he battled emotions that she'd thrown a spotlight on. Torn between wanting to go with the flow and needing to keep his distance, he felt buzzed, high on her energy, amazed that such fabulous fling material had materialized when he least expected it.

Chapter Nine

Last night has to have been the best take-me-I'm-yours moment of my life!

Layla woke up early to the sound of birdsong. She came to, gliding slowly into consciousness, total recall spinning her mind back to the place she'd been just before she fell asleep. Wave after wave of sublime sensation had washed over her body until she'd felt like he'd drowned her in pleasure. The fact was she'd never experienced anything like last night before.

The muddle of new emotions in her heart sank beneath a new complication – tangled limbs. Nick's delectable body held hers in place, gently, strongly. His stubble spiked her skin, heightening her awareness of his firm, masculine form, every muscle defined and perfect. The rough hair of one leg grazed deliciously against her thigh. Wrapped in his arms, against the perfect cocoon of his body, she'd never felt so naked, so deeply exposed in every sense.

'I need space.' She voiced her thought in a barely there whisper.

A blackbird chirruped. Slipping Houdini-like from Nick's hold, she tweaked the corner of one curtain, careful not to disturb either the sleeping man or the songbird. Outside her window it perched in the tree which separated her yard from Maggie's, and blasted the world with its call. The feast of colourful flowerpots below captured her attention. Somewhere amongst the petunias and geraniums there was an orange marigold and with it not just the buried past but her shining future.

The sky blazed red in the growing light. That wasn't good. Red sky in morning sailor's warning. She felt bad for the holidaymakers. Most likely there'd be rain on the way.

The house was silent apart from the soft sound of Nick's breathing. She crept to the bathroom, taking care not to step on any creaky floorboards. It was no different from any other morning. Except it was. His sexy sexiness had fried her brain.

After a quick shower, she scribbled a note on the back of a scrap of sample wallpaper. She slipped into the bedroom and placed the note in the dent her head had left on the pillow next to him. Closing the door carefully, so as not to wake him, she scooted off to her mother's guest house to help with breakfast.

113

Layla and her mum worked together like a well-oiled machine. She took orders and delivered pots of tea and coffee along with toast and smiles, whilst her mother rustled up full English breakfasts.

There was barely a moment to talk as she fluttered around the room with plates of bacon and scrambled eggs, ensuring that everything ran like clockwork. The B&B had only reopened a month ago, following her mother's accident. Reviews had been great, and she didn't want anyone giving them a bad one, not if she could help it.

After the last of the guests had set off for a day out, they cleared the tables in the dining room, bundling the tablecloths into a laundry bag and setting out fresh ones ready for the following day and the next round of breakfasts.

'A little bird told me you've got company at the cottage.'

Layla gulped, astonished that her mum would rather talk about Nick than the news that her dad and Jasmine were having a baby.

'Isn't he getting in the way? A man under your feet must be the last thing you need.'

'No-o,' she said, aiming to sound nonchalant, and feeling far from it. 'Nick's not a problem. Actually, he's been quite helpful. He helped me shift furniture. And things.'

Her mother frowned. 'He's not as nice as Alex. If the rumours are anything to go by, he's a bit of a one.'

'What are you saying, Mum?' She walked to the French windows, and flung them open to let in some air. Acting casual she tore up a leftover slice of toast and tossed the bits into the garden for the birds.

'I'm saying that he's got a reputation for being a player, so be careful!'

'Mother!'

'You've had a bad experience with Joe.' Shelly busied herself arranging salt and pepper pots, and adding sachets of calorie-free sweetener to the sugar bowls. 'I don't want some Hollywood Romeo taking advantage of you when you're on the rebound.'

'I'm a big girl. I can look out for myself.' She held back from observing that in the twenty-first century mutual-advantage-taking was a thing. 'I'm not on the rebound. I finished with Joe. It ended badly between us and I didn't tell anyone. The point is he's free. So nobody should feel bad about him marrying someone else.'

'Oh Layla, sweetheart.' Her mother folded her into a hug. 'You should have said.'

'I know that now.'

If her mother was shocked, it didn't show. Years of practice had fine-tuned her ability to mask her emotions.

'I should have guessed. I had an inkling that something was wrong when I came round after the accident and heard that he'd gone to Australia without you. I didn't want to pry. To be honest I felt responsible for him leaving and you having to stay behind.'

'You're not responsible for the choice Joe made. He is.' It dawned on her how infernally inconsiderate he had been. He'd set off when she needed him most. She'd been protecting him all this time, and he didn't deserve it. She'd also been protecting everyone else, and bottling up her feelings. 'He wanted ...' She made air quotes and pulled a sarcastic face. 'A *temporary break* until I could go out and join him, and I wasn't up for that, so I ended it. Only he didn't reply to my text, and I kept quiet about it.' She rolled her eyes. 'Evidently the message got through.'

'Would you like me to speak to his parents?' Shelly unnecessarily moved a sweetener sachet from one sugar bowl to another.

Layla kissed her mum lightly on the cheek. 'I'll talk to them myself. The atmosphere last night at the Lobster Pot was terrible. I need to clear the air.'

Shelly squeezed her hand. She glanced at her watch. 'I have to do a cash and carry run. If I go now, I should be back in time to do the afternoon shift at the kiosk. Are you still okay to work this morning?'

'Yes of course.' Paranoia about her night with Nick kicked in. 'Why wouldn't I be?'

'I don't like monopolizing you. I know how important painting is to you.' Shelly gave her daughter a pinched, apologetic smile. 'If I wasn't being so stubborn about rethinking the Kandy Shack, you'd have more time to do your own thing.'

'I fit it in when I can.' Following her mother into the kitchen, Layla waited while the older woman grabbed her phone and searched around for her car keys. Spotting them hidden behind a bowl of fruit, Layla passed them into her mother's hands. 'I'm fine,' she said. 'The question is how are you? Are you okay about Dad and Jasmine?'

'It's like the saying about waiting for a bus and then two come along.'

'First Joe. Then Dad. It's a lot to take in.'

'And a baby on the way.'

'Are you upset?'

'I just hope someone nice comes along and it'll be your turn next.'

Layla gave an internal groan. The subject hop was intentional and typical. Instead of discussing Ralph's announcement her mother had turned the conversation back to spotlighting Layla. A frivolous urge to reassure her mother that she had no intention of sitting about waiting for a husband to arrive overtook her.

'Someone nice has come along. And the timing's perfect. He's exactly what I need. And do you want to know the best bit? He's only for now.'

Porthkara Bay looked grey. Clouds had closed in and the beach was mostly empty of tourists. The hard core surfers and a couple of dog walkers had it to themselves. She'd hardly surfed this summer. Until her dreamy night with Nick had given her a wake-up call she'd been allowing one thing after another to take over her life, because she'd given up trying to organize it any other way. Going with the flow was one thing, but letting things happen because she'd stopped caring was another. She'd been intending to do something about clearing the memory of Joe out of her cottage for months, but she hadn't got any further than putting his stuff into big black bin-bags and picking up a few decorating samples from the DIY store so that she could make a start on redecorating her own place when she finished at Maggie's.

She needed breathing space. The kiosk could wait. It was going to rain and there'd be zero demand for ice cream.

Layla changed into her wetsuit at the back of the Kandy Shack. She kept her surf board propped up against a wall in there. It was mostly decorative, since she'd barely used it recently. Joe was majorly into surfing. He'd won trophies in local competitions. She'd kept a pile of newspaper clippings from his wins. She called them his smug shots. She wasn't into competing though, she just liked to surf. Basically, although she and Joe had lots in common, they were really very different.

She leashed the surfboard to her ankle and set off down the beach, loving the sensation of sand beneath the soles of her feet. No point wishing they'd ended things differently. It was too late for that. She waded straight into the sea, waited for a lull between the waves, and paddled out. She sat straddling her board, ready to catch a break. She liked the taste of salt on her lips, and the water felt fantastic.

Wet hair messy and body energized, she left the water after about an hour and sauntered back up the beach. She'd only caught a couple of waves, but she was okay with that. Exhilarated, ready for anything, she'd made her mind up to meet the future head on. Heavy rain soaked the soft sand and the beach was deserted except for the unmistakable shape of Nick, jogging, with a soggy Ophelia bounding along at his heels.

'Hey Layla.'

The hairs on the back of her neck prickled at the sound of her own name. 'I suppose there's no point offering you a bacon sandwich and a hot chocolate?' She paused, tipping her head to look up into his welcome smile. 'What with your strict fitness routine, and all.'

Wet through – again – his t-shirt clung to his muscles. She could practically see the cogs of his brain whirring as he thought about it, tempted. He pulled a face. 'The words Paris and promo shoot come to mind, but hey ... I'll have what you're having.' He gave her an incredibly readable look. 'We've earned it.'

'A bacon sandwich won't kill you, right?'

'It won't, but my nutritionist might.'

'I won't tell anyone if you don't.'

At the back of the Kandy Shack there was a two-ring stove, a kettle and a small fridge. Layla liked to think of it as her beach hut, although to be fair mornings when she could hang out and surf and eat sandwiches instead of serving ice cream were rare.

'You own this place?' He peeled off his t-shirt and she lent him a towel. He hung it around his shoulders like a scarf but it didn't cover enough of his distracting abs to stop her thinking about how she'd spent the night pressed up against them.

'My parents. I just work here. We sell sweets, ice cream, sticks of Porthkara rock, buckets and spades, fishing nets, postcards. All that kind of thing. It used to be a fun place to work but there's been a bit of hassle since my parents' divorce. They can't agree. Dad wants to buy Mum out and put the contract for running the kiosk out to tender. Mum is having none of it. She isn't ready to let go.'

'You're stuck in the middle?'

'They both have too much to do and I take up the slack. I clean Dad's holiday lets, I help Mum at the B&B and I

Reach for the Stars

hold the fort here most days. It's a lot and at the same time it's not enough.'

'Tell them.'

'I don't want to let them down.'

'They might be okay with it. It might help them come to a decision.'

She turned her attention to frying bacon and assembling sandwiches. It took a lot of effort to concentrate on anything other than admiring his physique. Fishing a couple of tin mugs out of a cupboard, he took charge of making the hot chocolate. As they waited for the milk to heat up it felt like nothing had ever taken so long to reach boiling point.

'The kiosk's the problem. They put making a decision on hold because of my mum's accident.'

Outside the rain poured down glumly.

'Cooo-eee!' Trish, Joe's mum, appeared huddled under a see-through plastic umbrella. 'Layla, honey,' she gushed, overly enthusiastic. 'I wanted to pop by and thank you for the way you stepped in at the last minute yesterday. You're a life saver.' She shivered. 'Brr! Where's the summer gone?' Taking in Nick, her eyes filled with concern.

'You're welcome.' Layla took a deep breath. 'Trish this is Nick – Maggie's brother-in-law?'

Trish smiled but there was undisguised mistrust underneath.

121

'We're about to have hot chocolate,' Nick said charmingly. 'Would you like some?'

'I'm in a terrific rush.' The doubt on Trish's face didn't budge. She looked flustered. 'Can I have a word?'

Mind whizzing, Layla caught the telepathic tell-her-now vibes Nick was firing in her direction. She stepped outside. The sun had begun to fight off the clouds and the rain had stopped. Trish lowered her umbrella and shook it vigorously. The shower of drops splattered Ophelia. She moved out of the way and lay down with her head between her paws.

'Of course.' Layla straightened her shoulders. 'I'm glad you're here. There's something I want to say. I can't work at the restaurant anymore.'

'It's Joe, isn't it?' The colour drained from Trish's face, and she dropped her umbrella on the sand. 'He's ruined everything.' Her voice wobbled. It smarted that Joe had married a stranger he'd picked up on his travels. But processing how badly he'd hurt his parents, Layla wanted to get him on the phone and give him what for.

She gave Trish a hug. 'It's not entirely Joe,' she said. 'If it's any help I saw a card in the post office window, someone looking for casual work. Her name's Emily. She might be a good replacement.'

Joe's mother gave a sigh that tugged at Layla's heartstrings. 'You don't have to quit,' she said softly. 'We can work something out. I thought you liked the work, with you needing to put money away.'

'I do. I did.' Layla shook her head. 'I'm going to concentrate on painting. The truth is we should have had this conversation months ago. I've been in limbo. Mum's accident was a line in the sand. Joe asked to be on a break and I wasn't happy.' Shades of confusion flitted across Trish's face. 'I'm kicking myself. I'm ashamed that neither of us bothered to put the people who care about us in the picture. I ended it the day he left for the airport without me. He didn't text back. And I haven't heard from him since. Not directly.' Her heart squeezed at the strain on Trish's face. 'I should have told you. I'm sorry.'

She'd wanted Joe to react to her text, come home, say sorry. He'd left profound disappointment in her heart and she hadn't been ready to accept that there was no way they'd be getting back together.

Trish grasped Layla's arm as if she wanted to hold onto her and never let go. 'He's made a stupid mistake. He shouldn't have gone. You needed him to stand by you. His dad's seething. I've never seen him so cross.'

Layla couldn't quite bring herself to free her arm from Trish's grip. 'He shouldn't be upset. Joe and I just weren't meant to be together forever.'

'He phoned late last night. It's the first we've heard from him.' Trish let go of Layla's arm and rolled her eyes skyward.

'He's run out of money. He's coming home soon. He's bringing Lainy to meet us. He wants a party at the restaurant. To celebrate.' She paused, on the verge of tears. 'You take care of yourself. If you change your mind, you know where we are.'

As she turned and walked away, shoulders hunched, Layla noticed the forgotten umbrella. She picked it up and ran to catch her up.

Trish shook her head in exasperation as she took the umbrella.

'Promise me you won't be a stranger Layla. If there's anything you need, you only have to ask.'

'Thanks.' She smiled awkwardly. She opened her mouth to say something more, realized there was nothing more to say and hurried off across the beach as fast as her feet would carry her.

Back at the shack Nick had finished making the hot chocolate. Layla took the mug he held out to her and inhaled the deliciously sweet smell.

'How much did you hear?'

'Some. Not all. Are you okay?'

'I've been better. He's coming home.' She felt as brittle as a bright pink stick of seaside rock; as if someone snapped her in two there'd be a seam spelling out her pent up feelings running right through her middle. *Rejected. Hurt. In denial.*

'When?'

'Soon. Trish didn't say exactly.' She blew on her hot chocolate waiting for it to cool. Now that the sun had come out people had begun to straggle onto the beach.

'I'd better stop lazing about and get things set up. Don't feel you have to hang around,' she told Nick. 'I know I offered you a bed, but you're welcome to come and go as you please.'

He gave her one of his looks, felling her with his burning eyes and that very sexy grin. Biting into his bacon sandwich he said, 'I think I'll stick with you. I like it here.'

Chapter Ten

'What in the name of Cornish pixies ...? Look at this.'

Layla's mother had given her a bundle of newspapers and magazines to use to catch paint drips. She opened one and whose face should greet her but Nick's.

He'd dusted off the coffee machine and grinder in Maggie's kitchen and bought some beans. The enticing smell of fresh coffee filtered through the house, mingling with sea air from the open windows, and a hint of paint.

As he stood in the doorway holding two mugs of coffee, she was doing her best to avoid the distraction of his very kissable lips. The corners creased and he smiled as she took her mug from his hand. She was getting too used to being the subject of that cracking smile. She'd been living in the moment since he'd arrived and one amazing night had turned into one more and then another and another and another.

'What?'

She'd reacted spontaneously when she'd spotted his picture. Taking in the gist of the article she wished she hadn't said anything.

'Nothing.' She shook her head, turning the mag over to put the page she'd been looking at face down on the floor.

He stole a kiss and took it deftly from her fingers. 'Let me see.' He gulped coffee and glowered at the story. 'What have they got? "*Where's Nick Wells?*"' With exaggeratedly dramatic emphasis he read out the words that had been jumping off the page. '"*While his socialite (presumably ex) royal girlfriend Toni Vanbrand flirts with her latest lover, Bertrand Flavio, former bodyguard to her father Crown Prince Ronaldo, actor Wells has vanished from the scene. Looking relaxed and happy with Flavio, now head of security at the mountaintop palace in the Principality of Monteluna, Princess Toni flashed a diamond as big as the ice cubes in her G&T onboard the family yacht in the South of France. The couple is reported to be expecting the patter of tiny feet early next year, and a private wedding ceremony at the family home is reportedly in the offing. Wells was unavailable for comment, however a close source said, 'Nick is thrilled for Princess Antonina. He wishes the couple all the best for the future.' The actor, also rumoured to have popped the question to the princess, has gone to ground after a scrap involving the enigmatic royal and a paparazzo. Here at Dazzle*

Magazine *we're wondering who's next on his alleged eligible spinster list!*"'

Picking up a small brush soaking in an old jam jar full of water, he dipped it in one of Layla's pots of non-toxic paint. He carefully painted spectacles and a moustache on the bodyguard.

'Is that true?'

'Which part?' He passed it back to her. 'I didn't ask her to marry me and there isn't a list.' Layla took the brush from his hand and painted a heart shape around the photo of the happy couple.

'I didn't think so,' she said.

'As for the wedding?' He stared without a flicker of emotion at the beautiful bride-to-be. 'It certainly looks like it.'

Layla and Nick had been having the best week. Both Trish and Shelly had hired card-in-the-window Emily. Layla had been working flat out on the mural, Nick's bruise was healing up nicely, and they'd been bonking each other's brains out. They were looking neither forward nor back.

Nervous tension prickled through her. It was none of her business. But a question had jumped into her brain, bursting to spill out of her mouth. Between sips of coffee she clamped her teeth together. It was no good. She couldn't hold back the burning question.

'You don't have to answer this.' She shrugged, acting

nonchalant. 'I mean, feel free to ignore this, but ...'

'Spit it out.'

She bristled. She was prying, the feeling too strong to contain, she couldn't help herself.

'Is there any chance that baby could be yours?' As soon as it was out she cringed at her nosiness. The atmosphere between them crackled like a lightning storm.

He ran an index finger back and forth over the furrows in between his eyebrows, then turned away from her and stared out the window at the sea beyond the rooftops like he was searching for something on the horizon.

'No,' he said darkly. After a moment of silence, he added, 'That's impossible.'

'Just saying.' Her attempt at nonchalance had failed.

'Toni and I.' There was a heavy pause. 'We were seen at parties together – but we were hardly ever together together. We didn't ...' Another pause. '... By the time we split we hadn't slept together in a long while.'

'Do you think she cheated?'

Nick shook his head. 'That's not her style. The press gets hold of a sniff of news, twist it into something it isn't and call it a story.' He paused, thoughtful. 'Toni's a party girl, but she has the greatest respect for her father. If she's getting married it won't be without his blessing. As for the baby rumour? Frankly, it's probably a fabrication. My guess is she's fallen in love.'

'So you and her weren't serious?'

'It's painful to admit this, but no, we wouldn't have led to anything meaningful. Toni flew in from Monteluna for the movie wrap party. The press pack called her my party princess and at the end of the day that's all she was. She's how I got this.' He pointed to his eye. 'There was a scrum of paparazzi outside a Paris nightclub. I'm guessing they got wind of that!' He snarled in the direction of Dazzle. 'I stepped in to protect her and got whacked in the eye by a long lens. I've no idea who the source is. Studio PR probably.'

Composing herself, thrown by the mishmash of truth and lies, Layla picked up her paintbrush.

'I'm sorry.'

'What for?'

'For being intrusive.' Whatever the facts, he clearly wanted to believe the best of his ex. 'I shouldn't have asked. I jumped to all the wrong conclusions. I feel awful.'

He placed his hand on her chin and gently turned her face up, dropping a kiss on her lips. 'You had every right.' Painful silence hung in the air. 'I did think about asking Toni to marry me. Some day. It ended without really getting started.' He turned to walk away, had second thoughts, and turned back. 'Anyway, something happened.' His voice had lost its confidence, it sounded like his words were trapped in his throat. 'Someone I knew years ago. She's going through a bad time at the moment and she got back in touch. It's complicated.'

A muscle twitched in his cheek and her heart flipped. Nick's real life had seeped into their bubble. Suppressing the question *'How complicated?'* she asked instead, 'Do you want to talk about it?'

He shook his head, his lips a thin line, zipped. Then he turned his back and marched out without a word, leaving her with an empty feeling, knowing she'd overstepped a boundary.

* * *

Hours later Nick leaned in the doorway of the nursery watching Layla paint. His face had healed sufficiently to reschedule Paris. He had a new date for the photo shoot. With a bit of luck and photo-shopping he'd pull it off. He'd kept things back from her, but he preferred not to drag her into his ugly mess unnecessarily.

Seconds before he'd seen Toni into a taxi outside that nightclub she'd air-kissed him sweetly. '*Au revoir.* Don't feel bad. I knew we wouldn't last. You aren't marriage material. It's not in your DNA.' His big stupid ego had ached to prove everyone who believed that wrong. He shared his DNA with Alex, and his brother had found forever. He never would. How could he when, in his

131

gut, he believed the rumours about him himself.

After he'd left Layla, he'd gone for a drive through sunken lanes with hedgerows full of wild flowers. On the open road he'd passed by the mysterious prehistoric standing stones that had stood on the edge of road for going back too many centuries to comprehend. He'd parked in the market square and stocked up on another bag of coffee beans and some picnic provisions at the deli.

He'd have to tear Layla away from her painting because he wanted to sound her out about Paris. Her reaction to the story about Toni grated. He'd like to deserve her trust. The flare-up of suspicion stung, not so much because of her questions, more because he hadn't been honest, he hadn't told her about Fran, and Beth. Mervin had summed him up when he'd called him unreliable.

Blanking it out, his eyes roved the seaside-themed painting. She'd blended deep sea greens and blues with lighter shades and pops of primary colours, filling the wall with waves and flowing seaweed shapes, dotted with starfish and an octopus and other fun motifs for the twins to discover.

She dabbed at the wall thoughtfully with a thin brush, absorbed, apparently unaware of Nick. Finally she stood back chewing thoughtfully on the tip of the brush and noticed him standing at the door. 'What do you think? Will Maggie and Alex like it?'

'They'll be thrilled. Blown away. They'll love it. I love it. I can see Maggie turning cartwheels of delight on the beach.'

The comment earned him a withering look.

'It's not that good. And even if it was, Maggie's never done a cartwheel in her life. The thing is ...'

He took the paintbrush from her hand and hooked an arm around her waist, drawing her close. 'What's the thing?'

'Will the twins love it?'

'The twins will turn cartwheels on the beach – in ...' He stopped to figure out at what age small kids would be capable of gymnastics. '... A few years, or so. Your work here is done.'

He kissed her, losing himself in her irresistibility and feeling the strong spike of desire, deep urgency and need that made him want to take her, right now, this minute. She kissed him back, reaching to push her fingers into his hair, and drawing his head down, molding him to her soft body, so that his brain ceased to function, thought driven out by heady arousal, the world closing in on them so that they only existed in the moment.

'I'm sorry I stormed off,' he murmured, breaking the kiss. 'I don't want to spoil this. Us!'

His fingers worked to explore the skin beneath her overalls. She wriggled and pulled away. 'I have things to finish.'

'Like what?'

'Tidying.' She bit her lip. 'And stuff.'

'Let it wait.' The kiss had left them breathless. He picked her up and she wrapped her legs around his body, hands hooked about his neck. Wanting to be inside her in that very second he half-carried, half-dragged her like a cave man out of Maggie's cottage and into her own place. Inside he closed the door behind them and pressed her hard against it, her sweet scent whirling through his senses.

His desire insatiable, all he cared about was her. She'd worked magic on him. No way was he ready to let this thing end. It damn well wasn't going to just fizzle out. He'd make sure she had a fabulous time in Paris. They'd have a blast.

He sought her lips, eager to get lost again, obliterate the brain cogs that threatened to whirr menacingly. He popped the fastenings on her overalls. They were so baggy he had no difficulty sliding them down over her thighs so that they dropped to the floor and he lifted her out of the crumpled leg holes like she'd been wearing a sack.

'I want you,' he drawled his words against her neck in a deep whisper. 'I need you.' One by one his fingers unbuttoned her shirt. 'And in the name of Cornish pixies I'm going to have you.' She spluttered out a giggle. His mouth found hers as his fingers worked to reveal the enticing lacy bra beneath the paint-splashed fabric. He pushed down the delicately patterned lace, exposed a breast and lowered his head to take the nipple in his mouth enjoying the feel of it harden beneath his tongue. With a gasp she twined her fingers in his hair and drew his head back to her mouth. Backing towards the staircase and pulling him with her she tore her lips from his.

'Not here,' she breathed.

'Yes here,' he pressed, his arms banding round her and holding her hard against him.

Kissing him long and languid, she slowed him down. He controlled his urgent need, until turning she drew him after her up the stairs. 'It's broad daylight,' she whispered. 'We need curtains.'

'And condoms,' he said, crazed by the fact that in spite of his best intentions he'd almost lost control because her sparkle had turned into something utterly overwhelming and unfamiliar.

Chapter Eleven

Later, much later, Nick and Layla and Ophelia set out for a very late lunch. She carried the picnic blanket and he had the hamper from the deli, so the dog trotted perkily at his side.

'Where to? The beach? We could walk over to the big rocks. It's less busy at that end.'

She looked at him curiously. The obvious way to get there quickly was via the cliff path which he'd so far avoided because of his problem with heights. 'Only if we take the shortcut, I'm starving, and the long way will take ages.'

He grimaced.

'How about a compromise?' Layla said. 'Picnic on the clifftop? I won't force you down the cliff-side.'

'I can't believe I'm agreeing to this, but yes, let's give it a go.'

They took the track behind the cottages and headed upwards, through the field, over the stile, past the bench

136

with the second-best view in Cornwall, along the path and through a kissing gate where the shortcut joined a small stretch of the scenic coast road. She couldn't resist pausing to kiss him. It was the most beautiful summer's day. White clouds floated across a blue sky and the calm sea, tide far out, spread out into the distance, sun glinting on the water.

'I love it here. The view from the meadow in front of the old farmhouse is bliss. The best view in Cornwall I reckon. You'll see.' As they approached the entrance to the farm Layla let out a gasp at the sight of a For Sale board by the gate. 'Oh my goodness. Cliffside House is on the market. I'd no idea.'

'It's important to you.' He spoke with a conviction that surprised her and she gave him a sideways glance. 'Your painting? In the bedroom?'

'That?' Wistful nostalgia rippled through her and a gull cried overhead. The house had belonged to the same family for generations. Her father was supposed to be distantly related to the owner. Second cousins or something. 'My grandmother was evacuated from London during the war. She was taken in by relatives who owned the farm. She grew up here.' Her heart thudded. 'It's silly really.'

'No, it's not. Tell me.'

'When I was little I used to wish that the farm would be for sale and that my mum and dad would buy it. I imagined us being a big family with sisters and brothers and a dog. That was before reality kicked in.'

Nick pointed to Ophelia, running ahead. 'Well, the dog part came true.'

'And I'm going to have a brother or sister soon. Better late than never.' She stared across the meadow at the house. 'I hope the new owners don't make too many changes. Or worse, knock it down and replace it with something slick and modern.'

After lunch they lay on the clifftop watching clouds, green grass beneath their backs, wild flowers scattered all around, not touching, but almost, nothing but the whisper of air and electricity between them. The last few days had been amazing. He wasn't just a marvel in the bedroom, he was the next best thing to a Michelin-starred chef in the kitchen. He'd eased up on his camera-ready diet, although he still had vitamin goo for breakfast. One lunchtime she'd persuaded him to go halves with her on a Cornish pasty. He'd eaten the smaller half and run Ophelia off her feet on the beach for a good hour afterwards. He seemed more at ease than he had done the day of his arrival. He was less uptight about his fear of heights too. From their position way above the beach a sailboat in the bay was toy-sized, the people dolls on the sand. All things considered he seemed pretty relaxed about sitting mere feet from the top of the path that zig-zagged down the cliff-side.

Five whole days – and nights – had gone by since Nick had arrived in Porthkara and he'd turned her world upside down with lust and loveliness.

'Upside down ostrich,' she said into the companionable silence.

'How so?'

'Can't you see it? That big cloud is its body and the long bit at the bottom the neck. The head is that little cloud blob and the teeny wisp is the beak.'

'What about legs?'

'Those trails of cloud at the top.'

He pulled a face.

She laughed. 'It's so totally an ostrich.'

The cloud shifted in the bluest of blue skies morphing into an altered shape. 'It looks like a fire breathing dragon to me.' Nick rolled onto his side, studying Layla instead of the clouds. 'Good game,' he said, 'It's a new one to me.'

'Can you honestly, truly say you've never spotted cloud shapes before?'

'I haven't lived.'

His eyes glinted, soft, seductive. Every time he looked at her like that she sparkled inside with flickers of the attraction that wasn't showing any sign of running out. He reached out a long finger and twisted a thick strand of her hair around it.

'Come to Paris with me.'

'That's a bit random.' Her heart beat faster.

'My photo shoot can't wait any longer. I'm leaving early on Saturday. Come with me.' He pushed the twisted tendril of hair behind her ear. 'Just say yes.'

'I can't drop everything and go to Paris on a whim.'

'Why not?'

'Too many reasons.' She counted on her fingers. 'One – I've got the mural to finish.'

'That's done.'

'Two – the B&B. Three – the Kandy Shack. Four – changeover day at the holiday lets.'

'Five?'

'There isn't a five. But give me a minute I'm bound to think of one. In all honesty, four's enough.'

'Emily's getting the hang of the B&B and the kiosk. Can't Jasmine manage changeover day?'

'She's got morning sickness and she loathes changeover day. I doubt Dad will cope without me.'

'Nonsense.' He broke off a small piece of freshly baked crusty bread and fed it to the dog.

'Five – Ophelia.'

'This is exactly why you should come to Paris. Nobody's indispensable twenty-four seven. Not even you. I bet your mum would be happy to mind the dog.'

Right there was the very reason she shouldn't go to

Paris. In less than a week Nick had become her definition of indispensable. While she'd been painting, the anticipation of seeing him lightened her heart. When he walked in the room she got a floating happy-in-her-skin feeling like she'd been filled with helium.

'Go on,' he urged. 'This is too good end now.'

She madly, desperately wanted what they had to last a while longer.

She'd only just got over Joe's wedding on social media. Nick's private life attracted publicity in a different league. She'd been discombobulated enough over the story about his ex. She'd hate to be any part of intense press scrutiny.

He cupped her chin and tipped up her face, forcing her eyes to meet his. Softly crushing her mouth with the indomitable power of his kiss, his persuasive lips worked their magic on her senses. Their lips moved together, a moment captured in time. Loathe to break away they lingered and lingered, his hands twisting in her hair, their mouths craving escape. Submerged in the amazing potency of their connection she pressed in closer and wrapped him in her arms like she'd never let him go. Two hearts and minds harmonized, her mouth searched his perfect lips endlessly as if they held the answer to an unasked question.

Finally, inevitably, the kiss broke, his breath fire on her skin. He'd unpopped the cork on her emotions and released her from the post-Joe stupor she'd been in.

'We've been lost in space Nick. It's been ...' *Heaven.*
'Good. But it can't go on.' She stared at the vast blueness of sea and sky.

'Look me in the eye and tell me you don't want to go to Paris.'

'It's incredibly tempting but I'm a home bird,' she said decisively. She picked a blade of grass, held it up to the wind coming off the sea and it fluttered. 'It's time to get on with our real lives.'

'Final answer?' Everything about him sparkled, wicked, provocative.

Tiny yellow seaside flowers dotted through the grass quivered in the gentle breeze. Around them, bees buzzed and butterflies flitted amongst the purple clover. Pulling away from him and kneeling in the grass she stashed the leftovers of their picnic in the wicker hamper. Resolute, she focused on tidying with the concentration of someone whose life depended on working out the answer to a difficult question. 'Yep,' she confirmed, heart quivering like the flowers. 'I can't go to Paris with you. Final answer.'

* * *

They strolled back along the cliff path in silence.

'You were impressively cool about picnicking on the cliff.'

'Anything for you. Evidently the feeling isn't mutual.'

'Don't sulk about Paris. It doesn't suit you. And it's not up for discussion. Let's leave it at that.'

'Can I say the offer's still open? If you'd like to think it over and get back to me ...'

She shook her head at his persistence, aware that he was wearing down her thin veil of reasons not to say yes.

'I leave early Saturday.'

'I'll bear it in mind.'

As they hit the stretch of coast road a white van bearing her dad's unmistakable logo approached over the brow of the hill.

'Ask him if he can get cover for changeover day.'

'Drop it, I'm not going.'

'If you don't ask, I will.'

'Control freak.'

'I can't help it. I'm addicted to you. And I'd love to show you Paris.'

The van slowed to a stop and her dad leaned out the open window. 'What brings you up here?' she asked.

'I've just been by the Lobster Pot to help fix a fridge. Someone said Cliffside's for sale, I wanted to see for myself.'

'It's for real. I hope someone nice buys it,' she said.

'I'd buy it in a heartbeat, but I'd have to win the lottery first, it's out of my league.'

They both laughed.

'Listen, I'm glad I caught you. Joe's coming home tonight. Bringing the missus.' His eyes rolled up. 'Apparently someone's giving him a temporary job troubleshooting for tourists at a camping and caravanning site near Newquay. She's going to work in their kids' club. They're not staying long.'

'With a bit of luck I'll avoid him.'

'Trish is beside herself. She's about ready to throttle him. He wants to celebrate the ...'

He stopped abruptly so as not to offend, obliging Layla to supply the word herself. '... Wedding.'

'There's a longstanding private party booked in for Saturday, an eightieth birthday Trish isn't prepared to back out of.' One arm resting on the steering wheel he ran the other hand over his chin clearly uncomfortable. 'So they've cancelled all their reservations for tomorrow night. It's all systems go for a shindig at the restaurant. They asked me if the band would play.'

'That's not on. You're not going to do it, are you?' The idea smarted like sea water in a cut.

'They're that stressed they're not thinking straight. I told them some of the guys are out of town. Gave them the number of some youngsters who do dance covers.' He

144

sighed heavily. 'There's no way I'm playing at the toerag's party.'

'You'll go though. You'll have to. Trish and Bob are your friends.'

'Will you?'

'Wild horses wouldn't drag me. But I won't be asked.'

'Sorry to be the bearer of bad news.'

'You didn't really come up here to see the For Sale sign, did you?'

She'd rumbled him. He shook his head. 'I've been driving around looking for you since I finished with the fridge. I didn't want you to hear on the grapevine, or worse, bump into him at the pub or somewhere by accident.'

'Thanks Dad.'

Ralph gave a disgruntled smile, put the van in gear and pulled away.

Nick slung an arm around her shoulders and pulled her close so that she slotted neatly into the curve of his body.

'You okay?'

'How perfectly lovely.' The words almost choked her and they didn't exactly answer his question.

Chapter Twelve

'Take me to Paris.'

'I thought "no" was your final answer.'

He'd stopped plaguing her about Paris after her Dad had delivered the blow about Joe. They sat together on a wooden bench at a table outside the ancient timber-framed seaside pub the next day. Halfway down the hill to the harbour, the tables out front had a picture postcard view. To the right the shining sea in the horseshoe shaped bay, to the left the fishing harbour with its quirky stone chapel, the white lighthouse and the pier. Layla watched the world go by, sipped her piña colada and ignored her ploughman's lunch.

Nick admired the ice-cold, amber-coloured pint of real ale in front of him. He'd been making like a true Brit and not a Hollywood actor. But his timeout had run out. He'd have to get back to work. He shuffled things about on the table, a beermat, his car keys, sachets of mayonnaise, mustard, ketchup. The beer had barely touched his lips, but for one sip.

The words 'Smugglers' Inn' were painted on the side end of the pub in bold black letters. A cloud blocked out the sun and a breeze off the sea fluttered the napkins on the table. Nick pushed his sunglasses onto his head. He raised the glass to his mouth and drank, a single cool swig of beer slipping down his throat. He pictured his nutritionist's face, tempted to text her a selfie saying 'Cheers' and asking for a calorie check. Then he set his pint on the table and stared at Layla.

'I've had a rethink.' She dabbed a yellow finger of cheddar cheese into a tiny pot of caramelized onion chutney and took a bite. 'I'd like to go with you.'

'Cool.'

'If the offer's still open?'

'Of course it is.' He stole some cheese from her plate and bit into it. 'What changed your mind?'

'Joe.' She shrugged.

'I knew it.'

'I don't want to have to prove my heart isn't broken. What's wrong with that?'

The flash of possibility that her heart could be beyond fixing bruised his ego somewhat. He thought he'd been doing an outstanding repair job. 'You want to come so you can avoid people. That's not a great reason.'

'I wouldn't say it's the only reason.' She held out her hands, palms up, and moved them fractionally in the air like they were a set of vintage weighing scales, drawing his eyes to the jingling charms on her bracelet. 'But in the toss-up between facing people and going away with you, you win.'

'At least you're honest.'

Having her there with him would make an otherwise dull trip more fun, but an under-the-radar fling in sleepy Porthkara had been easy, Paris might be more tricky and he didn't want to make things worse for her. Given her reaction to people seeing her ex's photos online, he'd hate for her to get papped.

'When do we leave?' Layla suddenly lifted her glass, held it in front of her nose like a shield, dipped her head and shrunk behind Nick. 'Hide me,' she whispered.

A car had screeched to a halt and was double parked in front of the pub. In a sudden gust of wind, the pub sign showing a keg of rum and a couple of jaunty chaps in three-cornered hats, creaked on its rusty brackets. A faint odour of burning rubber hung in the air. Around them, startled pub-goers looked up from their drinks to see what the commotion was about.

'Why?' He caught sight of a tanned, sporty-looking guy weaving his way through the tables and instantly knew.

'Layla!' Joe announced, clearing his throat, 'I'm glad I

148

spotted you. You do know you're on the guestlist for the party tonight?' A peculiar hush descended over the people in the beer garden, somehow sensing the aura of extreme awkwardness. 'You know how it is. We mustn't upset the parents.'

Nick barely held back from remarking that it was a bit late for that. His fingers clenched around his pint glass, tempted to fling its contents in his face. Joe stared at him, sizing him up. 'You're welcome to bring your friend.'

'My significant other,' Layla corrected. 'Nick, Joe. Joe, Nick.' Her eyes darted between the two men and she took a gulp of piña colada. 'Actually, we're off to Paris—'

'—in the morning,' Nick cut in, offering his hand to Joe and shaking it tensely. 'But we'd love to, wouldn't we ... darling?' He hammed it up and smiled adoringly at her, letting his eyes linger like she was the most phenomenal woman in a one-hundred-mile radius.

Not acting, Layla almost choked on her drink. 'We would?' She recovered and pasted on a smile. 'We would,' she agreed, nodding fervently to cover her lack of positivity. Assessing Joe, Nick doubted he realized that she was faking it.

'Great. See you guys later. Lainy's out shopping for a dress. She can't wait to meet you.'

Lainy? What happened here? Did the guy miss Layla so much he married the first girl who came along with a similar name?

A holidaymaker whose car had been blocked in by Joe's blasted his horn so he turned tail and ran. When he'd gone, Layla raised astonished brows at Nick. Pure fury burned in her eyes.

'*We'd love to, wouldn't we darling?*' She mocked his deep drawl. 'We would, would we? What the blazes was that all about? I need to go to Paris right now.' Her voice rose into a petulant crescendo. Eyes that flashed like two lightning strikes about to go to earth told him in no uncertain terms that he'd made a huge error of judgment. 'In fact, half an hour ago wouldn't have been too soon.' She stood up. 'Let's go. I need to pack.'

He regretted the panic in her tone. He'd been eaten alive by moments of helplessness since he'd found out he was a dad. He'd bottled it up so as not to ruin things with Layla. It wasn't her problem. When Joe had treated her as if there'd never been anything between the two of them, he'd recognized the pain on her face almost as if it was his own. He'd hoped that by going to the party they could shove it to the tosspot. 'How dare you accept the invitation on my behalf? What a prize-winning idiot! I wanted to curl up in a ball and hide under the table. Why couldn't you have said "No thanks buddy you know where you can stick your party!?"'

'Because real life doesn't have a script.' He gently took her wrist, his fingers catching in her bracelet. 'Relax,' he coaxed, 'Sit down. Finish your drink. We're going to rock this party. That guy's going to think you've forgotten he ever existed.'

'With a bit of luck.' Layla downed the rest of her ever-so-slightly-decadent lunchtime cocktail. '... I will have.' A trace of froth left a rum and pineapple moustache over her top lip. He ached to lean in and slowly, slowly kiss it away. Instead he handed her a paper napkin and she dabbed at it. He doubted that a weekend away from Porthkara would do much to wipe away the hurt, but he'd do his level best to help her forget about it.

'I wish you'd consulted me before you decided to offer yourself up as my plus one,' Layla continued.

'Significant other. Your words. Not mine.'

'Said in desperation,' she argued sulkily. 'It wasn't your cue to say yes to the party. You're about as much help as spare tyre with a puncture.'

'And almost as reliable,' he agreed. 'I should have kept out of it, but I reckon that Joe deserves to be reminded what he's missing out on.'

Stuck for a reply and hopping with nerves, Layla stood up and bolted, taking a random route through the tables to the pub door. She headed straight for the Ladies' and locked herself in a cubicle. If she was going to have a meltdown she intended to do it in private. She lowered the lid and sat down to consider her options. She picked ferociously at a hardened splatter of paint on her t-shirt. She had no decent clothes. Where was Maggie when she needed a fashionista to figure out the dress code? Miles away. Perhaps a video chat would help. She tried to call her but getting a signal in the village was haphazard at the best of times – in the pub loo it was hopeless.

The door to the Ladies' squeaked on its hinges as it opened, and the buzz of multiple conversations filled her ears, abruptly followed by the clear voices of the two girls who'd come in.

'My auntie lives across the lane from them, and apparently, he's not sleeping at Maggie's! He's staying with Layla! And get this! She says there are never any lights on in the spare room!'

Layla crumpled.

'Scandal.'

'Do you think they're ...?'

'Totally.'

'Go Layla.'

'Wouldn't it be awesome if they got married like Maggie and Alex?'

'That's never going to happen.'

'Why not?'

'It was in a magazine my mum read at the hairdressers, that he was dating some princess. He's a notorious player. He'll have his way with her and vanish into the sunset.'

'That's awful. Do you think Layla knows?'

'Maybe yes. Maybe no.'

'Maybe we should warn her.'

'Maybe she doesn't mind. Who'd blame her for going off the rails with Nick Wells after the way Joe treated her?'

'In that case, best not interfere.'

She stayed very still, both furious and nauseous at the latest village gossip. She was ready to burst out of her cubicle to vent on out-of-date magazines and not believing everything people read at the hair salon when she overheard the next snippet.

'What do you think of Lainy?'

'I haven't seen her yet. Have you?'

She stuck her fingers in her ears and studied a poster on the back of the door about sponsoring well-digging projects in Africa, but the girls were so loud she'd have heard them through a thick stone wall.

'She looks a little like Layla, I reckon.'

Layla couldn't help taking one finger out of one ear.

'Wow. Scarlet hair?'

'Not so much. I think she's a natural redhead.'

'Layla's a natural red. My sister was in her class at school. She had thick auburn hair down to her waist. My mum swears she's never seen a child with such beautiful hair. Not even in a catalogue!'

'Spooky! That sounds a lot like Lainy. There's definitely

something similar about her. A few people have said it.'

'Layla's lovely. She doesn't need to dye her hair to stand out.'

'Each to their own. Nick Wells definitely seems to like it.'

They erupted into giggles and Layla couldn't bear to hear any more. She quietly pushed open the frosted glass window behind the loo and climbed onto the seat. She stepped up onto the cistern, cringing when it rattled beneath her feet, and squeezed herself out onto the ledge. As she jumped onto the carpet of soft grass and daisies she was gripped by an overwhelming urge to paint. She was itching to start something new.

Irked beyond belief, she circumnavigated the beer garden and set off up the street, straightening out the chaos in her head.

'Layla, wait up.' Nick's mid-Atlantic drawl rumbled through her, filling her veins with electrical current. She quickened her pace. He matched it.

'Go back and finish your pint, Nick. I've got things to do. Maybe you haven't heard but I've got to go home and pick out a dress because the man I thought I was going to marry invited me to his wedding reception.'

'Strictly speaking it's not a wedding.'

'Oh yes, silly me, he's already married.'

'We can't change that. But we can make him regret it.'

'He's not sorry and nor am I.' She huffed out a breath. 'So why in the world would I want to do that?'

'What do you want Layla? Do you want me to go away?'

'Newsflash. I want to stop feeling like the local entertainer. It's like everyone around here has switched to Channel Layla. I need to get away.'

He drew her to him, and her bones dissolved as he ran his fingers through the hair at the back of her neck and held her firmly. Her body next to his gave her a natural high. He lowered his head and his lips crashed with hers, melting her fury. Her mind stopped whirring, the calm at the eye of a storm. 'Let me do what I do best,' he murmured. 'There's an upside to hiding a Hollywood fugitive. I guarantee you that tonight we'll put on a performance Porthkara won't forget.'

Chapter Thirteen

'You need a dress with the wow factor.'

'And where am I going to get one of those by sunset? I have no idea how to work a high fashion look.'

'Taxi?' He laughed. 'Luckily I didn't drink the beer. I'm okay to drive.' He tossed the keys to the sports car into the air and caught them with the other hand.

She dropped into the passenger seat while he held open the door. It clunked shut, and he rounded the bonnet, and slid in next to her. He started the engine. Its deep rumble was seductive, like everything about him. As his fingers gripped the gearstick, her eyes were drawn to the way his faded denim jeans hugged his thighs. He skillfully wove the car out of the village, collecting awed glances from strangers. He wound around the high-hedged Cornish lanes, shifting up a gear and increasing his speed when they hit an empty stretch of straight road. The wind whipped at her hair and sent it flying into her face. She felt so uncool next to the head-turning man in the driving seat. Behind dark shades, he fixed his eyes on the road, throwing an instinctive glance every now and then at his rearview mirror. Self-conscious about the comments at the pub, she dug around in her handbag for something to tie her hair back.

'Why are you helping me Nick?'

Focused on driving, he didn't look at her. 'Why not?'

'You don't have to. You could set off for Paris right away and leave me to it.'

'I want to.' Hitting the edge of town, he stopped the car at a red light, and turned momentarily to meet her eyes. She looked away. 'We're buying a dress. Don't over analyze it.'

That was typical Nick. He did nice things for her. He did explosive things to her body. But there was a defensiveness about him that warned her off as clearly as a 'keep out' sign.

He parked the car in the market square. Sitting amongst a couple of cafés and some small gift shops, a handful of chain stores dotted one side of the square. Picking one she liked, she pushed open the door. Nick touched her shoulder. His fingers slid to her upper arm, connecting with bare skin, and spinning golden threads of warmth through her veins.

'Not this one,' he said shaking his head. 'Let's try that one over there.'

In a restored Georgian building with a fancy façade and gleaming windows, a smart department store dominated the market square. 'It's rather high end. I never go there. It's not very me.'

'It's exactly what we're looking for. When I was a kid I went to boarding school in a little town about forty miles from London. My mother used to fly in to visit me and Alex. She'd take us out for afternoon tea in a store exactly like that. Alex would hang out in the audiovisual section watching TV while I spent hours listening to the shop assistants give her advice.'

Her heart fluttered. 'That sounds like an endurance test.'

He smiled. 'I didn't mind. I liked spending time with her – when she was sober. We didn't see her often.' He gently laced his fingers through hers and they walked across the square. Reluctantly she kept putting one foot in front of the other as if her legs were made of lead. 'The makeovers were nothing more than a quick fix. My mother had a hard time feeling good about herself.'

She stared at the window display, avoiding her reflection, and doubting that there'd be a single item inside that she could afford without blowing some of her savings. She pushed fluttery fingers into her windblown hair. They stuck fast in knots. 'I can't go in there. I look like I've been through a hedge backwards.'

Nick swept her ahead of him into the revolving door. Inside the store he pulled off his sunglasses and looked her up and down appreciatively. 'You look fine.' The wicked smile twisted his lips. 'Tousled,' he added. 'But fine.' He lowered his voice to a throaty whisper and adopted his best period character voice to suit the centuries-old building as if it was a stage set. 'And most charming, I might add, Miss Rivers.' She was grateful that he wanted to help, but it stung that this was her real life and to him it was just a bit of fun.

Ahead of them, through an ocean of perfume and cosmetic counters, a grand stone staircase oozed bygone elegance. Trying hard to ignore the half-pitying, half-disapproving stares from the pristine shop assistants, she looked straight ahead. Even so, the admiring glances reserved for Nick didn't go unnoticed. She avoided the other women's immaculately made-up eyes, embarrassed to look left or right and catch sight of a mirror.

Upstairs in the fashion department her heart beat faster. 'This is madness. I shouldn't be here. I don't need a dress because I'm not going to the party.' She spun around ready to run down the stairs and back out into the safety and fresh air of the street.

'Wait.' Nick grasped her arm, his touch firm and gentle. She turned back to face him, sucking in a deep breath. 'Chill. You can do this.'

She tossed her head and let her breath go irritably. 'You're wrong. I'm not like you. I'm not an actor. I can't switch my emotions on and off at the drop of a hat. If I go to the party I'm going to look like a wally, hanging around, waiting for whatever crumbs of attention Joe's prepared to give me.'

'That's not going to happen. You're with me.'

Her heart skittered. She looked away only to be caught out by the sight of her full-length reflection in an ornate mirror. Amazingly – bright red bird's nest hair aside – she didn't look as ridiculous standing next to Nick as she'd imagined. She hated to admit it, but he'd got it right. If she stayed at home, hiding, while half of Porthkara partied, everyone would think she was miserable. They'd worry. Like it or not, she'd have to put on a smile, go to the party, and act like she was having a good time. If she didn't people would be upset. Trish had worked her socks off to get everything ready at such short notice. Whatever she thought of Joe, his mum and dad were friends, they'd always been kind to her. She hadn't expected to be invited, but since she had been, she'd tough it out and put on a show of no hard feelings, to keep everyone happy.

'I kept quiet about finishing with Joe because in a tiny corner of my head I held on to the possibility that we might patch things up.'

'When all along it turns out you didn't want to?'

She didn't answer the question. She paced between the rails, collecting a selection of dresses, her choices based purely on the size printed on the tags and nothing to do with colour or style or whether she particularly liked them. She fumed with annoyance. 'I've been in limbo for months, waiting to hear back from him.'

'Marrying somebody new makes for a much more dramatic ending than simply 'fessing up and telling people that you and he fizzled out.'

'You make it sound like he only did it to get back at me. That's outrageous. Nobody could be that stupid. Not even Joe.'

Her arms too full of dresses to continue searching, he helpfully took them from her, forcing her to meet his eyes. 'Here, allow me!'

'The truth is I didn't know what I wanted.'

'You didn't want to hurt people.'

'I ended up hurting me.'

'I can't undo that,' Nick said solemnly.

'If this is what it takes to prove I'm over him, bring it on.' She tossed the words over her shoulder on her way to the changing room. 'I'm stronger than when he went away. I'm ready to turn my ideas into something concrete. As soon as I get back from Paris, I'm waiting for nothing. I'm getting my business up and running. By the time he gets off that campsite my life's going to be running on such a different track he won't recognize me.'

When she appeared in her umpteenth dress, Nick was reclined provocatively on a red leather sofa outside the changing room. It was actually only about the seventh dress, but to him it felt like more. His expertise was strictly amateur, and owed itself to years of assuring his glamorous mother she looked the part, but none of the dresses looked right on Layla. There was nothing wrong with them. They were lovely, and she looked good, but gut instinct told him that good wasn't enough. He wanted nothing short of spectacular.

'I look like a ballerina crossed with a cappuccino.'

In a froth of tulle layers in shades of light coffee and off-white he tried not to smile at her comparison, but felt a rogue wry twinge break across his lips regardless and had to laugh. He couldn't admit it wasn't the jaw-dropping gorgeous he had in mind without making her feel bad.

'Truthfully, I like you best undressed.'

'That's deeply unhelpful.' She withered him with gleaming eyes. The last few days had passed in a blur. He'd lost sense of time. She made him smile. More than that, she made it hard not to smile. He liked her unconventional dress sense, and her wonderful hair. But it wasn't about her look, because he liked her from the inside out and to top it all off her body without clothes did indescribably good things to him.

'Tonight, you're going to be one half of a Hollywood power couple.' She smirked like she'd never heard anything quite so hilariously unlikely. 'I'm not being funny,' he insisted, 'There may not be a limo. There may not be a red carpet. But when you walk into the party tonight, you are going to be the most stunning woman in the room.'

'I love that you believe I could be anywhere near that person, but, honestly, I just need to turn up looking present-able, say my hellos, hold my head high, and go.'

'And you will. Let's think about this. What would Maggie say? Let's call her.'

He pressed dial and speaker, handed her the phone and when her friend's voice answered she spilled her guts. 'It's me. Joe's home. And there's a party at the restaurant. And I'm in a shop. And I need help.'

'Why are you on Nick's phone?' Maggie asked.

'Because,' she said sulkily and pouted in his direction. 'It's all his fault.'

'Not Joe's?'

'His too.' Layla grudgingly admitted. 'Mostly his to be fair. What should I wear?'

'You don't want to look like you're trying too hard. In other words, you have to look like you're not trying too hard.'

She pulled a face. 'Oh my gosh. I'm losing the will to live. What's the difference?'

'The key thing is to arrive at the party looking absolutely amazing and as if it's taken no effort at all.'

Layla pinched the bridge of her nose and scrunched up her face. 'You've lost me.'

'Where's Nick?'

'Right here.'

'Are you and he ...?' Maggie asked.

'Sort of. Yes.' Layla said, raising her eyebrows at him. 'Not right this minute obviously.'

He stifled a guffaw.

'So, you worked out what to do with him then?'

'Funny! You could put it that way. I suppose. He's taking me to Paris.'

'Really?' Maggie's voice resonated with delight and surprise. 'Right. Give me Nick.'

Layla passed his phone back to him, and he switched off speaker, thinking he shouldn't risk any other raised eyebrows in the store. Layla swished the curtain on her changing cubicle and vanished behind it to take off the frothy cappuccino dress. By the time she stuck her head out from behind the curtain he'd deciphered Maggie's advice.

'Wait here.'

She rolled her eyes. 'I'm not going anywhere.'

'We need sophisticated understated glamour. She said along the lines of the dress she wore to the Wells Wish Foundation Gala at the Empire State Building. She looked awesome. In the perfect dress so will you.'

He took out his phone again to show her a picture of Maggie in New York. He speedily scrolled and held his mobile out for her to see.

'Who's the girl in the photo?'

Damn it, in his hurry, he'd hit the wrong image.

'No one important.' Completely thrown by his stupidity, he stopped dead, lost for words. 'Just the kid of ... of an ex-girlfriend, actually.'

'She sent you a picture of her daughter?'

He felt ashamed of the lie, claiming Beth was no one important. Damn it. This thing was bubbling just below the surface. He wanted to admit that Fran and Beth were the real reason he couldn't face the world right now. But it wouldn't be fair to dump his problem on her.

'We lost touch. I guess she decided it was time to catch up.'

'Pretty girl.'

'Yeah. I guess.'

He peered at the picture, taking in the features of the smiling girl for the hundredth time. She had messy-on-purpose shoulder length brown hair and a long slender nose, a little turned up at the tip, just like her mother. And her eyes ... looking at them was like hearing a whispered secret, seeing a memory of some part of himself that he'd rather forget.

He searched for the right picture, the one of Maggie, and held it out to Layla. 'See?' he said, 'The look's been tried and tested. We just need to find something similar.'

He did a circuit of the fashion department, stared at a store mannequin artfully draped in a silver gown, the kind of thing his mother loved, totally over the top with a price tag to match. He rejected it, cornered the nearest assistant and showed her the photo of Maggie looking stunning in a full-length sequined graphite and black zebra print dress, the back sculpted low.

'Okay,' he said, 'So not quite as formal as this, shorter would be good, and my ... significant other doesn't need to sparkle from head to toe, but the overall look ...'

The assistant nodded and politely listened to his floundering attempt at fashion styling. 'If it's a fab little black dress you're after, how about this?' She held up a dress with a flattering neckline adorned with shimmering diamante buttons. 'It has a certain *je ne sais quoi.*'

Layla looked amazing when she emerged to show off the dress. The column of black set off the colour of her hair.

'It's beautiful, I love it, but ...' She extracted the label from somewhere at the back of her neck and contortedly squinted at the price. 'It's not right for tonight.'

'What do you mean, it's not right? It's perfect. Trust me. I know what works.'

'It really suits you.' The assistant backed him up, adding in an effort to appear unbiased, 'I'll leave you to think about it.'

Layla disappeared and returned in her jeans and paint-spattered tee holding the dress at arm's length.

'What can I say to convince you?'

'I can't afford this,' she protested quietly. 'It was a nice thought. But I can dig around in my wardrobe. I'm sure I'll find something that will do.'

'Give it to me. I'll get the assistant to put it back.' As lies went it wasn't a bad one. There was no way she was leaving the store without that dress.

'I'll nip downstairs and see if I can find a new lippy. There might be something on sale. I'll see you down there.'

Five minutes later, she was chatting with the girls at one of the makeup counters when he joined her. 'Success?'

She beamed like the cat that got the cream, and held up a tiny bag. 'Yep.'

'Me too.' He pushed the strings of the carrier bag containing the dress over her shoulder. 'I got you this.'

'What the—?'

He cut her off. 'One the girls upstairs called the salon in the basement for me. They've had a couple of cancellations so you're booked in with the junior nail technician and the senior hair stylist.'

'What happened to not trying too hard?'

'Thanks to my crash course with Maggie, I gather looking effortlessly amazing doesn't mean no effort's been made.' She opened her mouth to argue, but he didn't give her the chance. 'I'm taking care of it. You've looked after me this week, now it's my turn to do something for you.'

Chapter Fourteen

'It's Friday the thirteenth!' Layla grabbed Nick's arm. 'Show me your watch.' He twisted his wrist and she glared at the numbers in the date box, the metallic strap glinted in the sharp rays of the setting sun.

'Forget about it. It's not important.'

A taxi had dropped them a few feet from the entrance to the beachside restaurant. The air was warm and the sun had turned the sky golden pink over the sea. Propped back with large wooden planters of roses and marigolds, the double doors to the restaurant had been flung wide open, and the sound of chatter and laughter, people having a good time, spilled out.

Layla drew in a deep breath and let it all go. 'I'm superstitious.'

'I know you are. Superstitions don't count for anything. I told you before, we make our own luck.'

'I beg to differ,' she argued. He radiated male vitality

and he looked stellar in the clothes he'd shopped for while she was in the salon. 'A party on Friday the thirteenth is bad luck.'

'What happened to sacking off the bad luck?'

'I said I'd try, I didn't make any promises.'

He squeezed her hand. 'I'm willing to bet that some-where in the world Friday the thirteenth is a lucky day.'

Her emotions had run high over Joe – anger, disappoint-ment, embarrassment. She straightened her shoulders.

Nick locked her hand in his. 'Ready?'

'As I'll ever be.' His firm touch filled her with strength. 'Let's do this thing.'

Trish greeted them at the door and pressed a blue cock-tail complete with orange straw and pink paper umbrella into her free hand.

'I'm so glad you could make it.' The hint of dark circles beneath her eyes had been skillfully concealed by flawless makeup. 'I'm so glad you could make it,' Trish repeated, all excitable and distracted. 'So, so glad!'

Joe's father shook Nick's hand over-enthusiastically. The impression that she'd stepped onto the set of a soap where the role of plus one for the groom's dumped ex had been written in especially unsettled her. She powered through and painted on a smile.

'You're looking well.' The older man's condescending tone, albeit unintentional, had the effect of making her feel like she'd been struck down with a bout of something contagious, and really shouldn't be out yet.

She slurped down half her lurid cocktail in one disreputable go, disregarding the straw.

'She looks stunning.' Nick's voice rumbled loudly through the restaurant stopping conversations mid-sentence. 'Absolutely sensational.'

Okay! Don't overdo it.

Surprisingly, heads bobbed in apparent approval as people got back to what they'd been saying. She downed the remainder of her drink, and plucked another one from a tray offered by Emily the new girl as the chit-chat built into forced jollity.

She scanned the restaurant. The table centres matched the planters and in one corner a hastily rustled up three-tier cake, complete with ivory fondant icing, orange ribbons and topped with yet more flowers, stood out.

When Layla's mother appeared, Nick casually withdrew the arm that had been protectively draped across her shoulders. 'I'll get some real drinks,' he murmured softly against her ear. 'More than one of those things and I'll be legless.'

'Lightweight.'

He laughed and went to the bar. Shelly hustled her into a corner.

'He's right.' She took the cocktail from Layla's hand and set it down on the nearest table. 'I've no idea what's in this, but it looks and tastes like mouthwash.'

'Mother! How rude.'

'There's a rumour going round that you and Nick are running away together. To Paris!'

'Mother!' she hissed. 'Please lower your voice.'

'Is it true?'

'Paris? Maybe,' she dithered. 'Running away? Not so much. I'll be back on Monday. You won't even notice I've gone. If I actually go, that is.'

'Are you going, or aren't you?'

Layla picked up her confiscated drink and twirled the pink cocktail umbrella. 'I haven't told Dad. I haven't arranged cover. And there's Ophelia to think about.'

'I'll mind Ophelia. And you can leave your father to me.'

'Do you think he'll cope?'

'It's a weekend off. Nick's not asking for your hand in marriage.'

'Been there, done that, and got the jilted-before-I-got-anywhere-near-the-altar t-shirt to prove it,' she sniped.

'There's no need to be prickly.'

Perfect! She was getting a telling-off. So much for sophistication. 'I meant how will Dad manage changeover day?'

'I'll give him Emily's number.' She discreetly pointed a manicured pink nail at Jasmine, who was vociferously regaling the new waitress with her own wedding minutiae. 'Failing that, he could ask Lady Muck to pitch in.'

'Mother!'

'Pigs might fly!'

'You're not wrong,' Layla said. 'Pulling her weight isn't Jasmine's forte. But she's got staffing issues at the gift shop and she's been feeling poorly. Pregnancy hormones kicking in.' A knot of emotion for her mother tightened beneath her ribs. Because she'd fallen pregnant Shelly had down-sized her dreams, only to find herself putting up with an unfaithful husband and faking contentment. And for what? In the end he'd left anyway. Layla crossed her fingers behind her back. She'd die if the party ended in a scene because either she or her mother lost the plot, incapable of stom-aching keeping up appearances a second longer.

Shelly stretched out her pink painted fingernails. 'Do I clash with the décor?'

Layla hugged her. 'In a good way.' Her mum had pretending that everything was okay down to a fine art. 'How are you feeling about it all?'

'I'm ...' Shelly gulped. 'I was about to say "fine" but the word's never felt less fine. I'm making a stab at acting cool with things but I'm only just holding it together. It prob-ably shouldn't, but Jasmine expecting and planning her wedding feels like déja vu.'

Their eyes rested, like a spotlight, on her father. Relaxed, a pint of beer in his hand, he was gregariously telling Joe's parents a story that made them laugh.

With a small smile Shelly shook her head slowly. 'Good luck to him!' She touched her daughter's arm. 'I mind that Joe's not marrying you.'

Layla sipped her reclaimed cocktail. 'This really doesn't taste good.'

'I'm cross with Joe. He's been so thoughtless. He treated you terribly. He's upset his parents. The more I think about it the more I wonder why we're here.'

Layla stopped herself from commenting that Shelly was the local expert at tolerating bad situations. 'We're keeping up appearances.'

'To pot with that.' Shelly stepped backwards and accidentally on purpose put a heel through a balloon. Oohs followed by laughter broke out above the loud pop. 'I thought the sun shone out of Joe, but he put himself ahead of you. I didn't say anything because you and he were making a go of things.' Shelly twisted her thumb and forefinger nervously around the empty spot where there used to be a wedding ring. 'Your dad and I weren't exactly a prototype for married bliss, so it wasn't my place to weigh in with an opinion.'

'Joe did the right thing the wrong way. We weren't meant to stay together.'

'Maybe you had a lucky escape. It's funny how things work out.' She looked around as if searching for someone. 'One blue drink was enough for me. It's gone straight to my head. Look. I match with the cocktail umbrellas.' She only diverted the conversation momentarily. 'There's no point promising to be together forever if you don't mean it.'

Layla's fingers worried at the clasp on her bracelet.

'Go and have fun. Starting with Paris.' Her mother picked a rose from the nearest table centre and pulled the petals off one by one, dropping them onto the floor around their feet. 'He loves her, he loves her not. He loves her, he loves her not.'

'Stop!' Self-consciously, stifled by the atmosphere, lost without Nick, Layla plucked the half-destroyed flower from her mother's hand and put it back in the vase. The volume of chatter had risen, ever more excitable as people knocked back drinks. Because he'd been swamped welcoming guests, she'd avoided Joe at the door. While he was circulating around the room she stole a quick glance. Grinning broadly, he looked nauseatingly content. In ankle-length ivory chiffon, red hair braided and twisted artfully around her face, Lainy rocked the bohemian beach bride.

'So about Paris? Is it what we used to call a dirty weekend in my day?'

'Mother! You're ruining my attempt to channel ice cold indifference. First off, it still is your day. And secondly, I've no idea what you're talking about.'

'That's a yes then.'

'I didn't expect you to be quite so on board with the idea of Paris. You do get that it's a fling?'

'You make a lovely couple. And I've seen the way he looks at you.'

'Now you're being fanciful. That cocktail didn't just go to your head, it scrambled your brain.'

'I plead insanity.' She dropped her voice to a whisper. 'Seriously though. Joking aside. He's a lovely guy. Much nicer than the papers make him out. But I'd hate to see you fall for another commitment-phobe only for him to waltz off with some other woman. Like Dad and Joe.'

She winced. 'Did you close your ears to what I just said?'

'Ignore me if I'm overstepping the mark. Pouring cold water all over everything isn't my intention. A weekend in Paris is fantastic. Don't lose your heart, that's all.'

Returning from the bar with two cocktails Nick cut in, 'Sex on the beach anyone?'

'Don't mind if I do.'

'Mother!' Shelly nabbed a glass and walked off giggling inappropriately. Layla glared disbelievingly. 'Is that what you call a real drink?'

He laughed. 'Your mother seems to think so.'

'My father's engagement has left her a sandwich short of a picnic.'

'Should I go after her and get that drink back?' Nick

looked perturbed. 'Do you think she'll unravel before the night is out?'

'Not a chance. Mum would rather stick pins in her eyes than let her true feelings show.' She blamed herself for the years of disillusionment her mother had clocked up. 'I'll pass on the sex on the beach thanks. I'm pacing myself.'

He cocked an eyebrow and drank it himself.

Cocktails gave way to plates of delicious food and wine, desserts, more wine. All the while, Nick stayed attentively at her side. Together they turned heads and she lost count of how many compliments the outstanding little black dress collected. Like compass points, Joe and Lainy and Layla and Nick remained strategically positioned on opposite sides of the restaurant.

'Are you avoiding them?'

'Way to go Sherlock.'

Ignoring her feeble sarcasm, he curved his arm around her waist. She stifled a yelp of protest as he propelled her across the floor to where Joe and Lainy were holding court in the midst of a group of friends. Instant silence descended. Someone cleared their throat. Someone else suggested more drinks. She shook her head, well aware that off-her-face at her ex's party wouldn't be a good look. In a split second the circle of friends vanished leaving just the two of them facing the bride and groom.

For the sake of any eavesdroppers she turned her charm

setting to maximum. 'Lovely party Joe.' She switched to Lainy and they air kissed without a hint of awkwardness. 'It's so good to meet you. You two were made for each other.' *Translation – You're much too good for him.* Like a nodding dog her head swiveled back to Joe. 'Good luck with everything. Have a nice time in Newquay.'

'I love your dress Layla.' Her attention bounced back to Lainy who sounded sincere, not at all like she was sizing her up.

'Oh, this?' She played down the designer dress. 'I found it at the back of the wardrobe. It's something I'd forgotten I had.' She crossed her fingers behind her back, hoping that telling a white lie to save face wasn't horrible.

Lainy linked her arm through her husband's and leant into his side. Emily passed out champagne, Joe's father called for hush, and Layla backed away melting into the shadows with Nick, side by side, bodies almost touching, silent.

'Raise your glasses, please, in a toast to the happy couple. Lainy and Joe!'

The room echoed with the mumble of Lainy and Joe. Overhearing someone mistakenly announce Layla and Joe, she exchanged a look with Nick, and held her glass high.

'The happy couple!' Her words rang out a little too loudly. She pressed her champagne glass to her lips. Inhaling the aroma, she sipped the bubbles. Nick touched her shoulder with one finger and trailed it the length of her arm. His free hand covered hers, their fingers meshing neatly. On the far side of the restaurant the groom kissed his bride and they posed for photos by the wedding cake. Layla looked on with the detachment of someone watching the scene on a cinema screen.

'Come here.' Nick spoke in a husky whisper. Warm salty air wafted in through open doors which led to decking overlooking the beach. Unresisting, she followed. Outside she practically swigged her champagne, remembering a second too late that she was meant to be pacing herself with the booze. She set the champagne glass on the wide wooden surface of the deck rail. 'It's lucky you're here. I don't think I could have done this without you. You're keeping me grounded.' He'd been more than a distraction, she'd gained perspective. 'You've helped me sort myself out. I can't believe I'm saying this but Joe and me ... we were perfectly okay together,' she said quietly.

'You were happy?' He tensed, and they stood not looking at each other but out into the twilight to the place where the red sun had dropped into the sea. A bank of cloud hung low above the horizon, its edges glistening pink and golden.

'I wouldn't go right to happy. I wasn't unhappy. I'd settled. We both had. The things we shared weren't enough. We were perfectly okay but we weren't perfect. When I saw him tonight I expected to feel something.'

'What kind of something?'

'Sad or numb. Instead I felt nothing. If he hadn't let me down when he did, it would have happened another time. Maybe a worse time.'

Nick stared at the sea. He didn't speak.

'You know what,' she said. 'I'm sick of defending him, being polite, saying nothing. My mother's accident was a seriously bad time. The worst. The doctors couldn't say if she'd be okay. He swept it aside like it was nothing. He's a selfish pillock. He sent me a text from the airport to say he wanted to be on a break, didn't bother to ask how Mum was. So I texted back that we were over.'

'Why didn't you say?' Nick turned to her, incredulity on his face. 'About the break?'

'I didn't swear to tell you the truth and nothing but the truth. It's a tiny detail. It didn't matter. He went away when I needed him to stay and if I had feelings back then I don't any longer. They've gone. You should know that.'

From inside the restaurant applause drifted out, along with the ripple of laughter. She looked in through the wide-open doors in time to see everyone gathering around Joe and Lainy, hands joined around a silver cake slice, ready to plunge the shiny blade into their cake. Her dad was standing behind Joe. Across the distance he caught her eye and for a comical half second held up the palms of his hands as if poised to give Joe a shove. He wouldn't have done it in a million years but the idea of Joe face planting his wedding cake was a funny one, and she appreciated the silliness of his dad joke.

'I'm tired of the Porthkara pressure cooker. Mum might be able to handle it. But I'm not sure I can. Is it too soon to slope off?'

'Say Joe made a mistake, he wants you back. What then? Would you have him?'

Emotional confusion twisted her insides. 'That's irrelevant.' She shook off his question. 'I'm different. I'm not the person he left behind.' Wide-eyed she gestured towards the restaurant. 'And, anyway ...'

Nick searched her face as if he'd anticipated a different reaction. He filled the void. 'I'd say the jury's out on whether he can step up to the plate for Lacey.'

'Lainy!'

'He's going to let her down. I'd put money on it.' In the darkening light his face was moody. 'A leopard doesn't change its spots.'

'Cynic.'

He nodded towards the couple inside the restaurant. 'Watch this space.'

Chapter Fifteen

'Ladies and gentlemen, a round of applause for the bride and groom.' The words fused with the sounds of the sea and the cry of a gull.

High over the cliffs Layla spotted the first shining star in the darkening sky. Inside the restaurant, the tables had been pushed back to make space for the wedding band. She wondered uncharitably how good they could be given their availability at short notice. Joe took Lainy by the hand and led her onto the dance floor.

Layla's heart wobbled, not because she'd lost Joe but because she felt wistful for the love they'd found. She hoped they were the real deal, despite everything. Despite Nick's cynicism.

A loud twang from the lead guitarist got everybody's attention.

As the band struck up, cheers, clapping, and a shrill wolf whistle made the initial bars of the couple's first dance difficult to recognize. Layla's cheeks burned. Was she hearing wrong? She listened more closely. It was their tune.

'How could he?' she gasped unable to contain her reaction. 'Why did he pick my song?' I-told-you-so was written on Nick's granite features. She recovered her composure struggling not to lose it completely while Joe twirled his bride around the dance floor like John Travolta.

'Whatever! Life's too short.'

'And too long to spend with the wrong person.' Nick slung a protective arm around her shoulders.

'I'm sorry things didn't work out with you and Toni. Moving on is hard.'

Inscrutable, he snatched up his champagne glass. 'I'm not having the slightest difficulty moving on.'

They fell silent.

She picked up her glass and twirled the stem between restless fingers. 'I – um – happened before my parents were married. I was a broken condom baby.'

'Ouch. Nobody should know that much about their conception.'

'Sorry, I don't know where that came from.' Her parents hadn't made the break years ago, because of her. Her dad was always off somewhere, out late, doing who-knows-what with goodness-knows-who. All smiles and charm in the outside world, while at home when things got tense they gave each other the silent treatment. Deadly silences got to her so much more than people hurling words around. 'Silence makes me twitchy.' It hadn't compelled her to lose control of her family secrets filter before.

'Did they really tell you that? Are they completely crazy?'

She shook her head. 'They don't know I know.'

'So how in the world did you find out? Did you read your mother's diary?'

'I wouldn't do that.' The words came out witheringly. 'One of my grans told me.' She pictured Granny Rivers painting at her easel in the drawing room window of the big Edwardian house that had become the B&B. While she'd alternated between dabbing paint at her canvas and staring at the grey sea merging with the sky Layla had sat at the table eating a cupcake from the village bakery and sipping tea from the best china. 'It was the day after my sixteenth birthday – a warning not to let it happen to me.' A shiver ran through her. 'Well meant, but plain wrong.'

'How did your grandmother even know that?'

'I know, right?' She cringed. 'My dad was meant to go away to study architecture at uni. He didn't go because of Mum being pregnant with me.' Her head and heart spun. The party had condensed years of deeply buried stuff. It bubbled over like a witch's cauldron spilling out of her mouth. 'I've never told anyone. Not Joe. Or Maggie. After Granny Rivers died I overheard a relative at the funeral say she'd called me Layla La Trap, but I can't believe she'd have been that cruel. She never said it to my face. Do you think she blamed her disappointment on me?'

She knocked back the last drop of champagne. He took the glass from her hands, drained his own and set them down.

'I doubt it.' A tower of strength he drew her close. Softly, silently, his lips brushed the top of her head. 'What you heard was a rumour. Chances are your grandmother didn't say it. And just supposing she did, people sometimes say things they regret.'

'Dad's motto is "fake it till you make it." He took it too far, like he wanted to prove my grandmother wrong, so he pretended to be happy when he wasn't. Things looking right was so important. He threw me fancy birthday parties with bouncy castles. One year he hired a magician. He made a rabbit come out of a hat. Granny Rivers didn't come to the parties. She got invited, and she always accepted. Then on the day she'd come up with an excuse and not turn up. When I was old enough to realize I wanted to hide. I felt terrible, thought she hated me.' He tightened his arm around her, holding her closer.

She stopped abruptly but the emptiness compelled her to keep talking.

'I sometimes wonder how my parents' lives would have turned out if that condom hadn't broken.'

Inside the party her father gyrated on the dance floor

to an eighties disco classic with his wife-to-be. Her heart lurched. He'd taught her the names of the planets and where to find the constellations in the night sky. He'd taught her to think big, shown her how to transfer her art skills into murals. And he was Mr Unfaithful – the man who didn't love her mum.

'You shouldn't think like that.' His arms a strong cocoon, Nick held her, his chin gently resting on her head. 'It won't change anything. It was a twist of fate. A good one if you ask me.'

'I know that now.' She pointed to the sky trying to find her way back into the bubble they'd been in before Joe came home and stirred everything up. 'That's the Plough.'

She had a lump like a beach pebble in her throat. Glancing back into the party, she spotted her mother dancing in the kaleidoscopic lights with Mervin, off-duty, out of uniform, shirt sleeves rolled back, totally chilled. Tall and lean, his dark hair was sprinkled with grey, especially at the temples, quite handsome.

Mum and Mervin?

'The policeman's flirting with your mother.'

'I'm so glad you said that. I thought it was just me. Now I know I'm not hallucinating.' Shelly was smiling and boogying on down. 'How embarrassing to have a mother who thinks she can bop for England!'

'Don't be mean!' Nick's eyes darkened. 'You know my

mother has done some outrageous things but I never hold it against her because I've seen her at rock bottom. I admire how she got her life back on track. I'd forgive just about anything as long as she's well.'

'Including dodgy dancing with your favorite policeman?' She half-closed her eyes because she couldn't quite bear to watch.

'Even that! I bet a few months ago you'd have been overjoyed if a doctor had told you that by summer Shelly would be grooving on the dance floor like her accident never happened.'

Her heart filled with gratitude to him for reminding her what was important. She shivered again. Nick pulled off his jacket and placed it around her shoulders. Still warm from his body, and imbued with his scent, she slipped her arms into the soft sleeves and lost her hands and fingers because they were much too long.

Standing behind her, his body acted like a shield between her and the party. He wrapped his arms tightly around her and she leaned back into his chest, a wall of rock.

'I used to think it was up to me to figure out how to fix my parents' unhappiness. I desperately wanted to please them.' She'd lie awake in bed at night, listening for her father's key in the lock, and dreaming up an imaginary world where she lived in the old farmhouse above the beach and their home wasn't filled with the unexploded tension of unspoken words.

'It doesn't work that way. Children aren't made of glue.'

'From now on I'm giving myself permission to feel what I feel. Even when I feel sad.'

Cut off from the noisy party Nick turned her in his arms to face him. 'Don't torture yourself. We'll go. I'm sorry I made you sad. I shouldn't have pushed you into coming here tonight. If I could snap my fingers and magically stop your heart breaking over this ...' He clicked his fingers, as if it was worth a try. '... I would.'

She stared up into the eyes she could lose herself in. 'That's sweet,' she whispered. 'But you can relax. I'm not sad. And you don't have to fix me. It turns out I'm okay. My future's my own. Things are clear in my head now.'

'That must have been awfully good champagne.' His voice rolled through her with a hint of mockery. Delicious tingles zipped down her spine.

'The best. The point I'm making, Mr Hollywood,' she said, retaliating, 'is that I realized something important today. I've been drifting.' She'd been locked in a pattern left over from childhood, too mollycoddled to see it, suffo-cated, convinced that everyone would be lost without her, when all along they'd been her safety net, helping her, giving her work, not because they didn't want her to be independent, but to ensure she'd have enough money saved to make her dream a success. 'It's finally dawned on me that I'm not responsible for anyone's happiness but my own.'

'Does this mean you're kissing goodbye to your people-pleasing tendencies?'

Reacting to his teasing tone she spun around the deck flaunting her disco moves, totally out of time with the music and not even trying to match the rhythm. 'I'm not giving them up entirely. Just aiming to use them more effectively.'

'Good to know.' He caught her in his arms. His devilish smile curved across his face. 'How about starting with pleasing yourself?' He trapped her against the rail with his body, their eyes locked.

She met his smile with bubbly anticipation. 'I only care about right now, with you, and the ways we please each other.'

The notes of a slow, sexy love song drifted out from the party, the beat clashing with the steady break of waves on the beach.

'Dance?' Nick drew her into his arms, where her body met hard muscle. Strong, powerful, possessive, he held her, moving in time. She lay her head on his chest and followed his lead, absorbed in the rhythm of the music and his pounding heartbeat. When the music stopped they stayed fused together, silent, lingering, listening to the indecipherable hum of party chatter and the shushing of the receding tide. His face was in the shadows, but her body responded to his touch.

Breaking the stillness Nick dipped his head and took her lips in a deep, burning kiss. On the verge of losing all sense of time and place, her mouth opened up to him, softly, hotly exploring him. His fingers caressed her neck and she melted into the moment, alive with new possibility.

'Hey Layla.' Joe walked onto the deck and they split apart like they'd been cut in two with an axe, the beautiful synergy shattered. 'I meant to say earlier – you look lovely. Like you belong in a magazine.' Her insides squirmed. He stared at them, his eyes adjusting to the darkening twilight, and cleared his throat loudly. 'I left some things at your place.' He looked around as if she might have stashed his belongings somewhere conveniently nearby. 'I don't suppose you thought to pack my stuff up and bring it down?'

'No Joe, I didn't. Because I don't suppose there's any etiquette guide in existence that covers turning up at your ex's wedding celebration with a load of binbags full of his assorted crap.' Straightening her shoulders, she looked him over like she was a trawler-man disappointed with a particularly poor catch. Pausing for impact she scanned the party to check that Lainy was out of earshot. 'Apart from anything else Lainy seems quite nice, so I wouldn't want to spoil her night.' His mouth gaped and she reined herself in. 'If you want your stuff, come and get it yourself.'

'Cool.' Conspiratorial, he lowered his voice. 'She thinks we were over a long time ago. She doesn't know we were living together – you know, before I went travelling.'

'Not my problem.'

'Just so as you know.'

'No Joe, I think you've mixed me up with your wife. She's the one who should know,' she said, determined to stay calm but close to failing. 'Because if you don't tell her someone else probably will.'

Joe's shoulders twitched and he looked at his feet. He shuffled awkwardly, scraping the toe of one shiny shoe in the sand that had drifted onto the deck until it turned dull and scuffed. 'Look,' he said, avoiding meeting her eyes, 'Lainy just happened. Alright? It was lonely out there. First off, I missed you. And one thing led to another. You know how it is.'

Chapter Sixteen

Layla trembled and Nick's fist clenched. He unclenched it and raked his hand through his hair to the back of his neck and turned away from the sideshow. He'd got himself into some situations but …

This guy takes the biscuit! He deserves a viewers' award. A definite contender for the Top Tosspot.

The moon shone like someone had painted it into a perfect sky spattered with glittering stars. Layla looked beautiful. In spite of everything that this night had churned up, she'd remained a picture of perfection. After the fabulous performance they'd put on, lost in a kiss, proving that she'd moved on, he couldn't stand by and see her unravel, her effort wasted.

Pent up with menace like his character in the action movie he butted in. 'We've got an early start.' He shook Joe firmly by the hand. 'All the best. Thanks for the party.' He didn't say 'back off.' Instead, he glowered at him, making sure he knew it had been implied. 'Give my regards to your wife.' He hooked an arm around Layla's waist and practically carried her down the steps to the beach. 'Don't let him see that he got to you,' he breathed against her ear. 'Don't give him the satisfaction.'

'He's infuriatingly insensitive. How did I tolerate him for so long?' She kicked off her shoes, and ran to the water's edge. He picked them up and followed. When he caught up the restaurant had become a distant splash of light and pulsing disco beats. 'Agggghhhh!' She yelled her trapped emotions at the sky, hitched up her dress and paddled up to her knees into the moonlit water.

For a few flickering moments like frames in an old film her despair reminded him of his mother's traumas. Talking about her family had picked at the scab of raw memories for him too. She stomped at the edge of the dark sea and he remembered a scream that felt as if the world was ending from long ago.

At their home in Beverly Hills he and Alex had run in from the garden to see what was wrong. Their mother couldn't find any vodka in her drinks cabinet because she'd drunk it all. In a tantrum she'd thrown the empty bottle at the wall and smashed it. Terrified, he'd reached her sitting room in time to witness her pour an entire bottle of orange liqueur onto the carpet for no other reason than she loathed it. She was padding about barefoot in broken glass, her feet bleeding, the cuts making red streaks on the carpet. He'd watched her cry, tears streaming down her cheeks, so full of fear he ached.

Alex had gone to get the housekeeper, and he'd run towards his mother, desperate to tell her he'd make everything that was wrong better, only she'd shouted, warning him to stay away. Looking back, he understood that she'd wanted to protect him from the glass. At the time, her screeches had been vitriolic, so out of control he'd been paralyzed with shock, afraid to move or speak.

The housekeeper had called their father at the studio, and sent them to play in their tree house until he arrived. Like two little birds they'd sat up in the silent tree house for what seemed like a lifetime, frightened, not knowing if she would be alright.

Finally, Alex had gone to see what he could find out. When he'd come back he'd reported that a doctor had come to the house. She'd bandaged their mother's feet and prescribed a tranquilizer to knock her out. The housekeeper had given him cookies and they waited, staring at the spaces between the planks in the floor and the long cracks of green light reflected up from the grass way below, the only sound their munching.

Sometime later their father had arrived, pacing back and forth at the bottom of the ladder ranting at the top his lungs that Cassandra was a bloody liability and that the studio would lose thousands of dollars because she'd run out of effing vodka.

'I can't sack the housekeeper,' he'd shouted. 'She's given her notice. And you pair are less than useless. Playing games while your mother's having one of her freak-outs. Get down here, this instant.'

So Alex had scrambled down the ladder and that's when it had happened – a debilitating sense of panic that stopped Nick climbing down from the tree house. He'd looked at the ground and frozen, unable to get his jellified legs to move. Thinking he was messing about, his father had flown into a worse temper, climbed to the top of the ladder and thrown him over his shoulder in a fireman's lift. It had felt like everything in the world was his fault; his mother's abject misery, his father's anger, the housekeeper's desertion – all of these things rolled into a ball of fear in the pit of his stomach. Wobbly, disoriented, when he'd been set the right way up on the grass, he'd vomited on his father's shoes.

He pushed down the memory and concentrated on Layla. 'Are you okay?'

She paced back and forth, wading in the black sea, painfully vulnerable. 'What the ...' she stopped abruptly, but the words burst out of her, 'fudge was he thinking saying he missed me? Why open the whole stupid thing up?'

Kicking off his shoes, he peeled his feet out of his socks, rolled up his trouser legs and walked into the water to join her. He took her by the hand and drew her back to the edge. She turned to face him, sadness brimming in her eyes. 'I nearly lost my cool with Joe – not that I ever really had any!'

She let go his hand and started to walk away.

'You're being too hard on yourself. You were going to marry the guy. He deserves to be called out. Just not tonight. When he swings by to get his things you can really go to town.'

'I mean how does somebody's wedding just happen?' She kept walking. 'Fate?'

'Or he made a mistake.' He grabbed their shoes and caught her up. 'I guess finding someone to spend a lifetime with isn't an exact science.' Ankle deep in the water they walked along the water's edge. 'For what it's worth you're asking the wrong person.'

She'd opened her heart, and as a consequence she had him dredging up things he hadn't thought about in years. He didn't know how to make things better. He remembered something now that lifted his mood. He and Alex had picked flowers from the garden and put them in a vase beside their mother's bed so they'd be the first thing she saw when she woke up.

He'd wanted to look after Layla for the same reason.

Being there for someone felt good ... until it went wrong. If he told her about his feelings he'd risk making things more difficult for her. He couldn't expect her to take on his problems. Discovering Beth existed and that he'd been excluded was a nail in his heart. Her rejection was a second nail, piercing in deeper, right next to the first.

His fingers found hers and he held her hand.

'It is not in the stars to hold our destiny but in ourselves.'

'You're full of wisdom all of a sudden?'

'Not me. Shakespeare. Julius Caesar. Courtesy of Alex.'

'Him and Maggie getting together again after all that time apart must have been written in the stars – they're so meant for each other, proof that sometimes destiny works out right in the end.'

He coughed, his throat scratchy like he'd swallowed sand. 'You really think that?'

'Yes.' She stopped paddling along in the sea and turned to him. She smiled and the hope on her face lit up the night.

His heart thundered. He couldn't bear to tell her that he'd taken Alex and Maggie's fate into his own hands. 'I don't believe in waiting for life to happen. I like to take control.'

'Some things are outside of our control.'

Breaking away from her spell, he stared off into the darkness and caught a tiny ball of light whizzing through the night sky. 'Wow! A shooting star! Did you see it?'

'Yes.' Her voice soft, the starry night stole her breath.

'If anyone had asked me, I'd have said they didn't exist.'

'You've never seen one?' She looked up searchingly. 'Destiny, you see?'

'I was meant to be here tonight on this beach with you to see a shooting star?'

He smoothed down her hair and his fingers caressed her temples. His lips found hers and his heartbeat pounded.

When she broke away from his kiss she looked down at the water. 'We're not fate,' she protested in a whisper. 'We're a fling.'

His heart lurched. The dial on his emotions was turned up high. All he wanted was this moment.

'What we are is fantastic,' he said.

He peered up into the star sprinkled sky wondering if he'd spot another shooting star. Did some people wait a lifetime and never see one? Something had happened here.

'Fantastic is good enough for me.'

She'd been the ultimate decompression, an escape from the mess he'd made. That didn't make him happy though, it throbbed painfully like the ugly bruise he'd arrived with. He'd stopped separating Layla from her feelings. And his own.

'Look I have to come clean,' he confessed, 'I agree that Maggie and Alex are made for each other. But I don't trust destiny. You can't rely on it. Here's the thing – I set them up. It wasn't fate. It was me. I asked a magazine to arrange for her to work on a fashion shoot with Alex and me.' She looked at him wide-eyed and a surprised *'Oh'* formed on her lips. 'I thought you knew.'

She shook her head slowly and bit her lip. 'Why?'

'Things were tense between me and Alex when *Vampires* finished. I was angry. Alex wanted to quit, and I blamed him for the show getting cancelled. In reality, it was time and he saw it first.'

'That's no excuse for meddling in his life.' Layla flopped down onto the sand and hugged her knees. She picked up a shell.

'I got thinking about how things started. I put a hell of a lot of pressure on him. He loved London. He was happy. His thing with Maggie was about to turn into something. He didn't want to leave for LA. Our mother was still living out there at the time and she'd got the heads up about *Mercy of the Vampires*. She was like a terrier with a bone – certain that Alex and I would be right for it.' He sat down on the sand next to her. She gathered a collection of pebbles and shells. 'I wasn't convinced. I'd done a little TV, not much, and Alex hadn't finished his degree.'

She didn't look up. 'What changed?'

'She wouldn't let it drop. She got me round to her way of thinking and quite honestly she'd been through such a lot of heartbreak – my dad leaving, her problems with alcohol, drug addiction, rehab – I wanted her to be proud of us.'

She touched his forearm. 'That's sweet.'

'Don't credit me with more kindness than I deserve.' His heart climbed into his throat. 'Sure, I wanted my mother's approval, but once she'd talked me round I wanted *Vampires* for myself just as much. More. I pushed Alex into dropping out of his drama course before he took his finals. It would have been a non-starter without him. The marketing concept behind us getting the parts of the twin vampires relied heavily on us being real life twins. Our mother had networked until she was blue in the face to get us considered. Given our lack of acting experience, I'm surprised the studio agreed to let us through the doors, never mind hire us.' He sighed heavily. 'They did and we'd have been crazy to pass up the opportunity.'

'Your mother's name opened doors for you?' She concentrated on the pebbles and shells, sorting them into separate piles.

'It's awkward to admit, but yes. Being the sons of Drake and Cassandra Wells definitely helped. We brought the Wells branding with us. She was beyond ecstatic when they signed us. There was no turning back.'

'And the rest is history. The show's a global hit. I'm sorry I haven't watched much of it. I'll have to get the boxset.'

He didn't care what she thought of the show, it was the impact of his admission that mattered. He reached out and touched her face, tipping her chin up so that she had to meet his eyes. 'You think badly of me?'

'I think you're driven to succeed.'

'Alex looked out for me when we were kids. I always looked up to him. And I couldn't forget the way he was forced to drop everything. He'd fallen for Maggie. I felt bad about it. So I fixed it for them to meet up again.'

'Ten years later!' Her eyes searched his face. 'Messing with people's hearts is risky.' She went back to fixing on the shells and pebbles. In an alternating pattern she arranged them in a circle on the sand. 'When Magenta – Maggie,' she corrected, 'came home to Porthkara after things turned bad with Alex it was like she'd taken a vow of silence. She hated the publicity circus. It hit her hard. She didn't want to talk about what happened in New York.' Layla paused, her interest in making a shell circle gone. 'What you did could have gone horribly wrong.'

'I wanted Alex to have a chance to see if there was still something there. I didn't count on things getting so complicated.'

She stood up and brushed the sand off her dress. 'Luckily it's worked out for the best. They couldn't be any happier.'

'Alex got everything he's ever wanted and more.' He got to his feet and picked up a pair of their shoes in each hand, hers swinging by their straps as they walked towards to the bottom of the cliff path. 'As matchmaking goes, I guess it doesn't get any better than that. But for the record I don't make a habit of interfering in other people's lives. It was a one-off.'

Her smile radiant her eyes twinkled. 'You tried to make good things happen because you wanted the people you love to be happy. There's nothing bad about caring.'

His heart thumped. He dropped the shoes, pulled her into his arms and wrapped her in his hold. He held her for a moment, breathing her in. Her electricity shot through him.

'The sooner I get you off this beach the better.'

'And if we don't go just yet?' The breathless charm in her tone excited him. Still wearing his jacket, she reached up, drawing him towards her, pulling him closer, their bodies pressed together tight. 'I want you right here, right now beneath the stars.' She whispered the words against his ear, her breath soft on his hot skin.

Aching hard, he moaned. Possessed with desire for her, a bubble of raw emotion grew from his gut and swelled in his chest. Closing his eyes, he searched his head for words. Her lips pressed against his in a soft urgent kiss.

Lost in the touch and the taste of her he broke away at last. Cradling her face in his hands he drew in a long breath and looked deep into her eyes. 'You're so beautiful.'

The words didn't come close to expressing the feeling she'd unleashed. She was a new storm in his world, good for him – *too* good for him.

Chapter Seventeen

Fireworks shot into the sky over the distant restaurant and the heat of the moment intensified as showers of explosive colour filled the night.

Nick reached a hand to the back of her neck, twisting strands of hair around his fingers, caressing her nape. She looked up into his eyes and his lips captured hers once more. She was totally, messily, melted. She'd go anywhere in the world with him if he asked her to.

'I want to make love to you,' he urged, gently shrugging her out of his jacket and letting it fall onto the sand.

Her heart warned her to back away. 'You don't have to use the "L" word,' she whispered. 'We're great together. That's enough.'

The sudden kaleidoscope of explosive colour ended, leaving behind electric silence. Far off, only the village lights punctuated the silvery moonlit darkness.

Nick was her avoidance of broken promises. She only

wanted to live moment by moment, right now. Because if she started to think any other way she'd be putting her heart in a danger zone she'd never get out of.

'It's just a word. I'm your quick fix. I get that.'

What had begun as frivolous had turned into something fabulous. And that was exactly it – he didn't get it, why would he? 'You're more than a quick fix. I don't want to confuse things by using a word you don't mean. That's all.'

'Okay, if that's how you feel then I won't use words.' He cupped her face in his hands and looked at her for a long moment, his eyes dark. His cheek muscle flickered tensely.

He kissed her again, long, slow and lingering, like they were discovering each other for the first time. His kiss reached deep inside her soul in a way that made her feel as if she was teetering on a dangerous ledge.

The fire between them had turned into something more dangerous, an inferno fuelled by emotion. Regardless of everything she'd said, she succumbed to the feeling that was so beautiful it was almost painful. All the while she ached to find her way back to the safety of that fleeting physical heat because discovering that she could fall deeply in love meant consequences.

The row of buttons just below her cleavage glinted in the moonlight, shimmering like a line of black diamonds. She ached with the temptation to feel his fingers unbutton her.

His hand cupped her breast and she threw back her

head so that his mouth moved to her neck, nipped at her ear and trailed hot and delicious kisses down to the curve of her shoulder. Urgent fingers tugged at the delicate buttons on her dress, slowly, oh-so-slowly, undoing each until in a final burst of impatience she arched into his touch, breasts tight with desire and he tweaked the last tiny jewel-like button so hard that it broke from its thread, getting lost in the sand. He smoothed the flat of his palm against her skin, parting the fabric and bathing her breasts in the pale light of the moon.

Feather soft, his mouth kissed her skin, moving intently down across her breasts, compelling her with desire.

'I have a confession' he said, stopping in his tracks and looking at her, eyes intense.

'We said no words.'

He ignored her. 'I wanted you the minute I first set eyes on you.'

'You did?' He didn't answer. His hand still cupping her breast, his lips returned to pleasuring her sensitized skin, his mouth unbelievably provocative, taunting, turning her on. She craved his mouth on her hard nipples and he satisfied her craving, driving her wild. 'Since you *first* first saw me?' she said, her voice raspy, breaking her own rule about no words. 'Are you sure?'

'Sure I'm sure. And when I *second* first saw you – the morning I woke up on the sofa?'

'Uh-huh?' The touch of his hands, his mouth, raised her levels of impatience and anticipation ridiculously high. His hands caressed her breasts and he circled his thumbs against her nipples.

'I wanted you twice as badly then!'

'Really?' Sweet delicious pleasure pooled with insane intensity at her core.

'Yes, really.' He pulled back, looking at her with an incredible intensity that made her desperate to feel him inside her, and then kissed her hard, his mouth hot, his tongue tangling with hers, intensifying their insatiable heat for each other.

'Do you want me now?' Her voice a whisper as she said the words, she knew 'want' wasn't what she was talking about. Was it actually love?

She trembled, her entire body tingled explosively and she curved close against him. He bit softly at her earlobe and his mouth trailed down her neck again.

'I think you know the answer to that.'

'I do?' Head thrown back, afraid of her feelings, more determined than ever not to define them, she ached for his ecstasy-inducing body.

'Oh yes, you do.' The arm encircling her waist pulled her down onto the sand on top of him. 'I have never wanted anyone more than I want you.'

'We agreed we're not doing words.' Arms around him

she rolled over, taking him with her, the exciting weight of his body on top of her.

'Right.'

'Ouch.' Against her back the soft sand was strewn with tiny, lumpy pebbles and shells. 'It's stony.'

Totally in control, he felt around with one hand for his jacket, spread it flat on the sand and shifted her onto the soft silk lining. His mouth connected with the jutting nipple of one breast, insistent, provoking her reeling senses, urgent. His hands smoothed over her thighs and tangled in the fabric of her dress pushing it upwards and pushing her need for him beyond patience. She fought with his belt buckle in a hurry to separate the smooth leather from the cool metal, and felt his erection strain against her hands as she undid his fly.

Impatient, he freed himself and paused to sort out a condom. The delay sky-rocketed her desire off the charts. She wriggled out of the lacey thong that felt more like dental floss than underwear, exhilarated at the idea of sex on the beach in the moonlight. Ready, he molded his body between her thighs and pressed the tip of his erection to her hot centre, holding off for a long, long moment, driving her crazy for him until, wired with desire and uncontainable lust, he entered her.

Falling for him deeply, enrapt, she burned, delirious with the good things his body did to her. She tugged at his shirt, her hands grazing feverishly up and down his back, nails lightly spiking his skin. Connected in delectable fusion, he was a dream. She pressed impossibly closer, drew him in, encompassing him with her legs, two bodies locked in one mind-blowing contortion. Her body responded to his deep rhythm, and he took her ecstatic senses higher and higher. He pushed back on muscular arms and without breaking the heavenly connection looked deep into her eyes like a mind reader, though the emotion on his own face was indecipherable.

The pressure of his body, his thighs touching hers, the feel of him so hard inside her – with his strength and power and vitality, he coaxed her willing body to go with him, driven to a peak of shattering passion, then, intuitively led by her soft cry of satisfaction as orgasmic frissons shivered through her, he followed fast, bonded to her by a heat that seared through their bodies with the shudder of a molten climax.

Reality hit him like a nasty headline. Groaning he fell away, releasing her from his arms, from his lunacy. Glaring stupidity lanced through him suddenly. The shock he felt couldn't have been greater if someone had driven onto the beach and caught them in their headlights. He stood up, straightening his clothes, fumbling to do up his belt. Thrown by the out-of-control passion that had driven him to tell her that he wanted to make love to her on the beach, that he'd never wanted anyone more, he reached out a hand, and drew her to her feet.

She stood, barefoot on the sand, dark eyes wider than ever in the moonlight, eyeliner smudged, trembling fingers quickly refastening the buttons on her dress. A ghostly trail of grey cloud drifted in front of the moon but there was enough light to see that the fabulously put-together woman he'd taken to the party looked a little wild – and very, very beautiful.

Silent, she smoothed her rumpled dress and dug her toes into the sand. He'd been lost in a kiss so full of hope and promise that he'd allowed himself to believe it meant something; and in the same moment he'd been torn to pieces by a lust that ran deeper than physical craving, reaching into him, pushing aside his resolutions, knocking down his barriers, cutting into his heart.

The moon slipped out from behind the spectral cloud bathing her in its mercurial glow. She looked changed, somehow different. He swallowed hard. He was seeing what he wanted to see, not what actually was.

'Just for the record,' she said, 'Sex on the beach under a sky full of stars is amazing.' She broke from his stare and bent to snatch up her shoes. 'With you,' she added, as if the statement needed qualifying.

He couldn't help himself. A possessive pang made him hope she hadn't shared that experience before. 'How did I rate compared to your previous sex on the beach moments?'

'I've never done anything so brazen.' She laughed. 'There haven't been any. You?'

He shook his head. 'Me neither.' He brushed the sand from his jacket and placed it gently around her soft shoulders.

'Another first!'

'Two in one night! I can tick "spot a shooting star" and "bang on the beach" off my bucket list.'

Uncertainty shadowed her face and she raised her eyebrows questioningly. 'Do you have one?'

'No.' It was his turn to laugh. 'But I may start one.' Sex on the beach had been all kinds of awesome. He felt secretly stupidly pleased that it was a first for them both. His attraction had turned into something more. She was so special; he'd work hard in Paris not to ruin it like everything else he touched and protect her from his undiluted chaos.

'I don't want to let you go.'

'It sounds like I'm fired,' she said, joking.

'Seriously, the days I've spent here with you have been the best time. Porthkara is perfection. I feel ready to face the world again.' He couldn't think of a moment in his life when he'd been happier, but it wasn't real. He was hiding from the harsh truth that he had a daughter he'd failed, she'd rejected him, and he was stuck as to what positive action he could possibly take to fix that.

She slipped her hand into his and pulled him towards the cliff path. 'Next stop Paris?

Chapter Eighteen

The shocking news that Beth was his and that he knew nothing about her had been the mental equivalent of going over the edge of the cliffs at Porthkara. Layla's unique brand of chemistry had seemed the easy answer. Suddenly it was too much. It was time to 'fess up. She ought to know the truth about why he'd come to Cornwall in a tailspin.

The idea of Beth and Fran suffering, and of Layla trapped in crossfire if some shark journalist found out and tried to exploit the information, filled him with dread. The idea of a random paparazzo patching together a few pictures and labeling any of them his next scandal set him on edge. He'd been in a media-free dream world because no one who cared to make some cash from photographing him knew he was there, but away from Porthkara that had the potential to change.

At the bottom of the cliff path he weighed up the choices.

Force Layla to trek all along the beach, past the ongoing party. Or brave the shortcut.

He had so much to explain. He plodded on, putting one foot in front of the other, bracing himself as they climbed the steps cut into the rocks leading up the side of the cliff.

'So, these photos you're doing in Paris. What are they for exactly? The film?' She threw questions over her shoulder at him.

His gut clenched. 'Publicity. Promotion. It's part of the job,' he answered, anxious to find the right moment to mention Beth. 'Acting is my whole world. It's all I ever wanted to do. It's what I live and breathe. Except for a long time, the edges between my real life and my professional life got blurred. I wasn't bothered by that because nobody – me included – cared what was true and what wasn't.' He stared at the back of her head and followed her upwards. 'Now I hate how it's chaotic. I have media training. I have a publicist. And my image is a total mess. Take that stupid spinster list.'

'The ultimate bad boy's bad idea?'

'Precisely. Rebooting my so-called image came up in conversation at a pre-shoot dinner in Paris with executive producers. A list of the world's sexiest married men had been published in a gossip magazine.' He gave a cynical snort. 'Alex, of course, was on it, along with several megastars. The headshots had captions from the guys' wives. Maggie said she wouldn't put Alex at the top of any *Hot* list because he was hopeless at reuniting his unpaired socks and there was nothing sexy about a man who can't keep his socks in line.'

'Too true.'

'Whilst Alex was on the *Hot* list, yours truly featured on the list of *Nots*.'

Layla's laughter sang out up ahead.

'The non-existent "spinster list" had the execs rocking with hilarity on their Louis XIVth dining chairs. There's a serious subtext. I need to clean up my act. If the public don't like me in this movie, I'll be replaced.'

His notions about tying the knot with Toni had been part of his short-lived move to clean up his act. That, and seeing Alex so happy with Maggie, he'd started to believe that if they could get it right then so could he.

As they reached the first bend in the path his stomach heaved. Carried on the summer wind, he caught the sound of the waves breaking on the sand far below.

'So, if you did have a list who would be on it?' Infuriatingly nonchalant, she tossed the question at him.

'I don't know. What's with all the questions?'

She laughed. Barefoot, she scurried on, hurrying off like a super-agile mountain goat.

He pushed the fingers of both hands into his hair frenetically. Frantic about the cliff rising upwards into the darkness, he turned around and paced back and forth on the spot like a caged animal. Perplexed, because he had something important to tell her, he willed himself to man up and climb the path. He couldn't back out, let her go on alone, the moon had disappeared behind a wall of cloud, anything might happen.

'For what it's worth you'd make an awesome Hollywood wife. We nailed it tonight. I'd pick the time we've spent together over hanging with any celebrity I've ever met.' He called out into the black velvet night seeking out the shadowy movements of her body.

Either she didn't hear him or she chose to ignore what he'd said. 'What you need is someone media savvy – who stands out, transforms you in the eyes of the press and catapults you onto the *Hot* lists, hopefully in at least equal place with Alex, or better still a notch or two higher,' she said.

'Not much to ask.'

He pulled his phone out of his trouser pocket and lit the screen using it as a torch light to find his way. He caught her up at the next bend. She turned to him and he captured her face in his screen light.

'While we're in Paris I'm going to make it my mission to identify your perfect woman. I'll let you know who I come up with.'

'That's not cool.' He gritted his teeth against his feelings.

It didn't work. Thrown by her ridiculous suggestion he snapped back, 'I'm fine thanks.'

He searched her face for a reaction. He didn't get one because she turned away from him and pressed on. 'Calm down. It was banter. I didn't mean anything by it. Are you coming?'

If he was brutally honest, she was like nobody he'd met before. She didn't stand to gain anything from being seen with him, and she wanted nothing apart from a good time, fun, living in the moment. He stopped, immovable. Looking into the distance he saw the village lights and an overriding feeling of sadness struck him; he wished he hadn't come to Porthkara, hadn't snuck into Maggie's house like a burglar in the night, hadn't stayed waiting for the bruise to heal on his face. Layla had triggered a need to lay himself bare. She made him feel things he'd rather ignore and want to say things that were easier left buried.

He lagged behind, the distance opening up between them as they climbed.

'It's not far now. Just a couple more bends up ahead and we're almost there.' Her voice was growing fainter the further ahead she got, and her voice sounded breathless and infernally sexy. She'd no idea of the effect she had on him, how much feeling she'd stirred up.

Angry at himself for how afraid he felt – of everything, not just the height of the cliff – every bone in his body seized up. Forcing one foot in front of the other he caught her up again. Waiting for him, unaware of his tense fragility, she took his hand. Neither of them breathed a word. He swayed like a clump of long sea grass moving in the wind and his heartbeat raced. She squeezed his fingers tight.

'You okay?' she whispered.

He gathered his nerve. Nodding slowly, he stared down at his feet unable to raise his head and look her in the face.

'Talk to me. Tell me something. Anything at all.' The tension coming from Nick was toxic. She'd hoped that in the dark, without being able to visualize the cliff clearly, she'd blast him with small talk and distract him into taking the shortcut he'd been avoiding. Her tactic had worked up to a point but now he was rooted to the spot. She felt terrible. She'd been tired and lazy and couldn't face the long way home with the added unwelcome likelihood of running into Joe again. But being stranded with Nick halfway up the cliff side in the pitch dark was ten times worse.

'I have a child.' His voice was hoarse and monotone. 'A girl. A daughter.'

She suppressed her reaction. Emotions, a fusion of surprise and confusion, wedged in her throat. In a split second she said flippantly, 'I was thinking more along the lines of a knock-knock joke to jolly things along. Not a bombshell.'

'It's no joke. It's the truth. I'm the father of child. She's eleven years old. And I didn't know anything about her until a couple of weeks ago. Her name's Be ... Be ...' He stumbled over the name like he was fluffing a line. 'Beth.'

'The girl on your phone?'

'She's my daughter.' He repeated it as if he didn't quite believe it.

'You didn't know?' Layla was so stunned she felt like she was trying to translate a foreign language.

'No. And she didn't know about me. And actually, it was better that way, because now that we do know she doesn't want to have anything to do with me.'

'When did you find out? Have you met her?'

'No, I haven't met her because when I tried she refused to see me.'

'Oh Nick, I'm so sorry. But how can anyone do that? Just turn around after eleven years and announce that you have a child together?'

Her heart hammered. It made sense. The girl in the picture looked like him. She ached to hug him, but uncertainty jabbed at her. She couldn't begin to imagine how he must be feeling. Half-truths, sudden subject changes, difficult silences – they'd been an all too familiar feature in her own childhood. Since Nick had been spending time out from his real life with her she'd started to believe that she could be free of all that. And now he'd told her this secret. What was she supposed to do with that?

'I know, right? I've done so much thinking since I got her mother's email.'

'You found out in an email? Crikey.'

'The truth is I was shattered. But I'm done analysing the ifs and buts and whys. The way she broke the news to me doesn't matter.'

'Eleven years of silence though. That's tough to take.'

'It doesn't sound great. I know. But she didn't storm back into my life and dump it on me without hesitation. She did it with good reason, there wasn't time for soul searching, and I'm dealing with it the best I can.'

'By hiding from it?' she said gently.

'I'm waiting for more news. I've said too much. I wanted you to know the truth. The reason I rocked up in Porthkara. That's all.' His voice robotic, his face all grim hard lines in the darkness, he held up the palm of his hand in a gesture that told her more clearly than words that he wanted to shut the subject down. 'I don't want you to feel that I'm involving you in my problem.'

She didn't want to pry. Inhaling sharply through her nose, she locked her teeth together, afraid to say the wrong thing. She exhaled sharply. 'Look. It's probably none of my business. But you've been hanging out with me, we've had a laugh, the last few days have been a blast. And all along it turns out you haven't just been hiding your face, you've been hiding a secret.' She pinched her forefinger and thumb together leaving a gap of air to indicate a small amount. 'It's kind of hard not to feel a little bit involved.'

Nick sank down onto a wide sandy step shored up with a wooden rung. 'You're absolutely right,' he admitted. 'I've been hiding from it.' Layla sat too, careful to leave a space between them on the step.

'The real question is what are you going to do about it?'

He closed his eyes and circled the tips of his forefingers on his eyelids deep in thought. After a long pause, he looked up. 'I don't actually know. Doing something means consequences. I tried to see her once. I failed. For now, I'm leaving well alone.'

'You know the farm at the top of the cliff? They used to keep a donkey. Billy.'

'Where's this going?'

'Listen. In summer he grazed the meadow in front of the house. And once a year for the village fair Billy gave donkey rides on the beach. Anyway, my point is he was a funny donkey. Obstinate in the extreme. So for every ride he gave he got a sugar lump.'

'I take it this is an analogy where I'm Billy?'

'No. It's me. I'm the donkey. When you got here I was like Billy, I wouldn't move forward. You changed that.'

'I'm cubed sugar?'

She laughed. 'Consequences can be good as well as bad you know. Think of the positives.'

'What are they exactly?'

'The birthday parties for a start!' She paused, weighing up his dilemma. 'And if you have a child, then Alex and Maggie have a niece and Phoebe and Horatio have a cousin. How great is that?'

Nick snorted.

'And Cassandra's been a grandma for over a decade. That's going to be about as popular as a wet Saturday in August.'

'Well if the photos Maggie's posted on just about every available social media site of your mother with the twins are anything to go by, I'm willing to bet she'll be thrilled to have another readymade grandchild to spoil.'

A sudden gust sent her hair flying across her eyes. He placed his hands either side of her face. His palms warmed her cheeks and he softly kissed her lips. Smoothing back her wild hair he curved it all into a long swathe, and his fingers massaged her nape as he pushed it off the back of her neck so that it all fell across one shoulder.

'If only it were that easy,' he said huskily.

A frisson from the touch of his fingers rippled through her body. Unable to resist she leaned into him and let him wrap her in his arms. Resting her head on his chest, she listened to the pounding beat of his heart. Still, quiet, they stayed that way.

'We'd better go,' she whispered, although not really inclined to move. For a while longer they sat staring out into the darkness at the black sea, watching the lights of a far-off ship inch across the horizon. Eventually his silence made her uneasy. 'We can't sit here like this forever.'

She stood up, but Nick didn't budge. Frozen on the step he started to tremble uncontrollably.

'I don't think I can go any further. My knees have turned to jelly.'

Her heart sank. 'Come on Nick,' she coaxed, remaining calm. 'We're nearly at the top. Don't freak out on me. You've got this.' She took hold of both his hands and drew him unsteadily to his feet. 'I know this path like the back of my hand. It'll be okay. I promise.' She positioned herself on the outside of the path and linked her arm through his, edging him forward. 'It's perfectly safe. The only awkward bit is the corner up ahead and it's securely fenced off. Once we get past that it's easy. To be honest, in the dark you can't really tell how far down it is.' That was the wrong thing to say because she felt him shudder like an engine that had just failed. 'Don't look down,' she said when he didn't speak. 'Look up, look straight ahead. And don't forget to breathe.' Slowly she half-shuffled half-led him towards the top of the cliff.

'It's the fear.' He flattened his back against the rock face.

She intertwined her fingers with his tightly and held his hand firmly. 'You can do it. You can't give up now.'

'I'm not a hundred per cent sure I'll make it.'

'You haven't got a choice. Besides, there can't be many things in life that anyone is ever a hundred per cent sure about.'

He let out a cynical snort. 'We sound like we're rehearsing lines from a script.'

'I hate to break it to you Nick, but this isn't a film set. No one's going to shout "cut" and swap you for the stuntman.'

'That's not helping.'

'Well, there's no way on this earth I'm calling out the rescue helicopter to airlift a hyperventilating celebrity from the cliff path. Apart from anything else it'll kill your action man image. And I can't have that. Not on my watch. Imagine the headline in the Porthkara Parish Magazine. No, on second thoughts, don't!' He gave a muffled laugh. 'You've come this far. You can make it the rest of the way.' She gave him a nudge in an attempt to diffuse the tension. 'I mean I wouldn't recommend doing this on a stormy night in January, but tonight we really truly aren't in any danger.'

Straightening his spine with resolve, he moved slowly forward. 'You know what? I think I can actually do this.'

'Course you can. All you needed was breathing space.'

In a sudden burst of energy, he strode on grittily. 'Come along. Keep up.' He shouted over his shoulder like a bossy tour guide implying she was the one who required chivvying.

Phew. She sighed with relief, happy to see him round the difficult corner and reach the final stretch.

'The cheek of it!' she yelled after him, overjoyed that he'd made it to top of the cliff.

'Stop dilly-dallying. We've got a flight to catch.'

Chapter Nineteen

'I can't believe we're here.' Layla brushed crumbs from her skirt onto the ground for the waiting sparrows. 'The city of romance.'

They sat on a bench in a little park in Montmartre, eating cheese and tomato *baguettes* and watching a young man take photos of his girlfriend in a variety of poses in front of the iconic Parisian 'I Love You' wall. A tree shaded them from the baking midday sun, its leaves fluttering in a hot gentle breeze. He'd suggested lunch at an upscale restaurant, but she'd had other ideas and he approved.

'So what's top of your list of priorities? Shops? Museums? Cathedrals?'

She swigged from a bottle of alpine spring water. 'The Eiffel Tower and the Lovers' Bridge and ...' She consulted her guidebook. 'I don't know. There's too much. You choose.'

'To be fair the ...' He made air quotes and pulled a face '... "city of romance" thing is nothing but a tourist trap.

What makes Paris more romantic than, say, London or New York?'

Layla smiled. 'I beg to differ.' She pointed at the wall.

'Well, you're here now. You can make your own mind up. But I can't promise romance.' *Hot sex and happy times? Sure.*

Layla read aloud from her guidebook. 'Listen to this. "Emblazoned with splashes of red paint to represent a broken heart the fresco says *Je t'aime* in over three hundred languages including some forgotten dialects." What's not to like about "I love you" in a zillion different languages?'

'Broken heart,' Nick repeated emphatically. 'I rest my case.' Despite his cynicism he scanned the wall, trying to locate a language he recognized.

She swallowed a bite of her sandwich. 'Okay,' she said, 'Explain this. How can a cheese and tomato sandwich taste ten times better in Paris than it does at home?'

'That's not in the guidebook. And I fail to see that it's got anything to do with romance. French bread? The *fromage* has holes in?' He shrugged. 'I don't know. It just does.'

'Exactly. It just does. Because we're in Paris.'

'And Paris is romantic right down to its sandwich fillings?'

'I believe so.'

'Why? Because it says so in that book?' With a magician-like flourish he took the *Ten Unmissable Paris Romance Hotspots* guide out of her hands and made it vanish into a litter bin along with their sandwich wrappers. It landed with a tinny clang.

'Smile, I'm going to take a selfie.' She held out her phone and leant close, filling his head with her sweet scent. He flinched, every muscle tensing. His heart sank a little, struggling to separate her desire to save a moment in a photo, and the ability of the world at large to intrude on his private life. Certain tabloids had turned grabbing a sneaky photograph and twisting the truth in a clever caption into an art form.

He gave an internal shrug. She wasn't into that nonsense. He trusted her. 'I'll do it. I've got long arms – made for selfies.' He whisked her phone from her fingers and took a photo of them grinning like Cheshire cats in front of the wall. Before he handed the phone back, he glowered at the picture. They didn't look remotely romantic. His long-armed shot included the young couple in the background, and a smattering of other tourists, all peering at writing on the volcanic lava tiles, trying to find 'I love you' in their language.

He couldn't show her romance, but she loved all things art – and in Paris, he could do art. Having wandered the narrow streets of Montmartre, they hopped on the Metro and headed for the Musée d'Orsay. After spending two appalling days at the former train station shooting rooftop scenes, he didn't care if he never set foot in the gallery again, but since he'd promised himself that Layla would have a lovely time in Paris, he'd made a couple of calls and arranged to be let in through a side entrance immediately after closing for a private viewing of the collection.

Discreetly shadowed by two security guards they wandered through the empty gallery in complete silence. He watched carefully for her reactions as she studied the paintings. When they emerged onto the high promontory that overlooked the vast space filled with art he leaned against a wall, fighting the beginnings of panic and seeking out something to grasp onto. Throat dry, he swallowed down a gulp of air and pushed back the sick feeling in his stomach.

'This is amazing. This whole place is unbelievable.'

'Yep,' he agreed through gritted teeth. 'I had a feeling you'd like it here.' He was dizzy and his guts churned with all too familiar irrational fear but it was worth it to see how she lit up.

'Like it? That's an understatement. I love, love, love it! I've seen these paintings in books. But seeing them for real? Oh Nick – I can hardly begin to put it into words. It's beyond amazing. Thank you for bringing me here.'

She turned to him and bit her lip, unconsciously sexy as hell, distracting him and reminding him exactly why he'd brought her to this place he loathed. She made him happy, and he wanted to make her happy, and right at this moment he longed to put his arms around her and hold on as if his life depended on it. A furtive glance at the security people, faces stony as sculptures, warned him off.

'Well if you've well and truly overdosed on amazing French paintings, I reckon it's a good time to show you where we shot my rooftop scenes.'

In front of the giant station clock face she handed him her phone and he snapped another selfie. Heads tipped together they studied the result.

'It's perfect,' she gasped, her voice breathily quiet. Impatience to be alone with her flickered through him. 'It looks quite arty with that halo of back-to-front roman numerals around our heads.'

He laughed, wondering whether she'd choose to share the selfies on the internet, use them to have a go at Joe. He hoped not. He wanted to keep these moments just for them, no one else. With Layla, every day in the Cornish seaside village had had a calm simplicity about it. She had a way of making just being enough. Around her he'd stopped trying to figure out how his life should be. He was content with the easiness of being together, spiked with the awesome anticipation of more phenomenal sex. Suddenly keeping his personal life private had never mattered so much.

'Come see.' He beckoned her over to the windows. The River Seine flowed below and way beyond on a hilltop in the far-off distance sat the white-domed shape of the Sacré Coeur. 'We shot a chase scene up there.'

'Wow,' she murmured. 'I think I'd get vertigo too out on that roof. How did it go?'

'Not so good. Most of the real work was done in a studio, but the time spent on that roof was the longest two days of my life.'

'I guess that's why they have stunt guys.'

He groaned. The combination of embarrassment and nausea he'd felt during the shoot flashed through his head like a recurring nightmare. 'The stunt team was awesome. But the heights thing is a real issue. It's limiting. And I want to do as much of my own work as possible.'

'Why?' Her warm smile washed through him like a ray of summer sun, but it did nothing to dispel the fear of failing as an action hero that plagued him.

'Because it goes with the territory. I've got to be able to convince cinema-goers that I have what it takes to play the character.'

'I bet you smashed it. But you're human just like the rest of us. So why not tell the truth in interviews and publicity and stuff. Admit you don't like heights – just be yourself.'

''Fess up to being a coward?' he asked incredulous, 'I don't think so.'

'Why not? People respect honesty. So what have you got to fear? It's a no-brainer. Deconstruct the image you created around yourself by revealing the real Nick Wells.'

'Suddenly you're a PR guru?'

'Nope. But I'm getting to be quite the expert in all things Nick Wells and in my considered opinion you're a pretty nice guy.'

'Being myself is risky. If the movie doesn't do well at the box office, I'll be dropped. I need to project tough and fearless.'

'No offence but what's the point in replacing one fake image with another?'

'I'm not tough and fearless? Thanks.'

She shook her head despairingly. 'The playboy love rat thing worked for you while you were in *Mercy of the Vampires*, but are you going to go through life reinventing yourself every time you take on a new role? It doesn't make sense, if you ask me.' She hesitated, adding with a giggle, 'Which I know you didn't, so I'll just shut up.'

'I'm not convinced. One.' He held up his thumb. 'I'm an action hero with a phobia. Two.' Up went his index finger. 'I'm afraid to go to the top of the Eiffel Tower for a few promotional photographs. And three, I've already delayed the promo. If I show up on Monday with my knees knocking and a face like a wet weekend word's going to get out that I'm a liability and the producers are going to lose faith in me.'

There was that heavenly hot bottom lip bite again. 'I believe in you. I know you can do it. Last night you faced your fear and went for it.'

She had a point. He'd focused, he'd breathed, and – apart from the bit where he'd felt woozy and told her about Beth – it had been okay. And although he'd convinced himself that he'd hated every minute of the museum shoot, thinking about it now – really thinking about it – he realized that there had been spells during that couple of days when the fear had been second to everything else, working with a brilliant director, the crew, the stunt team. If he'd been honest about his phobia he'd have made things easier for everyone.

'How about we go up the Eiffel Tower for a trial run? That way you'll know what to expect on Monday.'

'Good idea. It's worth a shot.'

'We can go tomorrow. And if all else fails,' she went on, 'I guess you could try medication. Or cognac. Or both!' She cut her words dead, holding a hand over her mouth to silence herself.

'Thanks. But no thanks!' he growled, unintentionally harsh. 'Drunk and drugged to the eyeballs isn't a place I want to go. Quite aside from the family history, it doesn't really say action hero to me.' The venom in his reaction shocked them both.

She mumbled from behind her hand. 'That was a stupid thing to say.' She shrank in on herself flattened like a lifeless subject in one of the paintings on the walls. Avoiding his glare, she added, 'Tactless.'

He stepped towards her. 'I shouldn't have lashed out. My mother has turned her life around. Her rough times are something I try not to think about. I don't want you to think badly of her.'

'I don't.' Injured her eyes clouded. 'I'm sad for what you went through. But I don't judge her. Do you think so little of me?'

A cold shiver ran down his spine and he pushed down the urge to try and explain that one of his mother's out-of-control episodes had been on his mind.

'I've told you too much. About everything. You didn't sign up to get dragged into my downers.'

'If you think I'll go to the press and tell them everything I know, you needn't worry. That's not my style.'

'I know that, ignore me, I overreacted.'

The first memory he had of his mother drunk was suddenly clear in his mind once more. He'd found her collapsed on the bathroom tiles. She'd been sick. His beautiful mother, always so elegant on screen, crumpled and incoherent, mascara streaked across her tear-drenched face. She was a wreck.

'My mother fell to pieces after my dad left.' Bitterness

batted back and forth between his parents throughout his childhood, mostly played out in the full glare of the media. Fatalistically aware that he was in danger of sucking all the fun out of Paris he added, 'He destroyed her.'

'That must have been hard.'

'The first time I saw her paralytic, yes. In the end, it happened so often I got numb to it.'

Layla touched his arm. 'I'm sorry,' she whispered.

The strangest feeling hit him. No one had ever said sorry before.

Sorry for being paralytic drunk. Sorry for going to rehab. Sorry for sending you away to school. Sorry for not being there.

It was easier to hate his dad for breaking his mother's heart, and hate her for not coping, than miss them. Most of all he'd felt a failure for not being able to make it alright.

'It's all in the past.'

He was beginning to see that love didn't always equate to high stakes and inevitable chaos. Just because his parents' happiness had been short-lived and highly volatile didn't mean it always panned out like that. Alex had found all that he wanted with Maggie.

He jabbed a finger at the button for the elevator. The doors slid open and he stood aside so that she could step in.

Inside, claustrophobically accompanied by the two

cheerless security guards, the silence intensified his bad mood. He was mad at himself for burdening her with the Beth worry and for being unable to keep Layla separate from the ugliness of his feelings.

Back on the ground floor Layla walked nonchalantly out of the elevator, apparently choosing to be unaffected by his moroseness.

'Look at these,' she called to him, artfully changing the subject, giving her attention to a row of glass cases displaying miniature set designs from the Paris opera house. 'The scenery is so detailed. It's awesome.'

The smile that twitched the corners of her lips masked the fact that he'd offended her, he'd hurt her feelings. Her delight with the model scenes gave him an idea. There was something he knew she'd like and he wanted to make it happen.

The agitated appeal of getting back to being carefree with Layla gnawed at him. The desire to hold her close and explain how he felt without words consumed him. He was impatient to be alone with her at the hotel and lock out the world.

'What do you say we give these security people the slip and go hang the *do not disturb* sign on the door handle of our hotel suite?' she whispered.

'I can't believe you said that,' he murmured back. 'You read my thoughts exactly.'

Chapter Twenty

Hot water would be coursing over his body, little rivers forming in the crooks of his arms, beads of moisture spattering his rock hard muscles. She was tempted to strip off and jump in the shower with him. Throwing herself wholeheartedly into enjoying his gorgeous hotness had been the ideal answer to her troubles. And sex was the best way she knew to make him calm. It was magic. She couldn't get enough of his relaxed, lazy smile, his kisses, and the way he held her tight in his arms. She wanted to get back to what they did best – being each other's ultimate distraction from life's problems.

The up-market, elegantly *art nouveau* hotel had bags of character and Layla loved it. Grand and imposing, it sat in a wide, tree-lined boulevard a couple of blocks from the Eiffel Tower. With its tall, shuttered windows and twisted wrought iron balconies, the hotel oozed old-fash-ioned charm. She kicked off her shoes and lazed on a chaise longue covered in kingfisher blue velvet in the sitting room of the superb suite. She spread her fingers and pressed her palm into the smooth fabric. When she lifted it away she'd left a handprint in the pile. Fidgety, she made another, and another. Brushing her fingers over the soft velvet to erase the marks she sprang to her feet and walked over to the window to see what was happening in the street. The evening sun beat down, creating pools of dark shadow on the pavement beneath the evenly spaced trees. Cars crawled towards the roundabout at the top of the road, and Parisians – effortlessly chic at the end of a stiflingly hot workday – marched to the Metro entrance. Behind the office block across the street she could just see the top of the tower. She wished she could magic up a bright idea to desensitize his fear of being photographed up there.

Turning her back on the window she picked up the boutique gin and tonic Nick had ordered from the hotel's cocktail menu. She raised the glass to her lips and an ice-cube slipped into her mouth. She kept the ice on her tongue, liking the cooling sensation as it melted. It slid down her throat and she sipped the drink. The heavenly flavours of Provençale summer herbs, wild thyme, lavender and rosemary, all handpicked on a sundrenched mountainside, swirled across her taste buds.

She bit down hard on her lip. She'd gone from forgotten almost-fiancée to fabulous fling with a film star and she'd come close to ruining it all because of a thoughtless throw-away remark. He felt he'd told her too much. It wasn't just confusing, she felt bruised. He didn't fully trust her. Each time he'd opened up to her about himself, he'd shut right down again, the things he'd shared gone, as if not speaking about them meant they didn't exist. Complex should be his middle name. He had unfathomable things going on beneath the surface and away from Porthkara she was out of her comfort zone.

She set down her drink, and pondered the world outside the window. Had he just been using her to hide from himself? That wasn't fair. She had no right to hold a grudge for him treating her the same way she'd treated him.

A sharp knock on the door rang out above the sound of the power shower streaming jets of water over Nick's body, bringing her back to reality and cancelling out her thoughts of leaping into the excellently-large and easily-big-enough-for-two shower cubicle. She quickly opened the door and a uniformed bellboy practically stumbled into the room overloaded with bags with designer labels on.

'*Bonsoir Madame* ...' His eyes flicked to her left hand where there was obviously no wedding ring and he ahem-ed self-consciously, adding '... *Mademoiselle*' with a flirtatious smile. 'I've brought the things *Monsieur* has ordered for you.'

'For me?' He nodded deferentially, so she took the things he held out to her and stood trance-like, puzzled and waiting for him to leave.

'The concierge asked me to tell *Monsieur* that he got the tickets. You can collect them from the box office.'

Tickets? Tickets for what?

'Oh right,' she said, attempting to look like she knew what all this was about.

The bellboy turned on his heels and strode out closing the door quietly behind him.

She opened a bag with a French designer name on it and, ripping into the rustling tissue paper inside, pulled out the most amazing deep green dress. Drop-dead-gorgeous shoes followed from the next bag. '*Ooh là là!*'

'You like?'

She spun around to find Nick watching her intently from the doorway. He looked divine. All tanned skin and wet hair, hard jawline, temptingly freshly shaved. *Ooh là là. Again.* She liked that his compelling smile was back on his face, even though he was being mute and mysterious about the 'I-have-a-child-I-didn't-know-about' revelation.

'I love!' She laughed. Making up her mind to accept his regret over telling her things about his life, and forget all about it, she added, 'What's going on?'

'The opera and dinner,' he drawled. 'I'm taking us to see *La Bohème.*' Suddenly self-conscious he ran a hand over the back of his head. 'Do you like opera?'

'I don't know.' She bit her lip. 'I've never been.'

'Me neither. It'll be a first for both of us.'

'Another one,' she hinted, deliberately a shade coquette.

'I figured it might be ...' He felled her with a smouldering look. '... Romantic?'

His far-too-bewitchingly-sexy smile curved impossibly wider across his lips. Electricity fizzled in the air, and they burst out laughing simultaneously.

Failing to control her eruption into fits of giggles, she managed to gasp, 'Great!'

'You realize I'm attempting to inject some romance into the weekend?'

Layla had realized which was why she was laughing so hard. 'I'm sorry,' she spluttered.

'Ludicrous idea, right?' He answered his own question. 'Frankly preposterous.'

Fighting her laughter, which was more tension than a rejection of his romance initiative, she said, 'It's a lovely idea.' Her giggles under control she added, 'And you definitely get points for effort!' She held up the shoes and dress questioningly. 'And these?'

'I remembered your sizes from the things you wore to the party in Porthkara. The concierge did the rest. I asked him to use a personal shopper. I hope you don't mind.'

Mind?

'Of course not.' She set them down carefully like they were the crown jewels. 'Why would I mind?'

'I don't want you to think I'm being controlling.'

'Aren't you though? Just a tiny bit? I mean this dress is fab but it's suspiciously similar to the one I was wearing the night we met.'

'You did something to me that night. I knew it at the time. But I didn't know how much it mattered.' He gulped. For a hesitant moment he froze in silence like he'd literally swallowed his words. His smile twisted back across his lips. 'You can't blame a guy for wanting to hold onto a special moment in time.'

She walked over to Nick, stood on tiptoes and kissed him. As his head lowered, wet strands of hair fell forward into her face. He returned the kiss, slowly exploring her mouth. Her stomach flipped as he whispered hotly against her ear. 'I can have the dress sent back if you don't like it.' His mouth recaptured hers and he kissed her so deeply that she tingled everywhere from her hair roots to the tips of her fingers and toes. It couldn't be any clearer that he was still into her, despite the fact he'd drawn a firm line in the emotional sands.

'The dress is out of this world!' Thrilled by him and the anticipation of the night he had planned she broke away, breathless. 'I'd better go get ready.'

Beneath the white towel around his waist he'd hardened

the microsecond her lips touched his. 'Go,' he groaned, 'Go, or we'll miss the overture and they won't let us in until after the interval and all the concierge's efforts will have been wasted.'

With a mammoth effort of her own she reluctantly extricated herself from the arms banded round her, holding her close.

'By the way,' she threw him an over her shoulder look as she scurried away to change. 'You're out of this world too!'

It was obvious to Nick that the concierge was suppressing a wry sneer when he called down and asked him if the car he'd ordered was ready. *'Oui Monsieur,'* he said curtly. *'Your car is here.'*

'Please ask the driver to wait.'

'Très bien Monsieur.'

So much for delivering romance! It had seemed like a good idea for all of about five minutes. They'd nearly split their sides laughing. He winced. *Let's face it! Even the concierge doesn't think I can deliver.*

He was low on romance, big on physical heat. Her body next to his had the power to drive him out of control. What she did to him was insane. But much more than that, she was important, she deserved the loveliest things, and he wanted her to know how he felt.

He flicked an impatient look at his watch. She was doing her make-up. How long could it take?

When she finally made an appearance, she was a walking artwork, enough to send his temperature soaring inappropriately all over again. She looked absolutely stunning.

The limo was waiting to take them across the river to the *Palais Garnier*. And yet he wanted to press pause, freeze the moment – splice it into his memory where he could hold onto her image forever. He wanted her just for him.

With Layla, his history had stopped mattering. Happy in the moment he'd forgotten the player with a past, the games he'd played with the press, the flirting with flight attendants, the hook-ups with women on set. She'd eclipsed the emptiness of his world.

Everything that went before had brought him to this time and place with this woman. She was an escape from the shallowness of Toni, the heartache of Fran.

She picked up the matching clutch bag he'd ordered and turned, fiddling with the clasp on her charm bracelet. Fixed in a knot at the back of her neck, and held fast with a handmade silver clip encrusted with shimmering precious stones, her red hair shone. She set his senses on fire. So strong was the urge to drag her into his arms, unclip her hair and let it tumble onto her shoulders, crush her lips with his and hold her close, that suddenly his hands felt awkward. He plunged them deep into his pockets.

'What do you think? Will I fit in at the opera?' Catching his gaze with glittering dark eyes made up to dazzling effect, she added mockingly, 'Or stick out like a sore thumb?'

Her beautiful rich brown irises enticed him with their sparkle. She'd neither blend in nor stick out. She'd fascinate. 'You'll turn heads. You look amazing.'

The shiny silver limo pulled up outside the *Palais Garnier* opera house. Suited and capped the driver held the door and in a little bit of a daze, Layla stepped carefully out to join her dream man. The fantastical building brimming with fashion conscious Parisians gave her butterflies. The one-off gala performance by a world-renowned soprano had attracted an elite audience. Nick must have paid a small fortune to get hold of last minute tickets. Goosebumps prickled her skin.

Somebody pinch me.

It was like walking onto the set of a glamorous film – and a long, long way from sleepy Porthkara.

Her heart in her mouth, she willed herself not to trip when Nick placed his firm hand at the base of her spine and guided her towards the impressive sweeping marble staircase that led up to the opera boxes. Awed by the grandeur her nerves skittered and she struggled to remain poised as her high-heeled feet touched the bottom steps. Nick smiled his fabulous smile, his hand pressing closer, his touch revving up her self-confidence. The green silk shimmered beneath the light of the candelabras and collected admiring glances as she passed by chattering groups of sophisticated opera-goers. Way more attention-grabbing than anything she'd ever worn, the dress demanded to be seen. Inhaling deeply, she straightened her spine and held her head high. With the tuxedoed Nick by her side, tall, gorgeous, charmingly disarming, she got away with it – just.

Reaching the top of the staircase they arrived in the palatial foyer without her having fallen over her feet and she heaved a sigh of relief. French chatter she barely understood a word of buzzed in her ears. The opera house was a feast of gold and gleaming light. She took in the mosaic floors and opulent columns stretching up to elaborate frescoes. Theatre box doors led to the auditorium. Nick cornered an usher and he pointed out which one they needed to take to find their seats.

Nick close behind her, she stepped through a door like she was about to enter a wonderland – and stopped, stunned. She buzzed with amazement. The circular ceiling of the auditorium was a riot of colour. Spread out above the light of a huge crystal chandelier, it took her breath away.

In astonished silence she gripped onto the back of one of the red velvet seats.

'Words fail me,' she gasped turning in time to catch him watching her, a flicker in his soft cheek muscle a striking contrast to his hard jawline. 'Oh Nick, thank you.' Somehow, she managed to breathe and speak at the same time. 'I thought the gallery was awesome. But without a shadow of a doubt this has got to be the most romantic place I've ever seen.'

Nick chuckled, and shot a winning smile at a long-faced woman impatiently waiting to get into the row where Layla had stopped, frozen in awe. He prized her fingers off the chair-back, gently squeezing her hand as he nudged her forward towards their seats. She couldn't take her eyes off the painting. 'The ceiling mural was painted by Chagall,' he said. 'Just so you know,' he added, smiling broadly.

When they took their places, she couldn't contain her effusiveness, 'If we leave now and I don't see the opera, I'll die happy.'

He leaned close, his breath hot against her neck, the light in his eyes, soft, teasing. 'Don't exaggerate Layla,' he whispered.

'I'm not!' She giggled. 'I could sit here all night and just gaze at the ceiling. It's fantastic.'

'Here's hoping that everything is fantastic. The orchestra. The music. The costumes. The performers.' Nick crossed his fingers. The gesture was a nod to her fixation with things luck related. It gave her a funny lump in her throat which was in itself a piece of luck because it stopped her embarrassing herself by blurting out that – marvellous art and Marc Chagall ceiling mural aside – he was the most fantastic thing about Paris.

By the time she was back in the bubble of the limo, gliding through the city streets en route to the restaurant he'd chosen for dinner, her head was awash with romance. She touched each of the charms on her bracelet and fidgeted with the clasp, which had come loose with all the opening and closing. The atmosphere inside the car was alive with the heat which raged between them as she rested her hand flat on the cool smooth leather seat. Her fingers almost twitched with the agonizing urge to touch him, resisting the burning temptation to kiss his lips and feel him kiss her back.

Chapter Twenty-One

Sliding her fingers across the soft grey leather to connect with his, she was on the verge of telling Nick how badly she wanted him when the limo came to a stop outside a quirky, vintage-looking restaurant called *Le Plein Soleil*.

Inside a woman with black wavy hair, gold hoop earrings and an antique watch chain looped around her neck showed them to a table at the back of the empty-ish restaurant. She had the air of a gypsy fortune teller. Layla wondered if she kept a crystal ball under the bar and did palm readings and tarot cards as a sideline when business was slack. She simmered in an invisible cloud of heavy scent, handed them menus with fingers that had neatly clipped, black-painted nails, and rattled off a list of specials. She had bright, beady, all-seeing eyes, and Layla couldn't help noticing that she slightly resembled the caged mynah bird at the corner of the bar which every now and then burst out with a few bars of *La Vie En Rose*.

'What's that weird bird whistling? Is it the French national anthem?' Nick whispered.

'No!' Layla nearly snorted her champagne. 'It's *La Vie En Rose*. With the odd line from *Je Ne Regrette Rien* thrown in for good measure.' The look on Nick's face told her he was none the wiser.

'When you've stopped splitting your seams you can help me out here and give me a clue,' he said.

'Edith Piaf,' she enthused. 'She was a famous French singer. There was a film about her life. Mum's got the DVD.'

Nick narrowed his eyes and straightened his knife and fork. 'I'm not sure about this place. The concierge recommended it. I asked for somewhere quiet. But this place is a bit too quiet.'

The tucked-away restaurant screamed retro. Yellow Tiffany-style shades hung low over the tables, illuminating them with a citrusy glow. The dark corners, the shabby carpet, worn in patches by the tread of many feet, the mirrored bar lined with golden-foiled bottles of celebration-ready fizz ... she could almost imagine that if she stepped through the door to the kitchen she might slip into a time-warp. Completing the mashed-up retro feel, an eclectic mix of pictures decorated the walls. The one above Nick's head shouted sixties style pop art – a giant plateful of spaghetti in psychedelic pinks and greens.

Layla glanced around. 'It's certainly different,' she

protested. 'I quite like it. To be fair to the concierge, it's more interesting than dining on nouvelle cuisine in some minimalist upscale restaurant. But if you're not keen we could pay for the champagne and do a runner.'

'If you're happy, I am too.' Nick flicked a glance at the chalk board marked *'Plats du Jour'*. 'Plus, I'm ravenous. And those specials look good.'

Layla checked that all the staff were out of earshot and whispered, 'Do you think the owner lady recognized you?'

He shook his head. 'I'm pretty sure we're off the press radar. And I'm not delusional. I don't imagine she's going to tip off a paparazzo to come and hang about on the street corner just because some actor who used to be in a TV series is eating dinner at her restaurant.'

'Not just any actor,' she remarked. 'And *MOTV* isn't just any series.'

'How would you know?' he mocked. 'You've hardly watched any of it!'

Her feelings bounced around like a ping-pong ball. She should be relieved, but nonetheless it stung a tiny bit that he was tactfully saying the celebrity gossip mags weren't interested in photographing him with her. She studied the menu in her hands and all the unfamiliar French words swam before her eyes.

'At the end of the day I'm a pretty shabby follow-up to dating a princess.'

'Why would you say that?' He closed the menu, which he wasn't reading anyway, and set it on the table. Underneath his cutlery jingled.

'What I'm trying to say is that it's good that nobody's taking photos of us together. And if you're at all worried about the selfies on my phone you needn't be. I'm not going to stick them up on the internet and make you look uncool.' She opened her clutch bag and pushed her phone across the table to him. 'You can delete them if you like.'

'I don't care about how you make me look.' His lips set in a solemn line. 'For what it's worth, I happen to think you look pretty cool. Sure, I'd prefer to keep a low profile while we're in Paris. But that's not about me. That's for you. After what happened with Joe I didn't think you'd want to find pictures of ...' He glared across the table at her, a deep furrow carved in his brow. '... Us plastered all over the internet, or anywhere else for that matter.' He hesitated. 'Of course, if you want to post a selfie or two to get back at him, I completely understand. At the end of the day that's what this – you and me – is all about, right?'

'Do you want me to use you to get at him?'

'Of course not.'

'Me neither.' Between them sat a small vase containing fresh summer flowers and a glowing, flickering tea-light in a glass holder. She pressed the palms of her hands together, and wrapped her head around what he'd just said.

'So,' she began. 'This isn't about Joe. I'm not sure it ever really was. It's you and me. Nobody else. And. Well. I won't take any more selfies anyhow.'

The corners of Nick's mouth twitched into a half smile that promised to erupt into a full on devilish beam. 'You can take as many selfies as you like. Knock yourself out. In fact. Let's take one now.'

He twisted in his seat so that he could take the picture. Grinning, happy that he was okay about her taking photos of them together in Paris, she leant across the table to get closer. A wisp of green chiffon from her dress dangled dangerously into the tea-light holder. Unnoticed, it smouldered and in a microsecond an acrid whiff rose from the table centre. Layla shrieked as she realized that the beautiful dress was singed.

In a flash Nick blew out the candle, leapt from his chair, removed the champagne from the ice bucket and dumped its entire contents of frigid water and ice cubes all over Layla. When she shrieked again with the shock of being doused in ice, he frantically clutched for the tablecloth, yanked hard, and like a magician performing a spectacular fail, sent a clatter of cutlery, side plates, and glasses smashing onto the carpet. Kicking the flower-strewn mess away he rugby tackled her to the floor and rolled her over and over until she was wrapped up in the tablecloth like an Egyptian mummy.

The raven-haired woman ran over from where she'd been polishing glasses behind the bar, flapping her dishtowel and brandishing a fire extinguisher. Without further ado she proceeded to blast Nick and Layla with a whoosh of foam.

At the bar, a portly elderly customer who'd been hunched on a stool and swirling amber Armagnac around a balloon glass, whistled through his teeth and muttered, '*Oh là là là là*' over and over like he'd never seen anything quite so entertaining in all his days. To top it off the mynah bird launched into a full and uninterrupted rendition of *Je Ne Regrette Rien*.

The old gentleman guffawed with laugher, knocked back his drink and hopped down from his perch. He winked at Layla and Nick and snapped a couple of photos on his phone, posing for a final selfie. 'No regrets!' he shouted. '*C'est bien vous? L'un des frères télé-vampire?*' He reached down to shake Nick by the hand.

'Yep! It's me alright, the telly-vampire!'

With a wave of his wooden walking stick the man pocketed his phone and exited the restaurant, still chuckling.

'Great,' Layla spluttered, struggling to stand up. 'What did you do that for? Bit of an overreaction don't you think?'

'That's gratitude for you.' He got to his feet and pulled her after him. 'I thought you were on fire.'

She unwrapped herself from the tablecloth and looked down at the bedraggled dress. 'It's totally ruined.'

'It doesn't matter.' His face was ghostly pale. 'The point is – are you okay?'

'I'm fine.'

'You're not hurt?'

She gently touched his face and wiped away a blob of foam. 'Nick, I'm okay. Honest. I'm sorry I scared you.'

The small gaggle of other customers in the restaurant cheered as he pressed a soft kiss to her lips and there was a ripple of applause.

'So much for romance!' The cold damp dress clung to her body and her teeth chattered.

'You're freezing. I'll ask if they've got anything we can change into.'

While a waiter cleared up the mess, the bustling owner relocated the couple into the storeroom where she produced two pairs of black and white checkered chef's trousers and t-shirts with *Le Plein Soleil* scrawled across the front in loopy letters and the restaurant's address on the back.

They changed sheepishly. Stuffing their wet clothes into a plastic bin liner Layla whispered, 'This is going from bad to worse. Do you think she's going to make us wash dishes?'

Nick smiled. 'I'll try a charm offensive. Promise I'll pay for the damage.'

Admiringly, she watched as he diplomatically smoothed things over with the restaurant owner. A frisson rippled along the length of her spine. She felt like someone had pushed her into the middle of the River Seine in a rowboat without any oars. Paris had taken her out of her comfort zone and Nick had stolen her heart. She had fallen in love with him.

Installed at a different table with a fresh bottle of champagne, they whizzed their way through snazzy starters followed by a traditional main course.

While Nick read the dessert menu she picked up the salt pot and spilled some onto the table. Absently she swirled her finger through it.

'Isn't that bad luck?'

She looked him hard in the eyes. 'It's salt. Anyway, I'm getting better about that stuff.'

He nodded, took a pinch of salt between his finger and thumb and threw it over his shoulder. 'Just in case.'

Layla's heartbeat skipped. She pinched some salt, and did the same. She didn't care that the night had turned into a fiasco. She was deliriously, irrationally, head-over-heals happy and she didn't want anything to change that.

Nick poured her some more champagne and clinked her glass with his. 'Cheers.' He passed her the menu. 'What are you having for dessert?'

'You!'

'No, really,' he said, plainly not taking her seriously. 'What would you like?' He pinned her with his gaze and she blushed. Heat spread up her neck, rose into her cheeks, and burned. 'How about *crème brûlée* to share, two spoons, one plate?'

'You know the way to a girl's heart.' The cheesy line was out before she could stop it.

'I have another irresistible suggestion. When we're done here let's take a tour of Paris by night.'

'Fab.'

When the waiter brought the *crème brûlée* she tucked in. Its deliciousness didn't sweeten the fact that Nick had sidestepped her attempt at skipping dessert and going back to the hotel. The direct approach was an epic fail. After a couple of mouthfuls, she set her spoon down. 'Beaten by dessert,' she confessed.

'In that case.' Nick pulled the plate that had been sitting between them closer. He loaded his spoon with another mouthful.

She raised an incredulous eyebrow. 'The words "photo" and "shoot" come to mind.'

'The hotel has a gym.' He shrugged. 'I'll work it off.' He scoffed the lot, 'That was *fantastique*.' He kissed the tips of his fingers flamboyantly into the air. 'Mwah!'

A tight knot twisted beneath her ribs. 'Do you think the pictures that man took are up online already?'

'Almost certainly.'

'Don't you mind?'

'For myself?' He gave a shrug. 'Not really. I've gotten used to it.' He reached across the table and touched her hand. 'For you though? Yes. I mind.' He sighed. 'The thing is I can't protect you the way I'd like to.'

'From what?'

'From my not-so-stellar reputation.'

'I don't care about your reputation. I know the real you. Anyway, I'm mainly interested in your stellar body.'

He reached across the table and his hand covered hers. 'I liked having you to myself – without people snooping and taking pictures.' He paused, gauging her reaction. 'Being together without ...' He paused, hooked his fingers in the air and pulled a mocking face. '... The "celebrity" magnifying glass was the most fun I've had in ...' He stopped abruptly and looked down at the table for a second. Raising his gaze to catch hers he added, 'I was going to say in a hell of a long time, but actually it feels like forever.'

A lump of emotion clogged her throat. She was a million miles from resembling the sophisticated women he was used to. She steeled her heart to prove that she could be the cool take-what-I-want-and-walk-away woman she had claimed she wanted to be.

'This is a moving on thing, right?' She leaned towards him and rested her palm against his smooth jaw. 'Short and sweet?' Her instincts tripped her up. She was saying one thing and feeling something different.

'I don't want to you to regret that I brought you to the "city of romance" without the romance.'

'I don't have any regrets.' He was a man in a million, so much more than a man-shaped sticking plaster and moving on sex. 'About any of this. Today has been brilliant. I loved being at the opera with you tonight. But if it's alright with you I'd like to concentrate on what we're really good at.' She fixed a smile on her face. Did she have to spell it out? She wanted to hide away with him in their fabulous hotel suite.

He narrowed his eyes and looked at her for a long moment, his face muscles taut. He was about to reply when the restaurant lady who'd been scrutinizing them from behind the bar whilst making a production of polishing an already sparkling clean glass approached the table and interrupted, *'C'est terminé?'*

'We'll have two espressos, *s'il vous plaît.*' His sexy smile pierced her heart. 'We're not quite finished yet.'

Chapter Twenty-Two

'Once upon a time my mother drank herself into a stupor and fell asleep in the bath with a lighted candle on the windowsill. It set the blinds on fire. If I hadn't smelt burning and woken her up I don't know what would have happened.' He paused, sliding into the back of the limo next to her. 'Well. Actually. I do.'

'Nick, that's dreadful.' Her hand touched his. 'How old were you?'

He swallowed as if to dislodge the lump in his throat; these memories were dangerous territory. He'd said more than enough already. It was becoming a habit. 'Nine or ten. I don't really remember.'

He heard her sharp intake of breath. 'I hate to think of you having to cope with that when you were so young.'

'Anyway, I'm sorry about going into panic mode back there at the restaurant.' His heart had nearly stopped when she'd screamed. He'd smelt smoke, feared the worst, and reacted on automatic. He tapped on the glass between him and the driver. 'Take a detour, please,' he said. 'We'd like to see the lights of Paris, before we go back to the hotel.'

With the flick of a button he closed the limo's privacy screen.

It was time to get his act together. And he couldn't see a way for her to be a part of that. What they had was red hot and combustible and on course to burn out. There was a slight irony in that. He'd wanted her to have a wonderful time tonight, but after the restaurant incident, he feared Paris had fallen short of her expectations.

He turned away, absently observing the sights outside the tinted windows. The car crawled past the spectre of Notre Dame, and then sped up, whizzing along the banks of the Seine where blurry strings of white lights punctured the darkness, circumnavigating the Place de la Concorde, and driving along the Champs Elysées to the Arc de Triomphe.

'Layla?' The lump in his throat swelled some more. He turned his head and watched for her reactions as she took in Paris by night.

'Yes?'

'What would you say if I said I'd like to keep you here, forever in this moment?'

Their eyes locked, the fire between them so far from burnt out that he ached. He needed to hear that she wanted him until the end of the week, or the end of time, or anywhere in between.

'Same. But that's just not possible. Right?'

'Right,' he agreed. The pull of attraction that buzzed between them couldn't be any stronger.

She snapped her gaze away. 'Apart from anything else, cruising around Paris in a limousine on a permanent basis might be a bit impractical.'

'Very.' He blocked out false hopes.

'I'm sure we could find ways to make it fun.' From beneath her lashes she sneaked a sideways glance at him. The car crossed a bridge and the Eiffel Tower stretched high above them, a pillar of light in the night sky. 'Wow!' The lights on the tower started to sparkle in the darkness. 'Paris by night is *très romantique*.'

In an instant she'd unsnapped both their seatbelts and was astride him blowing his mind with the burningly sultry look she was giving him, and her confusing contrariness. Her thighs pressed against him, her hands cradling his face, her lips gently crushing his, craving a reaction. His mouth sought hers and he nipped at her bottom lip.

She ruptured the kiss, breathed hot against his skin. 'Have you ever fantasized about sex in the back of a limo?'

'You have?'

She shook her head. 'Before tonight? No. You?' Biting her bottom lip she slid her hands inside his shirt, and as she flattened her palms smooth against his skin, her nails lightly grazed his chest. His heartbeat quickened under her hand. It felt as if her fingers were drawing on his skin, tracing like pencils, leaving their imprint – only it wasn't on the surface, it was deep within.

'Me neither.' She was like nothing he'd experienced before.

'That's good to know.' She pressed her lips to the skin below his Adam's apple and traced her mouth ever so slowly up over his throat, kissing along the line of his jaw, giving him such intense pleasure it was all he could do to stop from tipping her backwards onto the cool grey leather and taking her fast.

For a split second she pulled back and waited. That was it. Urgent for the feel of her, he trapped her mouth and she returned his kiss with matched passion. Straddling him she pressed in tight and he swelled and strained between her parted thighs. The tip of her tongue touched his and his fever to be inside her, to give her pleasure, climbed higher. Heat. Desire. Aching hard. He was lost, luxuriating in her sensuality.

'If you make me wait any longer I think I'll melt. Let's ...'

He groaned, desperate. Liking her sudden brazenness, he ached to do as she asked, be inside her. Now. She drove him wild.

A blur of headlights and lit-up shop fronts dragged him

into a drain of reality. Along with the sounds of the night – blast on a horn, distant siren – everything he felt for her was amplified. 'No.' He wouldn't exploit the moment for kicks. 'Not here.'

The atmosphere inside the limo felt dangerous. Like she might break him. Or he her. Or both. She'd been pure temptation and she'd turned into something more, someone so special, different. This was something he hadn't been afraid of failing at, until now. He wasn't playing games. His fear might be irrational, but he wouldn't risk her public humiliation by having sex in a chauffeur driven car no matter how badly he wanted to ignore the protective notion that drove him to hold back. After the scene at the restaurant he didn't trust anyone not to turn amateur-paparazzi with their smartphone, especially not an unknown driver with only a screen between them.

'You don't want me?'

'Don't think I'm not tempted.' Restraint had made his voice angry and she slipped from his lap and settled on the seat beside him tucking her legs under her as if she were curled up on the sofa in her cottage.

Fighting the aching in his groin, he took control and spoke to the driver. 'The hotel, please.'

She spiked her hands into her disorderly hair, unclipping and redoing the clasp that held it at the back of her neck. She'd possessed him and he couldn't put what he was feeling into words. He reached across and massaged the nape of her neck.

'Don't hate me,' he said, resolute that failing to fulfill her fantasy was the right thing to do.

Inside the hotel suite the door banged closed heavily behind them and he locked it. He reached out, spun her around and pulled her into his arms. His mouth crashed on hers. Holding her tight with one arm, he secured the bar that would prevent anyone on the outside with a keycard from entering.

Walking away after the weekend would be a struggle going by the strength of her feelings. Her emotions had soared when he'd said he wanted to make the moment in the car last forever. She hadn't known what to make of it, so she'd brushed it off and gone into *femme fatale* overdrive – not something she had previous experience of. She'd have to try supremely hard to be the wild woman she'd set out to channel at the beginning of this whole fling thing. Because right now it wasn't working out so well.

Security taken care of, he wasted no time in helping her strip. The baggy trousers were first to go. She trembled as his hands tugged at the drawstring waist, untying it so the trousers skimmed her thighs and dropped to the floor.

Still wearing the gorgeous green heels, she stepped out

of the black-and-white-checkered heap. 'Goodbye chef pants.' She tossed the words out nonchalantly and tossed her head at the same time. As he went to remove her t-shirt she automatically raised her arms and in one quick move he pulled it off over her head.

'Come with me,' he said, his fingers touching hers lightly as he drew her into the room like a magnetic force. She didn't know whether she was relieved or disappointed that he'd rejected her proposition back in the car, but he was driving her out of her mind now.

Without turning on lights he led her to the *chaise longue* in the centre of the room. Her eyes adjusted to the shadowy darkness and she looked at it, assessing. It was set back far enough from the windows not to be visible from the dark street far below. She glanced out. Across the wide boulevard, above the tops of the dark trees, offices housed behind a *belle époque* façade stood empty, vacant desks and chairs and blank computer screens, faintly lit and ghostly. Rising up into the night behind the shadowy buildings the lights on the Eiffel Tower sparkled.

'I'll lower the blinds,' he whispered.

'Don't. The lights are amazing.' He radiated hotness and she couldn't bear for their bodies to be parted. 'Besides it's totally dark in here. No one can see us, even if they are looking. Which I doubt they are. Nobody's out there.'

He kissed her deliberately and slowly, one hand at the back of her neck freeing her hair so it fell onto her shoulders, the other arm taut around her waist holding her tight against his hardness. Her breasts straining, she pressed closer and he strengthened his hold. Hooking his thumbs under her bra straps he slid them down over her shoulders, his fingers brushing her skin, melting her. Holding her close and kissing her provocatively, with one hand he pushed down the lace cup and rubbed his finger tip against her nipple. She moaned, buzzing, and aching to feel him inside her as he lowered the other lacey cup so that both breasts pressed against the soft layer of fabric between her skin and his.

He turned her away from him and she grabbed onto the *chaise longue*, its curved back soft beneath her hands, the sumptuous velvet a dark sheen in the barely-there light. He pressed tight against her and his hands cupped her breasts from behind until she virtually exploded with anticipation.

She closed her eyes, leant into him and unable to bite back her urgency said brazenly, 'Hurry up already.'

His hand moved lower, smoothed over her stomach, slid under her silky underwear and pushed inside her. Sweet heat swirled inside her body, her desire for him immense. Their bodies were pure heat; Nick was so in tune with her reactions, it was rapturous, instinctive. He held her close, one arm banded around her waist, and she went with it, leant back into his body, pressed against his hard erection, giving herself up to his touch as he heightened her pleasure, enticing her until she almost screamed. The touch of his fingers was so compelling, she wanted to have him completely inside her, but the desire to let go outstripped the longing, and high on his touch she shattered, orgasm ricocheting through her body.

All that pent up sexual energy spent, she was left with aftershocks of insecurity. She shouldn't have gone looking for the guy behind the image. She couldn't have the bad boy back. In his place there was an amazing man. And he did exquisite things to her.

Composing herself, dying to get back control, she slowly bit her lip, making a stab at channeling a demanding and seductive temptress. She wriggled out of her silky, lace-edged underwear, leaving it in a tangle on the floor. She popped the fastening on her askew bra and slipped it off. Pinching one silky strap between two fingers she held it up. Making like a burlesque striptease, she dropped it.

'I want to feel you. In me.'

Scooped off her feet and into his arms she squealed with sudden disorientation and surprise. He carried her around the *chaise longue* and laid her down, the velvet soft against her back. Unrushed, he knelt on the floor and tauntingly slowly, he gently slid his hands down her legs, undid the tiny silver buckles at her ankles and took off her shoes, dropping each one on the carpet, his darkened eyes not leaving her face for a second.

'What do you want from me?'

No matter how desperately she'd tried to hide it, her feelings were out there, obvious. From the start they'd had instant connection and intense chemistry. Her heart trembled, but her goal to exude outward confidence remained unshaken. The feelings laid bare beneath this attraction could ruin everything.

'I want a night of amazing sex.' She threw the words at him, fearing he could read the truth on her face.

'Coming right up.'

Everything outside the room spun away – hints of lights, the sparkling tower, the distant thrum of a car engine – and her control collapsed. He smoothed his hands over her skin and parted her thighs, pleasuring her so deeply that she was powerless against her reactions to the scorch of his mouth moving softly, then plunging deep, his tongue touching her and a sweet ache rocketing through her. She moaned, blanking everything that had been skittering in her mind, and yelled in pleasure as orgasmic deliciousness shimmered through her once more.

Nick stroked her thighs in the half-light. As her pulse settled and the world zoomed back into focus he stood up. A dark silhouette, she watched as he stripped.

Taking both her hands, he drew her to her feet and pressed a soft, hot kiss to her lips. His naked erection pressed hard and tight against her. Turning her around, cloaking her with the muscled wall of his body, he steered her out of the sitting room and into the bedroom. The heat of his hardness against her skin drove her crazy.

Nick closed the blinds and flicked a switch by the bed so low, warm lamplight lit the room. The bed was a gigantic four-poster, all shiny polished wood and cushions and billowy curtains, the mattress dreamily deep with the softest duvet and pillows as white as summer clouds.

He swept the cushions away with one arm and together they tumbled onto the big, soft bed, the white cotton cool beneath her back as he rolled on top of her, the weight of him exciting and passionate as rock hard urgency took him over.

She moaned, wondering how much more delay she could take as he lowered his head to her breasts. She tangled her fingers in his hair as he took her nipple into his mouth, twisting his tongue around it and driving her into a frenzy of need. Swapping breasts he caressed the one he'd pleasured first, overwhelming her with heat when he pressed his lips to the second. The touch of his mouth filled her with want.

Pulling back, braced, chest and arm muscles tight, he looked down at her.

'Have you any idea how much you turn me on?' With a groan he rolled away and lay on his side, his head on the pillow watching her face.

She laughed and ran a hand over his silky hard length. 'I have an inkling.' Rolled onto her side, lying facing him, absorbing the dark desire in his eyes, she smoothed the other hand over his shoulder and ran it down his muscled arms then brushed his thigh, his firm leg muscles. With a deep groan he wrapped his arms around her.

'We need protection.'

She sighed.

Reluctantly he let go of her and slipped from the bed. Her heart, her mind, her body were all past the point of no return and she was turned on beyond patience waiting for him. She craved his arms and his mouth on her lips. Quickly he was back, sheathed, and wrapping her in his sensational body heat.

The tip of his delicious erection connected with the fold between her legs and he entered her, pushing in and pulling out, slowly at first then driving deep, rhythmic thrusting. Heat wound through her body. Nick was perfect, filling her with more sensuous delight than she'd have believed possible. Moving in and out of her, taking her with him he rolled onto his back so that suddenly she was on top.

Both in control and out of control. His hands smoothed over every part of her – her shoulders, back, the round curve of her bum, her thighs, calves. She picked up the rhythm, tight around his length. He caressed her breasts, thrusting into her until her body melded to his in a fusion of intense ecstasy. Holding her close now, his desire built deliciously and she climaxed bringing him with her so that they both let go in the exact same moment and she cried out, high on physical pleasure.

Breathless, she stayed curled on top of him, head pressed to his chest, his heart pounding beneath her ear. Finally, she disentangled and lay back against the pillows. With one hand he gently brushed stray hairs off her face.

'I don't want tonight to end,' she said. She whispered the words into the stillness of the night as if they meant nothing.

'Don't speak.' His breath fluttered hotly against her ear and he kissed her there. For once, total silence didn't feel ominous and uncomfortable. If she closed her eyes and felt him it was as if his body was speaking to her in a million mingled sensations. She was all blissed-out emotion, simultaneously calm and electrified.

After he'd dealt with the condom, he came back and unfastened the ties which held back the bed curtains. He flicked off the light switch and drew the curtains around them as if closing out the world. They lay in the stillness, their breathing the only sound. Possessively, he gathered her, a limp, melted, hot mess, into his arms and kept her there tight all through the night.

Once she woke up and tried to wriggle quietly out of his hold but even deep asleep he wasn't about to let go.

Chapter Twenty-Three

'Eiffel Tower here we come!'

He grimaced right on cue. 'Yay.' His tone was not enthusiastic. 'The tower of doom.'

Beneath a cheerful blue sky, Paris was at its sunniest and most splendid. They'd spent the morning at the Louvre wandering through the never-ending corridors and rooms, taking in as much as was humanly possible in a single morning. As they left, walking away from the central glass pyramid, a saxophonist busking under an archway played a hauntingly beautiful tune. Nick dug his wallet from his pocket and dropped a note into an upturned hat on the stone paving. The musician immediately upped the tempo in a burst of gratitude. Nick took her hand, spun her out on one arm and twirled her around. The spontaneity of the moment made Layla laugh, but the sad strains of the original melody stayed in her head all the way to the River Seine. They walked for a long time and wound up wandering the *quais*, checking out the stalls of old books, before picking a café where they could collapse at a pavement table under the welcome shade of a parasol and get a much-needed caffeine boost.

Nick glued his dark shades to his suddenly tense, moody face. Her own sunglasses pushed up onto her head, Layla disliked looking at him and not being able to read anything in his eyes. It set her nerves on edge. He'd been avoiding her suggestion of a visit to the Eiffel Tower ahead of his shoot. But something else was wrong, it was more than an aversion to her relentlessly upbeat attempt to help him confront his phobia. The undercurrent of everything he had going on was hiding just below the surface. Studying him now from beneath evasively lowered lashes she warned herself to get real.

She'd woken up with her heart flying, and right then, surfacing from the whirlpool of emotions she'd been spinning in before she fell asleep, she'd made up her mind to get her feet back on solid ground. Her feelings were all in her head. A fantasy. She was being swept off her feet with the romance of Paris.

The reality was they were on course to fizzle out faster than a shooting star. They'd been nothing more than a time out for each other. At the outset she'd been clear that that was all she wanted. So how had she fallen so inappropriately for Nick? She opened her bag, pulled out a little notebook and pen and started furiously scribbling notes. She had a business to get off the ground. Starting now. The best thing would be to start focusing on the future, one that wouldn't involve Nick.

She itemized things she'd need to look into when she got home. 'Van. Insurance. Materials. Small business loan.' She added a long line of question marks.

'What are you doing?'

'Planning. Making a list of everything I'll need to set up my new business.'

'Right now?'

'There's no time like the present.'

'Can I see?' Reluctantly she let him scrutinize her scrawl. 'If you need money I could lend you some.'

She shook her head. 'That's sweet, but no – thank you. I've saved – quite a bit really. And I got money back from my travel insurance. It's not a massive amount but it should be enough to get me started.' She shrugged. 'After that I'll see what happens. Maybe apply for a loan.' Pulling her glasses off her head with twitchy fingers, she folded them and set them on the round bistro table. Its metallic surface shone in the sunlight. 'Besides, this is something I have to do by myself.'

The white-aproned waiter brought their order. *'Deux cafés,'* he announced. *'Un sandwich pour Monsieur, et une tarte au citron pour la demoiselle.'* He set a white plate and a small silver fork in front of Layla with a flourish.

'*Merci.*' Nick settled the bill right away, handing over euros and indicating with a thumbs up that the man could keep the change. '*C'est bon.*'

Layla carefully sliced through her pie, spearing a piece and popping it in to her mouth, enjoying the sharp citrus zing on her taste buds.

Nick picked up his phone and set it down again. Something was definitely bothering him. She fought the urge to ask what. She took a sip of coffee and silently ate a second mouthful of the mouth-watering pie. Untouched, Nick's baguette sat wrapped on his plate.

'Fran's sent me another email,' he said abruptly. 'She wants me to call her.'

'Beth's mother?' In silence he nodded. Her heart fluttered. He drank his coffee and she chased another piece of pie around the plate with her fork. The constant push and pull, getting close to Nick, letting him draw her into his heart, only to then feel that he was shutting her out was too draining. She'd been trying to keep things light, but whatever the deal with Fran and Beth was, it was cutting him up and the only thing for it was to offer a friendly ear. Besides, the silence got to her. She couldn't stand the awkwardness of unspoken tension. 'You want to talk about it?'

'It's complicated.' Nick's brows knitted into a frown.

'That much I figured out already.'

'I was nineteen. And she was thirty. She was talented. And ambitious. Assistant producer on a daytime hospital drama. I'd been shut away in a boys' boarding school for what felt like half my life. I landed the part of a teenager badly broken up in a motorcycle accident. It was my first real acting job. This might sound foolish, but she was my first love.' He paused and tension flickered in his cheek. 'Or more specifically – first lover.'

'Wow.'

'Yes. Wow.' His laugh had an acerbic edge.

'I'm sorry. That comment wasn't helpful.'

'No. It's me.' He reached across the table touching the tips of his fingers to the tips of hers. 'I shouldn't put this on you.'

'You don't have to tell me. Not if you don't want to. It's really none of my business.' It was horrible tiptoeing around like this. Everything that had seemed so easy at home in Cornwall was turning sour.

'I want to.'

She hated that he looked so troubled, but she hadn't the foggiest idea how anything she could say would help. She snatched her fingers away like he'd given her an electric shock.

'It was secretive and fun, a bubble in time.' He downed his last sip of coffee. 'Admittedly I had feelings, infatuation maybe. It didn't last long, ultimately it meant nothing. At least it didn't until now.' He rubbed a hand over his stubbly chin. 'I should have been more careful.'

'What happened?' She faked a sense of distance she didn't feel. 'Why didn't she tell you at the time?'

'Honestly. I don't know. Fran was in a terrible state when she contacted me. There wasn't time to talk about the past.'

'Why not?' Layla was way past trying to hide her astonishment.

'Because she had a health scare. She found a breast lump. She arranged tests straight away. And she contacted me.' He sighed. 'She was afraid. She figured that if the worst came to the worst Beth wouldn't have to be alone in the world. She wanted me to promise that I'd be there for her. I went to see them right away, but Beth stayed in her bedroom the whole time and refused to come out.'

Layla literally bit her tongue. Determined not to say anything tactless she stared at his granite profile.

'I know what you're thinking.'

The tense muscle in his cheek twitched almost imperceptibly. Layla didn't miss it. 'I'm not thinking anything.'

'Well I know what Alex thinks. He says get a paternity test and legal advice.'

'No prizes for guessing you haven't done either of those things.' She lowered her eyes and fixed on the leftover pie as if she'd found a hair baked into it.

'Correct. Beth's my child. Fran says I'm the father and I believe her.'

'Of course she is,' she agreed. 'She's the spitting image of you.'

'Fran's test results are negative. She's got the all clear. They did a biopsy. The lump is benign, but the doctor wants to schedule surgery and remove it – to be on the safe side.'

'The news you said you were waiting for? That's wonderful. You must be so relieved.'

With a solemn nod of the head he pinched the bridge of his nose. 'Here's the thing. Fran wants to see me again. She feels bad about keeping me in the dark all these years. She wants to give me a proper explanation about what happened. And she'd like Beth to get to know me.'

'That's good, isn't it?' she said optimistically.

'Beth didn't want to have anything to do with me. I totally understand if she sees me as a sperm donor, something biological, unemotional. I haven't got the best opinion of my own father. What a joy he turned out to be,' he scoffed. 'He drove my mother over the edge.' He set his cup down and the saucer rattled. 'Beth doesn't need me. Nor does Fran. She runs her own TV production company, based in Manchester. They have a lovely life. A beautiful house, holidays in Florida and Greece, and Beth's just about to start secondary school. The last thing she needs is a dad with a rubbish reputation. I think it would be best to go back to how things were. Without me in the picture.'

Layla was trying not to judge but it sounded like Nick was justifying things because he wasn't prepared to take on the responsibility of a child. 'Is that what you really want?' she asked gently.

He tore his sunglasses off, and set them on the table. 'It's best to keep things the way they are.'

'Couldn't you at least go and talk to her again? The scare must have been awful. It sounds to me like Fran's had a genuine change of heart. Think of what you could be missing out on if you don't go.'

He glowered, eyes darkening like thunder clouds. Radiating tension and his face stubbornly set like stone, he said nothing. So much for not getting involved. This was exactly what she'd hoped to avoid.

'My father's not the most reliable,' she attempted, 'but I've only got one and I wouldn't change him for the world. Warts and all.' She rolled her eyes. 'I can't believe I just said that.'

Even though he was scowling Nick laughed. Perplexed, Layla watched a sparrow scavenging beneath the empty table next to theirs. She tossed it a crumb of pastry. 'I don't know what more to say.' *And I don't know why I'm trying so hard.* 'Aren't you a tiny bit curious to meet her?'

Shadows darkened his face again like thick clouds

spoiling the sunshine. 'Honestly? I thought when I told you how I found out you'd back me up.' He jabbed a finger at the touchscreen on his phone and deleted Fran's last message. He dropped the phone on the silver-topped table and leaned back in his chair. 'I wish she'd stop hassling me.'

Her heart lurched. How could he imagine for one second that she'd agree with him on this? How could he turn his back on his own child? She'd been dragged in now. She couldn't let it drop.

'You could take it one step at a time. Beth might rethink things and agree to meet you.'

'What would be the point in me coming into her life now? It's too late to be a real dad. I missed eleven birthdays already. I can't change that.'

Her head felt muzzy. She was fighting Nick over something that mattered to her way more than it should. He was far too deep under her skin. 'Put yourself in her shoes. She's eleven. It was already an upsetting time and then the dad she's never met shows up. That must have been pretty daunting. Maybe she was testing you. Seeing how easily she could push you away.'

'Well it worked.' A splinter of emotion darted across his gaze. 'Dads aren't always all they're cracked up to be. She's better off without me.'

'That's not good enough. Stop blaming stuff you had

no control over in the past and work for the right to be Beth's dad.' She twined a long strand of hair around one finger before pushing it behind her ear. A rush of sadness flooded her heart. 'Man up, Nick. I know that your parents' marriage was a wreck, and that you had to deal with things no child should have to. But you're more than the sum of all that – so much more. None of it was your fault. Just like none of this is Beth's. She didn't get a choice. In her place I'd feel like half of me was a blank canvas. Face it – she turned you away so as not to risk being rejected. I hate to state the obvious but you're the grown-up in this scenario.'

Nick rearranged his props on the table. 'Growing up with my mother was like walking through a minefield. I loved her to bits. But I couldn't fix what was wrong. As I see it, if Beth doesn't get to know me, I can't hurt her.'

'As hard as that must have been,' she said softly, 'it's a sad excuse for ignoring your own child.' She couldn't help thinking that by failing to hear what Fran wanted to say, by walking away without giving Beth another chance, he'd be doing exactly what he hoped to avoid – causing harm.

Pocketing his phone and sunglasses he reached across the table, took both her hands in his and squeezed them. 'Some problems can't be solved. Trust me. I'm sure she's a great kid. But she's better off without me. Sometimes the best thing to do is nothing at all.'

Chapter Twenty-Four

'Real or fake?' he asked. Delaying, Nick stopped in front of a *patisserie* to admire an Eiffel Tower made of multi-coloured *macarons*. 'D'you reckon they're made out of cardboard?'

He looked infuriatingly like a little boy with his nose pressed to the sweet shop glass. Layla studied the tower of rainbow colours. She didn't like being annoyed with him. But if he was going to be this blind and stubborn about something so important, he should have kept his secret to himself. 'I've no idea. They look real to me.'

'I'll be back in moment. I'm going to find out.' He disappeared into the shop, and returned shortly later carrying a box.

'Well?' Layla raised an eyebrow. 'Real?'

'I've no idea. My schoolboy French isn't as good as I thought. They didn't have the faintest idea what I was talking about.' He held open the box, offering it to her and plucking out a strawberry one. 'I got these, though. On the house.' He took a bite. 'Mmm! Turns out the patisserie shop ladies are *Vampires* fans.'

She picked out a pale green *macaron*. 'Being a telly vampire has its perks.' She took a bite. Sugar and pistachio hit her tastebuds. 'What's *Mercy of the Vampires* in French?'

'I've no idea.'

They walked to the *Champs de Mars* and sat on a bench gazing up at the massive structure and polishing off the irresistible *macarons*.

'Better than vitamin goo?' she teased.

He answered her with a total non sequitur.

'Do you think you'll ever want a baby?'

'What? Where did that come from?' Dodging the pang of emotion that hit her with his unexpected question, she added jokily, 'Stop hogging the *macarons*.' He passed her the box and she picked out a chocolate one even though she didn't want it.

'I was just thinking. I mean, I didn't choose to be a dad.'

'To be honest, I'm not sure if I want a family,' she answered. She swallowed. Still startled by the question, it felt like she had a whole *macaron* stuck in her throat. 'It's strange, knowing I wasn't planned.' She hadn't discussed any of this with Joe, and here she was having another heart-to-heart with a man she'd really only just met. 'I love kids. But to tell you the truth I have a weird block

when it comes to imagining having children of my own.
I can't picture it.' Flustered, she added, 'Maggie's twins are
sweet. So who knows? Maybe someday ...'

She stood up, took the cake box to the nearest litter bin
and dropped it in, tossing her uneaten *macaron* in after it.

'You don't approve of me wanting to leave things as they
are as far as Beth's concerned.'

'It's not for me to approve or disapprove, is it?'

'I'd hate to be the reason for a messed-up child.'

'Not meeting you could be just as messed up – for her.
If I had a dad who didn't want to know me, I'd be hurt.'
Nick's fear of ruining his child's life made her sad for Beth
– and for him.

'I hadn't thought of it that way.'

She smiled. 'You're awesome. And you'll be an awesome
dad – if you stop inventing excuses.'

He stood and clasped her fingers in his, linking their
hands as if they were meant to fit together. Then he raised
her fingers to his lips and gently kissed them. 'Ditto,' he
said, adding in the voice that was an unraveling combination softness and gravel, 'You're awesome too. And some
day I bet you'll be a brilliant mum.' The gold charms on
her bracelet shone in the sunlight. He abruptly changed
the subject. 'This bracelet must be very special. You never
take it off. Not even when you paint.'

'Oh, you know me and lucky charms.' She shook her

wrist so that they jingled. 'It belonged to my grandmother.'

He pulled an awkward face. 'The broken condom story grandma?'

'Yep. The very same. She passed away suddenly. When my dad went through her things, he found an envelope labeled "For Layla". This bracelet was inside. With a note. In beautiful flowing handwriting. And decorated with little pictures she'd drawn of all the different charms. "Be lucky in love" it said. The funny thing is – until she died – I was fairly certain my grandmother didn't really like me.'

Nick studied the charms more closely, then he gave her a sexy half-smile. 'I think you got that wrong.'

Nick's heart hammered. Layla gripped his hand and they walked towards the Eiffel Tower. 'You can't put this off any longer,' she coaxed. 'You've distracted me with the Louvre, and with coffee and pie, and the best *macarons* Paris has to offer.'

'To state the obvious – it's a long way up.'

'I know you don't want to,' she whispered kindly. 'But we've run out of reasons not to go for it. We'll climb up to the first stage on foot, and take the lift to the top. The queues are shorter and you'll get a chance to acclimatize.' Her eyes sparkled, and she almost succeeded in making him feel motivated.

As his feet touched the first set of stairs, he wished he

hadn't eaten so many *macarons*. If his nutritionist knew she'd be livid. What was he thinking? Not about the shoot tomorrow, clearly. His stomach heaved. The first couple of sets of stairs were surprisingly okay. *So far, so good!* As they climbed higher, all he could think about were the gaping gaps in the metal structure that his irrational brain said he could fall through regardless of the fact that he knew he couldn't.

'My legs feel strange. I wish I had a double to fall back on.'

'Welcome to real life,' she teased. 'You're doing great.' She squeezed his hand.

Arriving at the first viewing level, adrenaline coursed through his veins and he searched for something to grab onto. Nausea clawed at his throat and every sense froze.

'Look I know you mean well,' he said, 'but I think this is far enough.'

She kept a tight hold of his hand. 'Breathe,' she encouraged. She chipped gently away at his boundaries. He was used to getting what he wanted.

While they waited in line to take the lift to the very top his heartbeat settled. *You can do this. And it will be so worth it. Because you'll know what to expect tomorrow.*

Inside the lift every muscle in his body tensed. When they finally stepped out onto the third viewing floor a mix of pure relief and trepidation flooded through him.

The viewing platform at the top of the tower was far bigger than he'd expected.

'Breathe,' Layla said again.

'Because I might stop if you don't remind me?' He only half-joked. He breathed in deeply like she'd suggested. 'This is my worst nightmare.'

'Okay?' She tightened her soft grip on his hand, and he felt surprisingly calm. 'How do you feel?'

'Not brilliant.' He nodded slowly, thinking about it. 'But okay!'

'I read up about it online. Once you get above a certain height the distance cancels out the vertigo – for some people. That's why often people who are afraid of heights are fine about flying.'

'Weird.'

She smiled. 'Let's get some champagne and celebrate.'

'I'll go. You – enjoy the view.' Relieved to have something to focus on he went to the champagne bar while she took photos with her phone. A strategically placed silver ice bucket full of beautiful red roses sat on the bar. 'For the sake of romance, I'd better have one of those too,' he told the barman.

By the time he returned with two glasses of champagne, one clenched tightly in each fist, the wobbly feeling in his legs had virtually gone. And he had a red rose jammed jauntily between his teeth.

Her dark eyes shone beneath fluttering lashes. 'Ooh, pink bubbles.' He unlocked his fingers to let her take a glass, surprised to feel her soft lips whisper against his cheek. 'Now you have a lipstick print to go with that fetching rose.'

He removed it from his mouth with his free hand and offered it to her. 'For you. This calls for a selfie.'

'I should get a selfie-stick.'

He frowned. 'That would be a step too far.'

She held up her phone, and he took it from her to do one of his long-armed shots.

'Say *Camembert*!' she cried.

'No. I'll look like I've seen a ghost if I say that,' he objected.

'*Gruyère?*'

'Not much better. How about "she'll sue"? It always works on the red carpet.' None the wiser, two little frown lines appeared between her brows as they knitted. 'Smile and pout,' he explained. 'You just keep saying "she'll sue" over and over until you're out of sight of the cameras. It's guaranteed to prevent the paps catching you making a hideous face.

He demonstrated, but she shook her head.

'I'm not convinced. And anyway, we're not on the red carpet, so I'll stick with "cheese", if it's all the same to you.' He took the picture before she could say another word, his own mouth poised in a perfect pout.

Taking the phone back, she laughed. 'You look like a pantomime dame!'

'Perfect, that was the look I was going for.'

'And I look sozzled – like I drank an entire bottle of pink champagne.'

'Let's take another,' he said, 'see if we can do better.'

The second selfie turned out half-reasonable. He braved more than a fleeting look at the view. The ground far below took on a feeling of unreality, the buildings, cars and people spread out below like a model city. She'd worked her magic on him and got him to the top of the Eiffel Tower. For the first time since he was a child he looked down at the ground and he wasn't afraid.

'Thanks,' he said.

'For what?'

'For this.'

She got it, she got him. 'I didn't do anything,' she said after a long moment, 'but you're welcome.'

He'd let her get closer than anyone, but she was just passing through. He put on the brakes before he could do anything rash, like ask her to stay – indefinitely.

They finished the champagne and he took their empty glasses to the bar. He didn't feel woozy, but Monday was only hours away and it was time for this to end.

'I think it's time to get back down to earth.'

Chapter Twenty-Five

'I don't want to be that guy.'

'What guy?' she mumbled, three-quarters asleep.

'The one you regret.'

'I've already had one of those.' She struggled to hide the tremor in her voice.

'I don't want to be another.'

'You're not. You couldn't be.' She was teetering on the brink of saying something there'd be no coming back from. She didn't want to go home. And if the things they'd both almost said – but hadn't – during that unforgettable night at the opera were to be trusted, he didn't want her to go either.

She'd woken up, face down on a pillow in the shadowy grey light of the Paris hotel suite, with the weight of Nick's arm pressed possessively over the small of her back. The hardness and heat of his body next to hers sent pulses of desire skipping through her veins, waking every nerve ending.

His erection stirred against her now and she turned into him, feathering kisses across his chest. The antidote to a whole heap of rubbish, she planned to enjoy every last minute of him. Raising her head, she nipped at his jawline. His stubble gently grazed her skin. He rolled her over and held her beneath him, kissing her.

When he finally released her from their dazed fusion she whispered, '*Lundi.*' Saying it in French didn't change the fact that the last day had arrived and she'd have to face it being over.

He banded her in his hold, keeping her close. The contact, skin-to-skin, bewitched her. She hardly dared admit it, but being together with Nick had made her outrageously happy. She played the notion that this might not be the end in her head like the repetitive music she'd got when she'd dialled room service late last night to order breakfast and been put on hold. It felt good that she'd helped him battle his fear of heights. And she hoped he'd make a go of getting to know his daughter. She resolved to hold onto the happiness and not let in the possibility that they wouldn't somehow be able to let this continue. She didn't want to let him go because behind the sex bomb celeb there was a decent, likeable human being that she was undeniably in love with.

Nick checked the time on his phone and groaned. 'I have to love you and leave you.' In the stillness she admired the handsome silhouette of his profile, imprinting him on her memory. The words he plucked carelessly out of the half-light gave her hope.

'Why so early?'

'They want to grab the sunrise,' he said. 'Plus, no crowds. Less hassle.'

'More romantic.'

'I'm going to take a shower.' He met her gaze. 'Join me?'

Having unwrapped a condom on the way to the bathroom she slipped into the shower with him and water streamed over them like hot, heavy rain. A zing of anticipation sparked through her. She pressed her breasts against his back and feathered kisses across his shoulders sliding her hands between his arms and his body to reach down and feel his hardness. He moaned, turned to face her and gently, provocatively, slowly, she sheathed his gorgeous erection.

He lifted her, hands cupped under her bum, her legs gripped tight around him, and her breasts bounced softly against his smooth, wet chest. Heat flickered between her thighs and, her mind melting, her body frenzied with desire, all she wanted was to feel him deep inside and for it not to be the very last time. What were the chances that the dreamiest man alive could be hers to keep?

Only one way to find out. Say something.

'I'm in love with you.'

Drenched in the spray of the rainfall shower he pene-trated her deeply and she lost herself in his powerful hold. His thrusts were urgent but he held back, prolonging his desire to ensure she found her release. Her arms curved tight around his shoulders, the fingers of one hand entwined in the soft wet hair at back of his neck, her mouth devouring him. The heat between her legs smoul-dered. The pressure of him tight inside her sent sizzling sweet spirals unfurling through her body over and over again taking her tantalizingly higher until delectable ripples spun her out of control again, her umpteenth fabu-lous orgasm. In an instant of perfectly synchronized shared pleasure, he let go too, driving into her, thrusting in ecstasy.

This beautiful man was a part of her, a feeling so essen-tial that she no longer knew who or what or where she was, only that she was with him, unable to contemplate letting him go.

Ready to leave, Nick came and found her sprawled on the velvet *chaise longue* in a bathrobe, devouring a croissant.

He poured himself half a cup of black coffee from the mini breakfast banquet left by room service. He drank it down in one gulp. The cup rattled as he set it back on its saucer.

'You can come and watch if you'd like to. I'll ask the photographer's PA to look out for you.'

His parting kiss was so, so sweet. He seemed reluctant to leave, kissing her again, so, so slowly. He hadn't reacted to what she'd said in the shower, but that was okay – she was getting better at handling unspoken feelings. With Nick, things left unsaid weren't confusing and threatening like in her childhood. His silence didn't faze her. She'd be patient, wait until he'd finished his shoot.

'You'd really better go,' she whispered. 'Or you'll be late.'

At last he moaned and broke away.

When he'd gone she poured a second cup of coffee and doubts began to sneak in. Was she being unrealistic hoping they could make this work with him in LA and her in Cornwall? With the best will in the world it seemed impossibly difficult. Yet the thought of ending something that felt so right made the idea of going back to Porthkara without a plan to see him again unthinkable – it felt like she'd be heading off into a wasteland. She forced herself to brighten up. He felt the same way. She was sure of it.

Excited to watch the shoot from the sidelines, she got ready quickly, hopping around the room in one shoe, searching for the other one and trying to remember where she'd left her bracelet. The clasp had been loose, she'd opened and closed it too much like the charms were worry beads. She prayed it hadn't fallen off her wrist. Having found the missing shoe but not the bracelet she set off for the Eiffel Tower.

Total astonishment swamped her when she spotted Nick, looking like a billion dollars, dressed in a designer suit and sporting an incredibly high-style silver wristwatch. It felt peculiar seeing him whisperingly close to a supermodel she instantly recognized. She hadn't expected there to be anyone else in the photos; he hadn't mentioned it. He was surrounded by the photographer and her assistants. The sun was rising over the *Champ de Mars* bathing everything in still pink light.

After introducing herself to the PA, a sylphlike girl called Louise with dark, shiny bobbed hair, a clipboard and designer sunglasses, Layla asked, 'They're doing the shoot here? At ground level?'

Louise gave her a warm smile. 'Of course,' she replied with a slight shrug, 'With *la Tour Eiffel* in the background. Where else?'

She didn't know whether to laugh or cry. 'It's just that Nick had the impression that you'd be doing the shoot up there.' She flicked her gaze skyward.

'I know. He's got such a great sense of humour. He told us as soon as he arrived about his fear of heights and how he went up there yesterday. He was very funny about it. The rose in his teeth! The selfies! He called you his phobia-buster. But you needn't have worried. The shoot was planned with the tower as the backdrop.'

The thought of Nick telling these strangers about their

time together made her feel small, no more than a hilarious anecdote. There were only a handful of people around, mostly dog walkers with tiny, pampered pooches. Some stopped to watch briefly, got bored and wandered off. A couple of the passersby photographed Nick being photographed.

Apart from the restaurant and the *patisserie* he hadn't been recognized, not openly. Seeing Nick looking like a star, stylish, professional, with a top French photographer and a team of people buzzing around him knocked her confidence. She didn't know how to be a part of this scene. She might as well be one of the random curious onlookers.

She hung around for a while, staying well back, trying to look as aloof as the French PA, instead of awestruck. Rapidly her excitement had turned into a numb mix of heartache and detachment. Reality hit hard. She didn't belong to Nick's celebrity circle.

Too uncomfortable watching, pointlessly hanging about like a leftover cupcake at a birthday party, she approached Louise who was writing something on the clipboard in purple ink. 'Excuse me.' She hated the tense, sharp sound of her voice. A reaction to how down she was feeling inside, she'd lost her breeziness. 'I'm going now. Please tell Nick I'll see him back at the hotel.'

Louise smiled. 'You can tell him yourself. *Tu sais?* You won't be interrupting.'

Since it wouldn't have bothered anyone, apparently, couldn't he have broken away for a couple of seconds to say hi? Instead he'd blanked her into a state of uneasiness, surplus to requirements and ready to run away and hide.

She couldn't help noticing Louise's perfect turquoise nails exactly matched her biker jacket and she had a trendy tattoo that started just above her collar bone and snaked around the back of her neck.

Her stomach tightened. 'I'd rather not,' she replied quietly, 'I'll catch up with him later.'

'You have plans? Sightseeing? Shopping?'

'Not really. This might sound silly. But I'd like to go the *Pont des Arts* before I go home.'

Louise gave her a curious look. 'The Lovers' Bridge?'

'To see the lovelocks,' she explained.

With a nod she turned away. 'I'll let Nick know when he's finished here.' She scribbled something on her clipboard in purple ink, jammed the pen between her teeth, and sauntered off to respond to a question fired at her by the photographer.

Layla walked to the *Pont des Arts* and stopped for a third coffee on the way. Sitting at a table in a café corner on her own her mood dipped lower. She had been prepared for this, but she hadn't expected to feel so out of it. It felt like the world Nick lived in was a remote island where people like her never went. It was different for Maggie and Alex, they'd known each other before his career took off and anyway she worked with famous people all the time.

When Layla had said she loved Nick she'd been in a dreamland. She really just wanted to go straight back to the hotel, pack up and go. Only, torturously, she couldn't allow herself to leave Paris without seeing the lovelock bridge that had started everything. It marked an ending, something she needed to get out of her system, so she finished her coffee and set off to find it.

Astonished by the sheer number of padlocks despite the city having removed thousands to prevent the bridge from collapsing under their weight, she milled around in the throng of loved-up couples, tourists, and business-as-usual Parisians using the footbridge to get from one bank of the River Seine to the other. The sounds of a string quartet giving a classical style performance of a pop song she loved lifted her spirits. Wistful, she tossed a euro into an open violin case. It chinked landing amongst the collection of coins on the silky lining.

The sunlight on the water, the boats cruising back and forth on the river, white fluffy clouds scudding across the blue sky, and the padlocks, each an individual declaration of love, squeezed her heart. Nick had shown her how different things could be, being with a man who was interested, who cared about what made her happy, not just himself. But something had happened at the shoot, she'd felt it like a sudden change in the weather.

She stood in the middle of the bridge looking back in the direction of the Eiffel Tower. The lovelocks were everywhere, jammed so tight in places there wasn't a spare inch of space. Padlocks from the DIY store, fancy engraved ones, heart-shaped ones, colourful ones. The sight of a bicycle lock made her laugh out loud. She looked at the names. Every one of these couples had a love story. She'd always known she'd adore this place.

'I knew this is where I'd find you.'

She jumped and spun around to find Nick, all tall and gorgeous and heart-stopping.

'You knew because the girl with the purple pen told you,' she pointed out.

'Louise.' He nodded and a lazy smile lit up his face. 'She said you'd snuck off here. But I'd have guessed – even if you hadn't left a message.' His incredible drawl didn't help one bit.

'It's so romantic.' She threw out her arms and did a little pirouette. She was drumming up cheeriness she didn't feel, over-compensating, just like she'd always done. 'It's a shrine to forever love.'

Nick tugged at a lock. '*Brad and Janet!*' he read. 'Really? I know I'm low on the romance-ometer but I'm not convinced.' He pointed at another one. '*King Kong and*

Cinderella?' He frowned. 'Some of these have got to be fake.'

'Cynic. You're not going to spoil it for me.'

'Take note,' Nick remarked, pointing at '*Claudine et Guillaume*'. 'Some people have used the ones with number codes.'

'Are you suggesting that's in case they have second thoughts?'

'You have to admit it's a practical solution for fickle hearts.' Nick felled her with his smile again. Butterflies fluttered in her stomach. 'It beats having to break out the pliers.'

'And hide the evidence in a flower pot.' She laughed. 'I'm so over all that. But – for the record, next time I pledge my heart I'll be sure to get a lovelock with a code. Just in case.'

He didn't reply with a comeback. If she hadn't been to the shoot she'd be happier right this minute than she'd ever been because he'd come to find her. But they were different with each other, tiptoeing on eggshells after what she'd said in the shower. So much for silent communication ... She hadn't improved at understanding silence one bit.

'What are you doing here, anyhow? Apart from spoiling my illusions. Did you finish already?'

There was an awkward expression on his face. 'No. Actually, I took a break. The shoot is taking longer than

expected. The studio asked for extra shots – different loca-
tions. I'm driving out to Versailles, I've got a taxi waiting.
The team's gone ahead and I can't keep them waiting so
I've come to say goodbye.'

Her heart almost stopped. This was it. Exactly as
planned. No big surprise. He was finishing with her. If
there had been an okay moment to tell him that she wasn't
ready for this thing to end, it had passed. He'd touched
her soul and the words *I'm in love with you* floated in her
head, resignedly ignored by Nick.

'Okay,' she said, all matter-of-fact as if she hadn't a care
in the world.

Nick put his hand in his pocket. He handed her a small
velvet bag.

'Open it.'

'What is it?' Avoiding his gaze she untied the silk string.
Confusion tied knots in her stomach as she pulled out
her bracelet, the gold charms shining in the sunlight.

'I asked the concierge to have a jeweller fix the clasp.
So you don't lose it.'

'Thanks.'

'And there's something else. There was a gap, so I took
a chance, and had something added.' Looking up from the
heap of gold in her palm she met his stare, a far off look
in his eyes, the emotion that had sparked between them
earlier gone.

She forced herself to speak, heart heavy. 'It's a star.'

'If you hate it,' he said, misinterpreting her numb reaction, 'I'll get it taken off. Right away.'

'I don't know what to say.' Misery engulfed her. 'It's lovely.'

'Give me your hand.'

His touch sliced through her leaving her cold as he robotically fastened the bracelet on her wrist.

'I'm not coming to the airport with you,' he announced, detached. 'I'm flying to LA tonight. Louise changed my flight. She arranged for a driver to pick you up at the hotel. Tell the front desk when you're ready to go.'

He'd been back in his own world for a matter of hours and he'd already arranged for her to be conveniently removed. Nerves stretched to breaking point, she backed away, recoiling from him, shunning all the magical moments they'd had together. The man she'd been with wasn't the real Nick after all. The time they'd spent together was pretend. She'd been living in the moment with him, but she'd been wrong to imagine that he returned her feelings. It was an actor's game. Standing with him now – remote, smooth, shallow – she felt sick and stupid. She'd been so taken in. And on top of everything, he was heartlessly running away, rejecting Beth, unprepared to go and see her in the UK, to give her another chance.

She turned her back on him, doing a mental handbag

inventory as she walked away. She had her passport, cards, money and the flight reference she'd need to get her boarding card, nothing to stop her going straight to the airport. 'That's very kind, but it won't be necessary.'

He ploughed the fingers of one hand into his hair and ran it to the back of his head, exasperated. 'Layla. Wait up.' He sounded arrogant and annoyed, like she was being a nuisance, not fitting in neatly with the plan. She felt dropped. She'd served her purpose and he was ready to have her spirited away.

And the star charm made her angry, not because she hated it but because she loved it. She kept on walking. 'Goodbye Nick. Have a nice life.'

'Where are you going?'

'The airport.'

'What about your things?'

'I'm sure if you speak nicely to the concierge he'll have them sent on.'

'If that's what you want.' His tone matched hers in condescension.

She inhaled a deep breath that filled her lungs. It nearly choked her as she let it go. *Of course it's not what I want.* 'I'm done with Paris. I want to go home.'

'Take your time. Have lunch at the hotel. Get your things. Let the driver Louise arranged drop you at *Charles de Gaulle.*'

She couldn't bear the mechanical way he treated her. 'Don't tell me what to do.' She stopped and turned to face him, knowing she was being irrational, but not knowing how else to be strong in the face of being given her marching orders. 'Don't follow me Nick.'

'I guess we'll run into each other again,' he attempted to say, 'With Alex and Maggie.'

'Yep.'

'Maybe I'll come and visit when they're in Porthkara. See how they like your artwork?'

Please don't.

If she could engineer things to avoid having that happen before Phoebe or Horatio got married, she would. That should give her ... what? About thirty years or so. If she was lucky.

'It's been fab.' She resisted her slap-on-a-sunny-smile reflex. Chauffeur-driven limos, designer dresses at the snap of his fingers, it had been mesmerizing, until the unreality of Nick's reality had slammed into her like an Atlantic breaker. She was so angry with herself for her confession that morning. But she'd get over it, she was used to relationships going wrong. 'What we had was a blip.'

'A good blip.'

'You can have too much of a good thing.' *And I can't be here a moment longer.* 'Enough is enough. I'm going home.'

Chapter Twenty-Six

'**D**on't you want to know what they're writing about you? This headline says "We'll Always Have Paris!" What a hoot!'

At the Kandy Shack, Shelly plonked a cup of tea under her daughter's nose and pushed a magazine towards Layla that she'd picked up when she'd fetched a pint of milk from the general store.

Her mother's tone was kind but the words twisted Layla's insides. She took a sip of tea and ignored the magazine.

More than two weeks had gone by since she'd come back from Paris and it was one of those windy, cloudy seaside days when the landscape in its entirety appeared grey. Her heart was lost and dismayed. She'd gone to Paris with Nick expecting a fling, and she'd known she was getting in too deep and too fast, but she hadn't expected to fall so hard. More fool her. She'd kept a lid on it and kept going with her ordinary life again, ignoring his calls, deleting his texts and emails without reading them. No point in prolonging the agony.

The minute she'd got home things had gone from bad to worse. News of their fling filtered into a tabloid, and spread like a rash to the magazines. Maggie called to talk about it but Layla couldn't. Everything was so wrong that at first, she hadn't realized that something else also wasn't right. She'd been in a state of denial for a few days.

'Sweetheart I think you're taking all this too seriously. Nobody pays attention to tittle-tattle. Mags are on the lookout for stories. Pretty soon they'll drop it, find someone new to write headlines about. You know how it is, A and B's Shock Kiss, X and Y's Baby Surprise.'

Layla drank her tea, hollow inside. Her mother had changed her tune. What had happened to the reigning queen of keeping up appearances? Had she abdicated and handed back her crown?

'So how are the business plans coming along?' Shelly changed tack brightly and opened a packet of biscuits.

'Dad knows someone who's selling a van, low mileage, reasonable condition. He's arranged a test drive, reckons it's a good price. And I had a call from the village pre-school. They made more money than expected at the summer fair. The committee wants to redecorate. They've asked for a continuous mural on all four walls and a ceiling like a sunny day.'

'Right up your street.'

Layla tried to raise a smile, and failed.

'What's wrong love? Is there something you're not telling me? Something about Paris? And you-know-who? I can't remember when I last saw you so down-hearted.' Shelly dunked her biscuit in her tea.

'I'm a bit blah. Being in magazines is a shock.'

'Silliness sells newspapers. Daft headlines on the cover. And half-baked stories inside. Nick could breathe half a dozen unconnected words in as many different languages and it would be news. It'll blow over soon.'

'He's hard to forget. Especially as it didn't end well. I miss the person he was when he was with me, but he wasn't the real deal. And thinking about him every day makes me sadder than I thought possible.'

'Is that why you're not speaking to him?'

She studied her beloved charms – pixie, heart, four-leafed clover, horseshoe, padlock, key. And the star ... Deep sadness flooded her heart.

'When he gave me this, he wasn't the same Nick. He was cold. Couldn't wait for me to leave. And condescending. As if I was a bad smell under his nose.'

'Adding a new charm to your bracelet doesn't strike me as the action of someone who thinks you smell bad.'

She sighed. 'Believe me, it's how I felt.'

'You smell lovely, like summer flowers.' Shelly kissed the

top of her daughter's head. 'Sweetheart, you were both on the same page, neither of you expected the weekend to turn into anything more, I don't see how he could have behaved any other way. He had to work.'

'You think I'm being unreasonable.'

'I think you got in out of your depth.' She finished her biscuit and took another one out of the packet. 'When you and him were getting on so well I was happy for you. I hoped he might blow away the cobwebs – after Joe.'

'It went sour very quickly.'

'He seemed smitten to me, but with all that's been written about him over the years, there's no smoke without fire. I can't lie – I doubt someone like that can change, not unless they really want to.'

'The thing is, it's possible I might be pregnant.'

Shelly dropped the biscuit into her mug, sloshing milky tea onto the counter top.

'It's *possible*? Have you done a test?'

'No, not yet.' Her voice trembled, and not for the first time since she'd walked away from Nick, she wanted to cry, afraid of the way he'd reacted to Beth, how easily he'd rejected his daughter. 'I'm scared. I don't want to find out, because if it's a yes, I'll have to tell him, and then it's all going to kick off.'

Shelly emptied the unfinished mugs of tea into the sink. 'We're going into town, right now.' She ran the tap, flushed

311

the biscuit mush down the plughole, then set about closing the kiosk.

'It's probably a false alarm.'

'That's what I thought, and I ended up with you.'

'I know. And Granny Rivers made sure I knew it. And now look.'

Shock registered on Shelly's face. 'She told you?'

'Uh-huh.'

'About the ...?'

'Condom failure. Yes.'

'The witch. When?'

'The day after I turned sixteen.'

'Let's go.' Checking the time on her mobile, Shelly grabbed her keys and Layla slung her handbag over her shoulder. 'If we leave now, we'll make it before the chemist in town closes.'

Shelly marched her to the car and gently ordered her into the passenger seat. She drove the car in silence weaving along the lanes to the main road. She turned the radio on and pop music, all love songs as luck would have it, filled the loaded silence in the car.

By the time they arrived in town Layla felt ill. As Shelly parked the car heavy rain began to fall.

'Have you got an umbrella?'

Layla shook her head.

'Me neither.'

They waited for the shower to ease off, aware of the minutes ticking away on the dashboard clock. Incapable of getting out of the car, Layla watched rivulets of water trickle down the windscreen. Making their watery descent, the trickles divided and forked, creating new streams, setting off down the glass in new directions.

'You'd better go.'

'I can't. I feel sick.'

'Well if you can't, then I will sweetheart.'

Her mum hurried across the market square in the rain holding a magazine over her head. Layla's mind whirred, struggling with the big what-if. Her mum had put her well-being ahead of her own since the day Layla had been conceived. If she was pregnant, more than anything in the world, she'd strive to do the same thing. She'd put her feelings for Nick aside, and first and foremost figure out what it meant to be there for a child; something he'd proven he wasn't capable of.

Arriving back at the car, Shelly slid into the driver's seat and dropped a wet plastic bag into Layla's lap. She opened it and peered in fearfully. 'Six? Was it really necessary to buy up the entire stock?'

'Best double check. What if one of them is faulty or you do it wrong?'

She held back from asking if that's what her mother had done, checking and rechecking, hoping the first result had been a mistake. It was a gloomy thought.

Shelly started the engine. 'You mustn't do anything stupid.' She'd gone into maternal overdrive. 'You can't tie yourself to a man who doesn't love you back, no matter how much you think you love him.'

'A baby's a strong reason. It's what you did.'

'And we raised a lovely daughter. But if he doesn't love you and if you don't trust him, then keep your freedom and focus on bringing up a happy child. That's my advice. No matter what he says.'

'Look, we're getting ahead of ourselves. The test might be negative.'

Her mother pulled carefully out of the square and turned towards Layla's cottage. 'Your grandmother wasn't a witch. I shouldn't have said that. But she shouldn't have told you that thing.'

'It doesn't matter.' She didn't want to hurt her mother's feelings, but even without the too-much-information details it had been obvious she was unplanned.

'Granny Rivers had a difficult start in life. Her older brother was killed in the Second World War. She was evacuated from London to live with relatives at the old farm on the cliff, then stayed on after the war, didn't go home, because her mother died in a bombing and her father didn't want her back. He didn't think he'd cope with a child he barely knew, he needed a fresh start. She was devastated, never really came to terms with it all.'

'Why didn't anyone tell me?'

'It wasn't talked about. And it's not the sort of thing you tell a child.'

'Poor Granny, I'd no idea.'

'It affected the way she lived. She didn't make friends easily. I think she was happiest when she met your grandfather. The bracelet was her most precious possession, a present on their wedding day. Those charms were important. She loved him with all her heart, he died much too young.'

Layla clutched the plastic bag dripping in her lap. 'Do you think she blamed me? For Dad missing out?'

'Why would you think that? She thought the sun shone out of your dad. She had big dreams for him. Bigger than he really wanted for himself. And she loved you to bits.'

'She didn't show it.'

'That's how she was. But she loved you all the same. On your first birthday ...'

'She didn't come to the parties.'

'True. But she always marked the occasion. That day she stopped in after everyone left, explained about the bracelet, said she was putting it away to keep safe for you.' They reached the main road and drove in silence for a while until finally Shelly added, 'She was cross with Ralph for being careless. He was too young and too fickle to settle down when he married me. She knew it. She didn't want me to get hurt, and she was afraid to get too close to you – convinced we'd split up. My mother loathed her. That's why she didn't come to your parties – because she was afraid there'd be arguments, that Ralph and I would fight and I'd leave and take you away. After what happened over our wedding, she didn't want any upset.'

'What do you mean?'

'Granny Rivers told us to wait until Ralph had been to university to get married. My mother said he might not come back. That's how our mothers fell out. It escalated, got seriously unpleasant, both of them starting rumours and making accusations. Someone said she said I wasn't good enough for her son, that I got pregnant on purpose to keep Ralph from leaving. We told her about the contraception fail in our defence. Eventually we got sick of our mothers rowing and eloped. We got married in the registry office with a barman and a waitress as witnesses then hid out in a hotel in Newquay for a couple weeks. We ran up an enormous credit card bill.'

Layla gasped. 'No celebration?'

'Nothing. No wedding dress. No flowers. No champagne.'

Anxious, Layla twisted the plastic bag. 'I didn't know.'

'We're not proud of it. It's not exactly something we

advertised. We tried to make up for it by making your birthdays special.'

'It might have been an idea to explain why my grannies didn't get along. I thought it was me Granny Rivers hated.'

'It didn't occur to me,' she said, 'Your dad and I were always papering over the cracks, too preoccupied with putting on a show to think about how any of this affected you.' After a long pause she added, 'I'm sorry.'

'It's okay.'

'She wasn't spiteful, but she was very disapproving. What I find strange is that after so much tragedy, Ralph failing to live up to her expectations was just a disappointment, but she reacted as if it was the end of the world.'

They arrived back in the village and Shelly pulled into a parking space in front of the cottage. 'Do you want me to come in and wait while you pee?'

'Thanks but no thanks.' Layla grappled with her seatbelt, opened the car door and jumped out. 'I might need to build up to it.'

Shelly lowered the driver's side window and gave her daughter a reassuring wave as she put her key in the lock. 'Don't leave it too long. And let me know as soon as you know. And remember, whatever happens don't do anything crazy. Like say you'll marry the man.'

'Mum, stop! What makes you think he'd even ask me?'

'You might ask him.'

'In your dreams,' she said bleakly, 'I haven't spoken to him since Paris. It's over. And baby or no baby, marriage isn't what I want. I can cope without Nick's input.'

Her mother must have a screw loose. She was warning her off proposing? *As if!* If the comment was a motherly attempt at lightening the mood it fell flat.

'A little bird told me he'd been sending you gifts. That doesn't sound to me like a man who knows it's over.'

'Whoever your source is, they have it wrong.' She wanted to bury her head in her hands. She held up the bag containing the pregnancy test selection. 'Thank you for these.'

Once inside the cottage she let the dog out into the yard, fed her and made a much-needed cup of tea. Evidently her mum had talked to the neighbour because Nick *had* been sending things by courier every day. The first offering had been an irresistibly delicious Eiffel Tower made out of mini *macarons*. She'd allowed Ophelia to have one, but it was a lot for one person and a dog so she'd taken some across to her neighbour. The rest of the gifts were hidden under the bed in the spare room, amongst them a beautiful art book from the *Musée d'Orsay* and a large framed photograph of the amazing Chagall ceiling at the opera house. She wished he'd stop. She detested that he wanted to buy her off, compensation for the ridiculous media frenzy.

She flopped onto the sofa, opened her handbag and took out the magazine she'd shoved in there.

Inside, there was a zoomed in picture of her hair that appeared to have had the brightness dialled all the way up to accentuate its redness.

'Great. Listen to this, O.' Ophelia tilted her head to one side, eyes like a couple of shiny brown buttons. She read out loud to the dog.

'"*On the rebound, jilted playboy actor Nick Wells has been photographed in Paris with a striking mystery red head.*"'

Ophelia lay down with her head on Layla's feet, and huffed out an empathetic canine sigh. She silently read the rest of the article, rubbing salt into her wound. The ludicrous item had evolved from the old man at the restaurant's pictures. It named her and mentioned them meeting at Maggie's wedding. According to speculation, the journalist claimed – allegedly – wedding day shenanigans between her and Nick had driven Toni into the arms of the security guard.

She wondered if her mother had properly read the piece. It didn't paint her in a good light. Heart-battered, feeling like a fool, she tossed the magazine onto the growing pile and set the bag from the chemist's on top. The thought of doing a pregnancy test curdled her stomach. Given what she'd just read all she wanted was to crawl under her duvet.

319

The doorbell rang and her irritation bubbled up. Another pointless item? So annoying. Where were the things she'd left in the hotel? She'd borrowed the snazzy little suitcase from Maggie's loft so she'd have to replace it. The rest was all clothes, nothing special. What would he try and pay off her humiliation with today? A chocolate model of *Notre Dame* complete with bells and an edible Quasimodo?

Ophelia jumped up and ran to the window with an unusually ear-splitting yap. After another nerve-jangling ring of the bell Layla got up off the sofa. Alternating between emitting nervous yelps, and turning in circles, chasing her tail, the dog got under her feet. 'What's going on?' she asked, side-stepping so as not to trip over. She peeked hesitantly out the window. 'It's late for a delivery.'

Her heart sank to an all-time low at the sight of Joe on her doorstep. She nipped across the room and quickly hid the bag of pregnancy tests under a cushion. Bracing herself, she opened the front door.

'Joe,' she said frostily. She bit back remarking on the fact that he'd finally deigned to show his face and remove his belongings. 'Your stuff's ready. It's in the cupboard under the stairs.'

He marched in like he owned the place. 'Lainy's not with me. I don't know if you've heard. We're getting a divorce.'

Chapter Twenty-Seven

Nick waited for the electric gates to Fran's chic new build to slide back, and drove across the crunching gravel with a ball of trepidation in his gut. He swung around the turning circle with a fountain and sculpted topiary at its centre, parked and cut the engine. He twiddled with the dashboard controls, stalling. He checked his phone. Still nothing from Layla. It hadn't properly sunk in that they were over. He'd tried to make contact, she'd cut him dead. Her suitcase was in the trunk. He'd been lugging it with him, postponing sending it on because as long as it was in his possession he had a reason to continue trying to reach her.

He quickly read a text from his brother. He'd sent Nick that Shakespeare quote he was so fond of – typical. '*It is not in the stars to hold our destiny but in ourselves.*' The irony jarred. Alex didn't know he was in Cheshire. He'd decided to keep quiet about the meeting with Fran and Beth until it was fait accompli.

Alex's words referred to Layla but Nick had a strong feeling that that ship had sailed. It was for the best he told himself, it's what they'd agreed. Once he'd talked to Fran, and met Beth, he'd sort out how to deliver the suitcase.

Fran's house had a grand entrance, mock classical pillars, steps up to the front door and a golden lion's head knocker which stared him in the face while he steeled himself to press the doorbell, the high tech electronic chime setting his teeth on edge.

Fran opened the door, and his trepidation ramped up a notch. 'It's good to see you. Come in. We can hang out here for a bit, pick Beth up after school, go for pizza. How does that sound?'

'Whatever you think best.' he croaked, uncertain how to handle the formalities and also relieved she was on top of it. 'How does Beth feel? Is she okay with this?'

'Absolutely,' she said reassuringly. 'Things have settled down, she's looking forward to meeting you.'

He followed her into the vast kitchen. While she made tea, he walked over to the wall of bi-fold glass doors and pretended to admire the view of the garden.

'I was in a spin the last time you were here,' she said. 'I wasn't coping well. I shouldn't have dumped everything on you the way I did. I'm sorry. I have a lot of apologizing to do.'

Listening with his back turned, he sucked in a deep

breath and let it go slowly. He appeared calm on the outside, but beneath the surface he was an undetonated bomb. 'There's no need to apologize – an explanation would be nice. Why didn't you tell me about Beth in the first place?'

He turned to confront her. Her gaze bored into him. He couldn't have been more uncomfortable if she'd produced a high-pitched dentist's drill.

'What we had was supposed to be a no-strings thing, nothing serious.' The corners of her mouth drooped sadly. 'There are things I didn't tell you, not excuses, but I'm hoping they explain my decision.' She closed the space between them and handed him a mug. The heat seeped into his palms. Seething with questions, he sipped the tea and gazed out at the meticulously landscaped garden. 'I had a broken heart. You were the cure. I didn't tell you because you not knowing about it, well, that was kind of the point of us.'

'For you,' he remarked, wondering if his feelings had been taken into account at any point.

'I'd been planning a big wedding. It was all arranged – dresses, bridesmaids, caterers, marquee on my parents' lawn. You wouldn't believe how thorough the details were.'

He didn't react, suppressing the urge to say he didn't care.

'I'd been planning the day for over two years. I was bridezilla!' Mirthless she laughed. 'I'd ordered a cake shaped like a gigantic pile of teacups. I must have been as mad as a hatter.' She took a sip of tea, and almost snorted out another unfunny laugh which she stifled just in time to prevent a disaster. She set the mug down on the kitchen table and straightened her back, composing herself. 'Needless to say the wedding didn't take place. The guy I was going to marry tried to get my bridesmaid into bed. She was mortified. She didn't know what to do, but in the end she told me, and three days before the wedding I called it off. I'd already forgiven an affair, and turned a blind eye to other ...' She hesitated uneasily, and Nick sensed that she wasn't sure if she could trust him, like she hadn't been able to trust her fiancé. 'Indiscretions,' she said. 'Anyway, when I heard he'd tried it on with my bridesmaid, I knew he'd never change.'

'You must have been devastated.' It was a major letdown and an explanation for throwing herself into a just-for-fun fling, but how could he sympathize when he was the one who'd been damaged? 'But why keep our child a secret from me? Didn't you think I had a right to know?' All the anger he'd bottled up in the weeks since he'd found out broke his control. 'We weren't serious. I didn't expect us to last any more than you did, but for all that, I fell hard for you. I'm gutted to look back knowing that you didn't believe I could step up to the plate.' He hadn't told her, it would have been too uncool, but the feelings he'd had were real, and if he'd known he was nothing more than moving on sex, he'd have held back, the way he'd been doing ever since.

'I wasn't ready to find someone new, someone reliable, start a family – all the things I'd planned for. I was in a different space.'

'It didn't stop you having the baby and shutting me out. You've taken something away from me I can't get back. Eleven years of my child's life? Have you any idea how bad that feels?' The chaos of his emotions crashed into him.

She put her hand on his arm, and he didn't flinch or back away. He didn't resent her, didn't hold this against her, but the knowledge that she'd chosen to freeze him out tortured him.

'You had an absolute right to know. I regret my choices. I don't have any words to defend myself. By the time I found out, you'd gone to LA. I didn't tell anyone who the father was. Time went by and being alone got easier. I had lots of support from family. And Beth is the sweetest child anyone could wish for. It's not that I didn't think about getting in touch ... I'd see pieces in the tabloids, and get cold feet. We were only together for a few weeks, I didn't really know you.'

'And being Beth's dad doesn't count for anything?'

'I put it down to contraceptive failure.' Her voice faltered.

'My failure. I'd taken antibiotics for a throat infection and the midwife reckoned they must have reduced the effectiveness of my pill. When I discovered I was pregnant I realized I desperately wanted a baby. It wasn't something we'd discussed. I saw her as my responsibility. I decided not to ask you for anything.' Her hair flopped into her eyes and she pushed it back behind her ears with trembling hands. 'Look I wouldn't blame you if walk away but I really hope you won't.'

'I'm not going anywhere.' He set his mug down and folded his arms across his chest, his concerns about Beth meeting him after so long still strong. 'When did she find out I'm her dad?'

'A couple of months ago. She's pestered me for a name the last couple of years. I got very good at avoiding the question.' She turned away. 'I didn't feel good about it. She'd get upset during the dad's race at school Sports Days. Her granddad used to enter in place of a dad, but he always came last and it made her so miserable that I had to ask him not to come this summer. Worse than that, every year the school fair was on Father's Day and she didn't have one.'

The image she painted of a little girl who desperately needed a dad cracked his heart. As difficult as the situation was, its biggest impact was on Beth.

'This scare's been awful. The lump's removed, everything's okay. We can go over the past and what's brought us to where we are a million times and it won't change anything. Keeping her from you is indefensible. I'm genuinely sorry Nick. Honestly.'

The bitterness he'd been fighting with full-scale denial for the last few weeks began to diminish, cancelled out by Fran's remorse.

'Let's look on the bright side,' he said. 'We should grateful for being forced to face up to this. For Beth's sake.'

She turned back to face him and paused for half a moment, regret written on her face. 'And yours. I want to sort it out.'

Cautious, but trusting Fran's readiness to make amends, he asked, 'So why wouldn't she see me last time?'

'Any number of reasons. Because she's confused. Because she's missed out on having a dad. Because she needs you to prove that you want to be part of her life. Not just because I asked you to – but because you really care.' She started walking towards the kitchen door. 'Come here.'

He followed her across the wide chandelier-lit hallway to the dining room. The long mahogany dining table that wouldn't have looked out of place in a stately home was covered in Beth-related memorabilia – photo albums, school reports, a favorite teddy, souvenirs collected on holidays. His heart swelled and he didn't fight it.

'We got this lot ready for you. She's been adding to it all week.'

He picked up two tiny red shoes. 'Lucky your dining table's so big.'

She laughed. 'Her first shoes. Would you like me to talk you through it? Believe me. I've wanted to make this as easy as possible. The last few weeks have been horrendous.'

For more than an hour Fran reminisced about the collection, from photos of Beth's first baby smiles to the picture of delight on her face at her eleventh birthday, a retro themed dance party, complete with deejay, disco lights, glitter ball, and all thirty of her classmates. Spread out in front of him, he absorbed moment after moment of his daughter's life. Dying to meet her for real, it was hard to take in; gymnastics certificates, swimming badges, an award for tap dancing.

Eventually Fran sat back in her chair and looked at her watch. 'That's enough for now I think,' she said, 'Beth can show you the rest later.' She leaned in and squeezed his hand. 'Come on,' she said, 'it's time to go get her.'

Parked around the corner from the school he waited for Fran to bring Beth to the car. His fear and reluctance had morphed into better feelings – ones he couldn't pin down. Excitement. Joy. He couldn't wait to meet his daughter.

When she hopped in, shoving her backpack onto the

empty seat beside her, he turned and looked at her.

'Hey.'

Shy, she smiled. 'Hi.'

Fran slid into the front passenger seat. 'Pop your seatbelt on hun,' she instructed. To Nick she said matter-of-factly, 'Turn left at the end of the road, take the second exit at the big roundabout, drive up the hill, you'll see the car park for the pizza place on the right. It's not far, two miles tops.'

The people in the restaurant were friendly. They knew Fran and Beth and showed them to their favorite table. They ordered drinks and then Beth disappeared to change out of her school uniform in the Ladies'.

'So what do you make of our little girl?'

'She's great. I don't know what I was expecting. Big introductions! Big emotions!' The emotions lay below the surface alongside a side-order of relief.

'I was hardly going to make a dramatic announcement. Meet your father!' she teased. 'Parents are embarrassing enough.'

He smiled, happy to follow her lead. 'I appreciate your no fuss approach. How am I doing?'

She reached across the table and touched his hand. 'Brilliant.'

'Is there anyone I should know about,' he asked. 'A significant other?'

She shook her head. 'She's a little young for a boyfriend.'

He hammed a comedic shudder. 'I meant you.'

She laughed. Her eyes sparkled. 'There's no one. Just me and Beth. And my work. That's how I like it. It's enough.'

'For now.'

'We have a lot of catching up to do.'

'It could take all night.' He smiled, keeping it light, determined to make a go of it. 'By the time the hospital drama we worked on aired you'd finished with me. How long ago was that?'

'Too long,' she sighed. 'Twelve years.'

When Beth joined the table, she'd transformed to a super trendy tween.

'What are you two having?' She shuffled onto the bench next to her mum. 'I'd like bruschetta, a quattro stagioni pizza and pistachio gelato with chocolate sauce for dessert.

After the meal they skipped coffee. Nick asked for the bill and drove them home so Beth could tackle her homework. Perched on a high stool at the kitchen island she worked away at English, Maths and Geography while Fran and Nick had a glass of red wine and chatted about the other people in the show they'd worked on and what had happened to them since.

'I can't do this. It's difficult.' Nick turned to see his daughter staring sadly at a French textbook.'

'What's the problem?' Fran asked.

'I hate French. We have to revise the difference between *être* and *avoir*. I don't get it.' Beth slumped over her book in frustration. 'I can't tell the difference.'

'Can't help hun,' Fran said, 'Not a clue. French wasn't my best subject.'

'Can I help?' Nick offered. 'I've been working in France. My French isn't exactly brilliant, but I know the basics.'

Beth pushed the book towards him, eyes wide and hopeful. Nick studied the questions. Twelve sentences to complete, six using each verb. Thankfully his rusty schoolboy French was up to the task. 'So,' he said, '"To be"...'

'Or not to be,' Fran interrupted.

'That's not helpful Mum, shush.' Beth complained.

'Let's have a go at one of these questions.'

Encouragingly Nick helped her translate the questions and patiently waited while she wrote the answers into her exercise book. Hesitantly she passed it across the worktop for him to check.

'Brilliant. You nailed it.'

'It's not as difficult as I thought.' She looked up at him and smiled confidently. 'Thanks Nick.'

The homework finished, they all went to view the impromptu museum of childhood in the dining room. Overwhelmed once more, Nick was relieved when Fran suggested that it was time for Beth to get off to bed.

'Say goodnight to Nick,' she said.

Beth looked at him thoughtfully. 'Would it be alright if I call you Dad?'

Staggered, Nick couldn't believe his ears. His heart felt suddenly too big for its allocated space in his chest. The instinctive connection he felt blindsided him. 'Of course you can.'

Beth approached, put her arms around his middle and gave him a hug. Automatically he hugged her back. 'I've been waiting for you,' she said. 'I'm happy you're here.'

'Me too. I'm sorry I'm late. I'm sorry I missed you growing up. But I want you to know, I'm here for you now, and I will be – always.'

A second later she asked if he could get her on the guest list to a London premiere and he said yes, discovering that he could deny his daughter nothing. It was a great feeling. Fran scolded her gently for being cheeky and scooted her off to bed.

'Sorry,' she said smiling. 'I told her not to.'

He laughed. 'I'll see what I can do.'

'Stay for another glass of wine. You're welcome to stay over – if you like.' It would be so easy. Fran was more attractive now than she'd ever been. They had a daughter together. It was hard to imagine anything more important than that. She picked up the bottle of wine. 'It's an awfully good vintage,' she coaxed, 'Like me.'

'You're as incorrigible as ever.'

'You never were any good at saying no.' Her voice was as gentle as a cat's purr. 'What if we let bygones be bygones?' She moved so whisperingly close her strong perfume wound through him. He hadn't registered her gold painted toenails and her six-inch heels when he'd arrived, but he was noticing now. 'Take it slow this time? You could buy a place nearby.'

He nodded. 'I've been thinking about a UK base.'

'You're going to need one.'

'It's all so new,' he admitted, tempted by her offer of a refill.

'There's lots to discuss,' she ventured. 'Finish the bottle. Call a taxi. Pick up the car in the morning. If you'd prefer not to stay over, that is.' Her powers of persuasion were superlative. 'We were fabulous together. We could be again.'

In twelve years he'd mastered a skillset of his own. But she was his child's mother and he couldn't afford to forget it.

She poured herself another glass waiting for him to make his mind up. 'I used to tell people you were my candyfloss.'

He met her smile because she made him laugh, like she'd done before with her crazy ideas. 'Because I was bad for you?'

'Because you were sweet, and indulgent, and much too much of a good thing.'

'Ah.' He was lost for words.

She poured him a glass of wine and he leant in and brushed his face gently against her cheek.

'Goodnight Fran.'

'You can't blame me for trying.'

'I don't. I'll be in touch.'

Chapter Twenty-Eight

'I've brought you a magazine.' Joe assessed Layla with a rapid onceover.

She was still processing the news of his divorce but glanced at the collection piled on the coffee table. 'Because I don't have enough?'

'You look amazing in those.' He pushed the one he was holding into her hands. 'This one's different. Light at the end of the tunnel? See for yourself. Page fourteen. Did you know he has a kid?'

Grudgingly she flicked to where he said. She failed to ignore Nick's wayward smile beaming out from between the covers. He'd been photographed accompanying his mother to a red-carpet event with Beth between them smiling as confidently as her dad. The picture knocked her sideways. Tight-lipped she checked the date on the cover.

'Some of the papers slagged you off. Said you're not good

335

enough for him. If you ask me it's the other way around – he's not good enough for you.'

He sat on sofa in the spot that had always been his. 'Thanks for that.' Deflated, defeated she walked over to the under-stairs cupboard eager for him to take his things and leave. Guilt jabbed at her. She changed her mind and sat down next to him. The bag she'd hidden rustled under the cushion behind her back. 'What happened? With you and Lainy?'

'She left me.'

'I'm sorry.' Ophelia had been lying in front of the fire-place. She got up, stretched and pottered across to sit next Layla, leaning against her legs. She reached down and tousled her fur.

'I shouldn't have got married in the first place. It was a mistake. My parents are furious.'

'Why did you?'

He sighed, got up and headed for the kitchen. 'Got any beers?'

'A couple in the fridge.' She did a double take at her automatic response.

'Want one?' The familiarity of the sound of Joe opening a drawer to get the bottle opener and popping the top stunned her.

'No!'

Slugging the beer, he slumped back into the space beside her. 'I missed you.'

'So you married my double?'

'I know, right?' He chortled.

She couldn't believe her ears. 'It's not funny.'

'And that lot is?' He pointed at the coffee table. 'I'm back for good. Why don't we draw a line and start again?'

'You mean, when your divorce comes through?'

'Why wait? The divorce is just a detail.'

'A significant one.'

Thinking it over, he knocked back another slug of beer and made himself comfortable stretching out his legs in front of the fireplace and crossing them at the ankles. He was settling in as if he was at home. 'Aren't you happy? I thought you'd be up for it.'

'You want a second chance?'

'You forget Lainy and I forget ... him. It'll be like they never happened.'

'I can't forget.' Her head was spinning. There was one sure way to kill off Joe's ideas of getting back together. 'And another thing – I may be pregnant.'

Flummoxed he stared at her. 'You're kidding.'

'I don't know for sure. I might not be. But the point is – it's a real possibility. It's not ...' She hooked her fingers in the air '... just a detail!'

'Does he know?'

She shook her head, sorry she'd said anything.

'Face it. He's gone. He's not coming back.'

She trembled. It was true, but hearing him say it knifed her in the soul. 'I know,' she whispered.

'It's early. You could terminate. If you want to.'

'I'm perfectly aware of my options,' she said frostily.

Joe stood up abruptly, set his beer on the mantelpiece and started pacing the living room. 'We can work it out,' he said. 'Maybe you're not. We need to find out. If you are …' He stopped pacing. '… Why tell him? He doesn't need to know. No one does. Have the baby and we'll bring it up together. We'll get married.'

'When your divorce comes through.' It was stating the obvious, but the fact needed clarifying.

'A proper wedding. Not a silly after party.'

'You're unbelievable.'

He reacted as if she meant in a good way. 'I know. We'll sort it, one way or another. If there's a baby it can be our secret. What do you say? You and me? The way we were before. Let's unpack my things.'

'Stop.' She jumped up from the sofa and held up the palm of her hand like she was directing traffic.

'Too fast?' He looked optimistic, like a more measured approach might work.

'I love him.'

'No, you don't.' He paced again suppressing her words. 'I thought I loved Lainy. I didn't. I love you.' He wheeled round, and stared at her intensifying her confusion.

338

'I'm not in love with you,' she said as clearly as possible.

He started moving again, walking back and forth, tracing a triangle between the spot where she stood, the front door and the kitchen. 'You're angry. You're possibly hormonal.' He paused, briefly computing what she'd said. 'What's your problem? You should be grateful I want you back. What more do you want from me?'

Frazzled, she didn't answer. The room felt too small and a nasty silence hung in the air. She wanted to throw him out and fling his bags after him. She hesitated.

He stopped pacing and confronted her. 'You can't rely on him. He used you. Like he does. He's a player, he's well-known for it.'

'You don't know him.'

'You're deluded.'

The conversation she'd had with her mother rattled in her head. She'd thought her dad was unreliable – he was the opposite. The intensity of young love had burned out, but he'd stuck with his decision, taken the responsibility of becoming a dad seriously, and done the best he could – for all his flaws.

'Maybe I am. I know one thing for sure though. You don't love me. If you did, you wouldn't have gone away when I needed you. And you wouldn't have married someone who isn't me.'

'How many times do I have to say it? I made a mistake.

So did you. The way I see it, we're even. Admit it, Nick Wells doesn't give a toss. Get over it and get back with me.'

'Be Lucky In Love!' Despite everything, her grandmother had held firm to the hope that she'd found true love and that Layla would too. She counted to three in her head. 'I'd like you to go now. This – what you're proposing, isn't going to happen, not now, not ever.' Nick had gone, but in their short time together he'd shown her more kindness, cared more about her happiness, than Joe. That part, she knew, he hadn't faked. 'Be honest. This isn't about what I want. It's about you.' She opened the under-stairs cupboard. 'Your things are ready.'

'You don't know whether you're coming or going.' He started to pull the bags out of the cupboard. 'Think it over. You'll see it makes sense.'

Fury boiled inside her. She opened the front door as wide as it would go and stepped outside so that he could squeeze through with the overstuffed binbags. She breathed in the fresh sea air. She wasn't going to lose it, she'd tell him once and for all. 'For starters, you didn't only hurt me, you hurt your parents, getting married without telling them.'

'They didn't say.'

'Because instead of saying they were upset they worked like crazy to organize things. They practically stayed up all night to get your "silly after party" ready. And as for me?' A seagull's squawk from the roof distracted him. She stared hard at him, trying to figure out what she'd liked about him, how they'd got into a relationship and at a loss as to why they'd stayed together so long. 'I'm not going to think it over. I don't need to. The only place where what you're saying makes sense is on Planet Joe. And I don't live there anymore.'

Three binbags clenched in each fist, he loitered in front of the row of white cottages glaring like thunder. Like a little sentry on duty, Ophelia waited in the doorway.

'If you think a baby's going to make any difference you're dreaming,' he shouted.

'Goodbye.' Out of the corner of her eye she caught movement nearby. When she spun around to see who was watching the scene with Joe unfold, she found herself looking into the eyes of the man she'd become used to seeing only in magazines. 'Nick!' He was trailing the suitcase and holding a bottle of champagne.

'What's going on?' he asked, eyeing Joe scornfully. 'Are you okay? What's the yelling about?'

'Joe came for his stuff. He's just leaving.' She narrowed her eyes and fired off a look as if she could zap her ex with telepathy. 'Go on,' she said, 'don't stand there gawping.'

Barking and jumping so that all four paws left the ground at once, Ophelia rushed into the lane to greet Nick. He bent down and rumpled her fur.

Joe smirked. 'Oh, to be a fly on the wall,' he sneered before loping off.

She turned from his retreating figure to Nick, her chin jutted out as she weighed him up. 'Don't ask me if I'm more pleased to see you or that suitcase.'

'Is it a toss-up?' A muscle twitched tightly in his jawline.

'I'd like to say the suitcase, but as it happens, I may need to talk to you.'

'You may?' The familiar smile curved across his lips. 'You didn't answer my calls. Why have you been hiding?'

'I wasn't. I've been right here. Making plans. Getting on with my life.' She put extra emphasis on 'my'. 'The only person I've been hiding from is me. Not anymore.'

'It wouldn't have hurt to answer one of my messages.'

She looked away unable to explain because that was it precisely – it would have hurt. She'd thought she could handle no ties, but Nick was something else.

'Let's go inside.' The champagne and the suitcase balanced in one hand, he placed the other on the small of Layla's back and directed her into the house, closing the door with a thud. He went into the kitchen to chill the bubbles.

Relieved to be back inside the cottage, not putting on a show for the neighbours, she jabbered. 'So since you're here ... And if Joe's got anything to do with it the rumour will soon be spreading round the village like wildfire ...'

The fridge door clunked closed and he came back into the room. 'What?' His eyes flashed like a lightning strike.

'... I might be pregnant.' She dug under the cushion for the bag from the pharmacy.

Shock drained the colour from his gorgeous face. 'I wasn't expecting a life-changing announcement. More something along the lines of "Cup of tea?"'

'Sorry. My manners have gone out the window. Would you like tea?'

'No. I'd like to know why he's the first to know.' He threw a glance through the window.

'He's split up with Lainy.'

'Hah! I knew it.'

'It just came out. And he was here.'

'Well I'm here now.'

'He wants us to try again.'

'That's what you want?'

'Not in a million years.'

He drew a deep breath. 'Let's back up. Have you got a pregnancy test?'

'Lots.' She held up the crumpled plastic bag pathetically. 'In here. It's probably a false alarm. We were careful.'

'What about the green condom?'

She clapped her hand to her mouth. They'd been a little drunk and a lot crazy for each other the first night. 'Maybe it was past its use by date. I didn't check.'

'Same.' He pulled an apologetic face. 'It wasn't top quality in the first place.'

'If I ever get a novelty condom in a goody bag again I'm binning it.'

'No point beating ourselves up over how it may or may not have happened. Let's find out.'

'Right.' She'd run out of reasons for putting off the moment of truth.

'I'll put the kettle on. You ...' He took her by the hand, led her to the bottom of the stairs, and gave her a gentle push towards the first step. '... Go do what you have to do.'

Numb she ran upstairs and locked herself in the bathroom. She balanced on the edge of the bath and opened all the packages. Drained and wondering what he was doing here and why on earth he'd brought champagne she perused the instructions that came with the various test kits.

Dread filled the place of her heart. A pregnancy wouldn't trap her and Nick like it had her parents. Since Paris she'd done lots of thinking, realized the only person holding her back was herself. She'd changed everything about her work life. Her business plan for 'Layla ♥ Art' had fallen into place. And now she felt so positive about the future, a baby wouldn't hold her back. Why should it? She felt strong. And her family and friends would support her when she needed help. They always had done, although she hadn't fully appreciated how much, feeling suffocated by their good intentions, not processing how much they cared. From now on, she'd make sure they knew how much she loved them.

While he waited, Nick picked up a magazine, scanned an article, and threw it down again. He could throttle the journalist who'd run the imbecilic story. 'These belong in the trash.' Ophelia looked at him blankly. He scooped the whole lot up, carried them into the kitchen and dumped them in the recycling bin.

In Paris, about a minute after he'd told Layla about the change of plans, he'd regretted it. With her, everything had been right with the world, too right, he'd needed distance. He could have asked her to go with him to Versailles, introduced her to everyone properly. Instead he'd taken the easy way out, caught in an emotional stranglehold. He'd behaved despicably, like he'd frozen over.

In LA he couldn't shake off the memories. His feelings paralyzed, afraid to go forward or look back, he couldn't get her out of his head. Alex had been in touch, demanding to know what the hell had gone on, and warning him that the British press had been publishing stories.

She'd been so right. About everything. He'd realized that when he'd first been offered the action movie role he'd grabbed the chance, hadn't given his phobia a thought. It was only later that it had kicked in. He'd worked too hard, he loved his career too much to bottle it, let the fear take over. So after he'd tied up some loose ends in post-production, he'd talked things over with his agent, started to get his life in order. He'd discussed the contract for the sequel and secured a tailor-made pre-production training program to help with the vertigo.

He'd spent nights lying awake picturing Layla, lonely, desperate, gutted to realize what a gaping empty hole she'd left behind. Eventually exhaustion would force him into a few hours' sleep. When he woke up again she was the first thought in his head. It was agony not hearing from her.

He'd fantasized about Cornwall while in LA, the view from the top of the cliff, the spectacular sunsets, what it would be like living there, coming home to her, holding her, talking to her every day. He looked around. She'd redecorated, changed some things. The painting of the old farm on the cliff-top was hanging above the fireplace. The sight of it panicked him and tightened the muscles in his chest. When he arrived back in the UK he felt wretched. The discussions about the next movie had made him excited for the future. She was the first person he wanted to tell. It killed him that she didn't want to know.

Before anything else he'd wanted to put right the situation with Fran and Beth. Now all he could do was put one foot in front of the other and hope that Layla would forgive him for the insensitive way he'd acted. They'd held onto each other, seen each other through a tough time. She'd opened his heart, shown he was wrong to drop trying to get to know his daughter. His heart thumped waiting to tell her how alone he'd felt without her.

His mind was blown. She'd been sunny, funny, red hot energy in bed. If the test result turned out positive and Layla was pregnant, he absolutely wanted to be included.

He walked to the window and looked out, anxious for an answer. Outside in the lane one of Joe's plastic bags had burst spewing the remnants of his life with Layla onto the road. He chased a shirt, and as his fingers stretched out it billowed in the breeze and flew away again. Nick went to the kitchen drawer and grabbed a roll of bin liners. Followed by Ophelia he went to help. Joe took hold of a new bag, grunted and together they wrangled his stuff.

'Everyone loves her,' Joe said. He looked down at the dog. 'I've screwed up. But I'm here for Layla now. I love her, and I want to be with her all of the time.'

'That makes two of us.'

'You're not what she needs.'

'What makes you think that?'

'I want to marry her. Do you?'

Nick side-stepped the question. 'That's got a name buddy. Bigamy. You're already married.'

'Do you want to marry her or don't you? Because if it's a "no" you should take a hike. I've been stupid, but I care about her, I only asked for a break. I didn't want to finish with her. She knows it. And she deserves better than a man like you.'

Shaken by the fear that Joe was right, Nick turned his back on him, avoiding making the argument worse. His head pounded. Ophelia sloped back into the cottage, and he went too. As there wasn't any sign of Layla he made tea and dug out the digestives. Two mugs hooked in one hand and a packet of biscuits in the other he hurried into the living room to the sound of feet on the stairs.

'I'm pregnant.'

Chapter Twenty-Nine

'For real?' He cleared his throat. 'You're sure?'

She nodded. Stunned into a fusion of unreality and agitation she couldn't speak. The universe had caved in and they were looking vacantly at each other over mugs of tea.

'Marry me.'

Jolted out of inertia she blurted, 'Typical. I wait ten years for one man to say "marry me" and two come along on the same day.'

Nearly spilling the tea he set the mugs on the table. 'Be as flippant as you like, you're not marrying him, you're marrying me.'

The knot of tension in her stomach tightened. 'Wait just a minute.'

'If you don't marry me you'll be doing what Fran did, keeping me away from my baby.'

'I'd never do that.'

'Marry me.' His rich drawl ricocheted through every part of her.

'Tying ourselves down isn't the answer. If I say yes, it'll be a nightmare.' Her voice wobbled, stinging emotion burned behind her eyes. 'We'll end up resenting each other, feeling trapped.'

'How can you say that?'

'How can I not?' She'd learned it growing up. 'It's what I feel in my heart. Think about it. Cornwall? LA? London? Paris? And wherever else? I'm a home bird.'

'And I'm what? An itinerant? No fixed abode?'

'You're a wandering star.'

'You're wrong. I've got a UK base. I bought a place. I want to put down roots. Say yes and this will fall into place, I promise.'

She ached to believe it, for him to pull her against his body and wrap her in his arms. 'I won't lie, there was a moment in Paris when I hoped we could be something more.' She swallowed, forcing back tears. 'Now? No. Not anymore.' When he'd been outside she'd opened the bathroom window. She'd heard the raised voices clearly, every word. 'Joe asked if you want to marry me, you didn't say anything. You're only proposing because there's a baby.'

'I didn't answer because it's between you and me – nobody else.'

Tense and put on the spot she whispered, 'This baby means everything to me.'

'There's a "but" coming.'

Sadness weighed her down. She sank onto the sofa. 'I can't marry you.'

He sat beside her and passed a mug into her trembling hands. She instantly looked away.

Head exploding, she leaned into the sofa cushions. The positive test had changed everything.

'There's too much to take in,' he said, 'I shouldn't have jumped right in. Let's rewind. Talk it over.' He offered her the biscuit packet.

'No thanks.'

He picked one out for himself. The silence was beyond awkward, the only sound in the room was the ticking of a vintage clock on the mantelpiece. Ophelia sat at his feet, one paw raised imploringly. He broke the biscuit and fed her a tiny piece.

Layla's nerves jittered. When she'd read the result, the floor might as well have fallen away beneath her feet. It confirmed what she'd suspected for days. She felt swamped. As if the negative comments in the papers, plus Joe's half-crazed ideas, weren't enough to cope with, Nick appearing out of nowhere in time to find out about the pregnancy and insist that she marry him freaked her out.

'The appalling publicity after Paris has been cluttering

my head for days. I wanted to apologize. But since you wouldn't talk to me.'

'We'd finished,' she snapped. 'I was getting back to normal.'

'I sent you things that reminded me of the brilliant time we had. I hoped you'd realize I was thinking about you, about us.' He threw a glance around. 'Did you get them?'

'Yes.' She didn't admit she'd hidden his gifts out of sight.

'The papers twist things. I've thrown them away. If what they wrote upset you, I'm sorry. I didn't expect to have to share you with the world. I wanted to keep you to myself.'

Echoes of her childhood whirred in her head. 'They pretty much nailed it. We're a mismatch.'

'I don't think so.'

She set down her mug. 'You went to see Fran.'

His tense lips twisted into a whisper of a smile. 'Beth's great. She's met my mother, who adores her. You got that part right.'

'I saw the photos, she looks sweet. She has a cracking smile.'

'Thanks for getting me to see sense.'

Her head was a mess. His world was in a different stratosphere. She was relieved that Beth had accepted him. Heavy-hearted, she wondered if he might still have feelings for Fran.

'Look, the pregnancy is very new, but right upfront I have to say I don't want to be shut out this time.'

She stared at him for a long moment. 'Do you really think I'll close you out? That's not me. You ought to know that by now.'

'So let's get married.'

'I can't be in your world.' He incensed her. He'd proposed out of desperation. He was going to have to be a big part of her new life, but her heart would break chained to a man who'd be happiest free, he'd have a never-ending hold on her emotions.

'Rubbish. I want you with me.'

Unnoticed, the dog nudged a biscuit that had escaped from the packet off the coffee table and snaffled it.

'It's about what you want, what will work best for you. Where do I fit in? What about what I want?' Her words spilled out irritably, overwhelmed. He didn't love her.

'It wouldn't have to be forever. If that's not what you want I totally understand. We could work out a pre-nuptial agreement, if that's what you choose. You wouldn't be locked in.'

More miserable than ever, hearing his Hollywood spiel offering a disposable marriage, she felt trapped and crushed with the weight of what lay ahead. Deeply, hopelessly entrenched, she loved him. She looked at him sadly. It was crystal clear, he wanted his baby, *just* the baby and

he'd go to any length to get what he wanted.

'We're having a baby for all of five minutes and your lawyers are drawing up a pre-nup. Correct me if I'm wrong, but wasn't it you who said that "sometimes the best thing to do is nothing at all"?'

'It's the obvious solution.'

'We don't need a solution. Getting married isn't the only way forward.' Her voice rose in a crescendo of outrage. 'I can't commit to sharing my life with you.'

'Give me one good reason why not. Is it because you regret finishing with Joe when all he wanted was a break?'

'Because it wasn't important. You know what happened.'

'Run it by me again, because it seems you don't want to be with me and he wants you back.'

'He texted from the airport to say we were on a break. I was hurt. It wasn't what I wanted. I texted back and ended it. Does that change anything for you? It doesn't for me. Over is over and that goes for Joe and me, and me and you.'

'And the baby?'

In Paris he'd transformed from the gorgeous man she'd fallen for into a dispassionate robot. There'd been a chasm of emptiness between them as wide as an ocean and nothing he'd said since he'd turned up uninvited convinced her that anything was different.

'We're having a baby. That's amazing. But I'm not getting

married without love and that's final.' As she said the 'L' word her throat constricted unpleasantly.

'Have it your way.' His face stony and unreadable, his voice a low growl, he added, 'At the very least we should have a plan. There'll be appointments to schedule. And I'd like to be present at the birth – if you don't have any objection, that is.' He stopped abruptly, she supposed to do a quick mental calculation, work out the dates, so that he could slot it in to his hectic lifestyle. She closed her eyes, shutting him out, breathed in and counted forward in her head to April.

'I haven't thought about any of this yet,' she sniped, hating herself.

'Will my name be on the birth certificate?'

'Of course.' Tentatively she whispered, 'Assuming that's what you want.'

He softened. 'We don't have to make decisions yet. I'll stay at the hotel tonight. We can talk more tomorrow.'

Choked, she fought the desire to feel his arms close around her and the thrilling touch of his lips, reminding herself that what they'd had amounted to a supreme performance by a good actor. She couldn't make him happy. They'd been so close and he'd smashed it to bits. Being a single parent would be difficult, but nothing compared to living with a man who didn't know how to love.

In agonized silence she got up, went into the kitchen,

lifted the champagne from the fridge, returned to the living room, handed it to him, walked to the door, and held it open, silently inviting him to leave.

'I'll just go, shall I?' He caught her gaze.

'Go,' she whispered, crestfallen and almost hoarse with suppressed emotion.

He leaned down and as his face brushed hers, the way she responded to the graze of his face against her cheek nearly killed her.

'See you tomorrow?'

She nodded and her head swam. He opened his mouth to speak again. Afraid she'd cave and ask him to stay, she silenced him with a softly spoken, 'Don't.'

Before she closed the door she watched him walk away, his long back straight and proud, his fair hair brushing his collar. Her heart was in her mouth and the tears that she refused to let him see stung the backs of her eyes. Fighting the intense, unwise urge to run after him, throw herself into his arms, feel his kiss on her lips, she couldn't stop herself from calling out, 'Nick?'

He spun around, his face inscrutable. 'What?'

'You didn't come all this way to deliver a suitcase.'

Eyes emotionless, he ran a hand over his head to the back of his neck. 'No.'

'So why are you here?'

'I had something important to tell you.' He stopped,

and stared absently towards the cliff path which ran up the hillside behind the old cottages. 'It can wait.' He searched the skyline. 'It hardly matters anymore.'

Chapter Thirty

Nick stood on the bridge, contemplating the brook far below, unclear how he'd managed to ruin everything that mattered the most in the world to him. He'd overdone it with the instant marriage proposal. Joe had wound him up, made it feel like a competition, and he'd panicked. He'd said the wrong things.

He'd been cowardly, should have come after her immediately. If he'd done the sensible thing, there was a chance she'd believe he badly wanted to be with her, he wasn't only hell-bent on staking a claim to the baby.

He'd lost his grasp on happiness like watching the tide go out. On the day of the shoot he'd pushed her away, convinced that ending it was the only way to go. He'd been afraid to do any differently, hadn't trusted his feelings. When she'd said she was in love with him, he'd known he felt the same and he'd been scared, afraid to give in to loving her.

She was his everything. He'd untangled the truth in his emotions and it was too late. He wished he'd put Los Angeles on hold. He'd wanted to do the right thing, get his life in order, come back one hundred per cent clear about not dragging her into a mess.

Because of Layla he believed in himself in a way he hadn't before. He didn't want her as part of a crazy package deal – the freebie mother that came with the baby. That she thought so poorly of him cut like a knife.

Destroyed, bitter reality pulled him apart. The unbearable loneliness of missing her was nothing compared to the desolation of hearing her say she didn't love him. For once he believed in forever. And apparently she didn't.

He leaned on the railings of the bridge. He'd have to accept it, as fast as they'd fallen in love, she'd fallen out of it.

Whizzing down the hill on his bicycle, Mervin rounded the bend in the lane and jammed on his brakes to stop on the bridge. His face dropped as he recognized Nick. 'Well Mr La-di-da from Hollywood. What do you want?'

Pain bit into him. Blind stupidity had made him think he could shake his image, turn his life around. 'Hey Mervin. It's great to see you too!'

'That's not for me, is it?' The policeman chortled and nodded at the champagne bottle he clutched.

'Your powers of deduction are mega.' He smiled half-heartedly.

'Celebration?'

'I was hoping, but my luck ran out. Would you like it?'

'I won't say no if it's going spare. As it happens I've got something to celebrate. I've asked Shelly out on a date.'

'I had a feeling about you two.'

Affection for the over-protective policeman hit Nick quite unexpectedly. He popped the champagne bottle in Mervin's bicycle basket.

The shock of the positive pregnancy test had sent him into an emotional vortex. He wholeheartedly wanted to be a good dad but that wouldn't be enough, not now, not ever.

'I asked Layla to marry me.' He'd wanted their life together to start right away, not waste another minute apart. Without her love the future stretched out into nothingness. It broke his heart. 'She turned me down. She doesn't love me.'

'She said that?'

'Pretty much.' He thought back over it. 'I won't marry without love, she said.'

'Do you love her?'

'Totally.'

'Did you tell her?'

'I messed up. I made her angry when the most important thing in the world to me is to make her happy.'

'Sounds like crossed wires to me, more like a "maybe"

360

than a definite "no". The older man sighed exasperatedly. 'She's a rare treasure that one. You've more chance of finding a diamond in the sand on Porthkara beach than you have of finding another one like Layla.'

'Tell me about it! She's in my head all the time. I can't think straight.'

Mervin got off his bike and balanced it against the railings. He put a friendly hand on Nick's shoulder. 'What are you going to do about it?'

'Not a clue. I'm wracking my brains for a bright idea.'

'Well you could start by telling her why you love her.'

For a difficult few minutes the two men glared over the side of the bridge, the only sound the chirping of birds in the tree branches above them and the babbling rush of the stream flowing down to the sea. All of a sudden, Nick turned to Mervin.

'Can I borrow your handcuffs? I need you to lock me to the bridge.'

'If that's a good idea I'd hate to hear a bad one.'

'Please Mervin, trust me. I know what I'm doing.'

Mervin studied Nick with an air of suspicion. 'I don't know about this, by jingo. Shelly told me you're the twenty-first century's idea of an action hero. There'd better not be any high jinks and no Houdini impressions. You were only two shades from a stark staring lunatic in the first place, but since there's a chance she might say yes if you're lucky ...'

'Thanks!' he said dismally. 'That accurately sums up what'll become of me if Layla doesn't say "yes" this time.'

'And you'll stay handcuffed to the bridge until you get the right answer?' Nick nodded silently, jaw resolutely clenched. 'Nice one. Right then, we'd better give it a go.' Fixing one handcuff to the bridge, he secured the other around Nick's wrist. He looked at his watch. 'It's getting late. What's the plan if Layla doesn't find you? You could be there until morning.'

He smirked. 'I'll cross that bridge when I come to it.'

'I like what you did there. Funny.' Mervin slapped him heartily on the back. 'At least you haven't lost your sense of humour. I'll check back later and see how you're getting on.' He looked sceptically up at the sky. 'It looks like rain and I can't leave you standing there all night with a face like something that got washed downstream in a storm.'

Striking a nonchalant pose Nick waved him off with his free hand. 'I've got this.' His heart thumped. 'I'll wait as long as it takes.' He'd been so desperate for Layla's love he'd forgotten to tell her he loved her too. He'd never felt like such an idiot.

On the way to the bridge of lovelocks he'd made up his mind to be immune to her, no matter what. As it turned out immunity to love isn't a thing. Still he'd hardened his heart, focused on not giving way to his feelings. If he'd secretly been hoping for a reaction from Layla to the star charm, a flicker of emotion to challenge his decision, it hadn't come.

He stared bleakly over the edge of the bridge. He'd covered up his fears his entire life. Love had damaged his mother, and her catastrophic breakdowns had affected him, driven him into himself. He'd strenuously avoided commitment. Confident he'd changed, Layla was the one he couldn't turn his back on; he'd be strong and not run away, if only she'd give him a chance.

At the cottage Shelly had come back to check on Layla. 'I have something to tell you,' she said. 'Mervin's asked me on a date, a proper one.'

'What, no hiking boots? Not just quiz buddies?'

'A romantic dinner at the Manor House Hotel.'

Layla hugged her mum. 'Go you!'

'So? Any news?'

'It's positive.'

'Oh my gosh. I'm going to be a grandma?' She clapped her hands excitedly as Layla nodded solemnly. 'I hope it's not a secret because it won't stay that way. Nobody can keep a secret in Porthkara.'

She didn't have the energy to mention that Nick was in the village and that she'd refused his proposal. She didn't want to ruin her mum's happy mood.

'I'd better run.' Shelly hugged her daughter tight. 'See

you tomorrow.' She stepped through the door, suddenly hesitating on the doorstep. 'Listen, I don't know if you've heard.'

'About Joe and Lainy breaking up?'

'Can you believe it? Trish told me he's back to stay.'

'He's been by to pick up his belongings.'

Her mum touched her arm reassuringly. 'It's time for a new beginning.' Shelly walked to her car, and waved cheerfully before she climbed in and drove off.

Ophelia had fallen asleep in front of the cheerless, unlit wood-burning stove. Whimpering and twitching her legs, she was chasing a rabbit or a squirrel in her dreams.

Nick had made Layla deeply unhappy. A strange thought crashed over her like a breaking wave. Someday, she'd read about his wedding, to someone ultra-glamorous and she'd handle it, because she would have to. She'd refused to say yes to him, yet she felt queasy at the thought of him marrying a woman who wasn't her. She pictured their future child as a pageboy or flower girl. When the time came she'd go away somewhere remote with no wi-fi for a month of meditation and silent yoga until the fuss died down.

Pleased that things were looking up for her mum, and determined to keep calm about the pregnancy, she decided to walk down to the beach and clear her head. She'd make an appointment at the doctor's surgery and take it from there. She snatched the lead from its peg near the door and whistled. 'Come on O. Let's go.'

Outside spits and spots of rain spritzed her face. She looked up at the white grey sky, then down at the dog. Two brown eyes stared up at her. She stuffed the lead in her coat pocket. 'It's only a light shower. We won't dissolve.' The dog barked, did a tail chasing pirouette and took off. After locking the front door, she turned to see her running down the lane.

Suddenly she felt no enthusiasm for the beach, alone, just her and the dog. She wanted Nick with her. She couldn't give in to her feelings, she'd be risking everything, and more than anything, she refused to put their baby through the same tense, uncertain childhood she'd experienced, fraught with unspoken truths and shattered dreams. The Layla she was before she met Nick might have crossed her fingers and gone along with his marriage proposal.

Sense warred with optimism, certain he could find it in his heart to love their baby, but clear he was too broken to love her. The heartache ahead gave her shivers of apprehension.

'Come here O,' she called out. 'Not that way.' She had a hankering to go by the cliff path. Ophelia sat down, not going anywhere, apparently. 'What's wrong? You're not normally this mischievous Mrs!' She pulled the lead out of her pocket and walked towards her.

The dog yapped, pirouetted excitedly and scurried off a little further. 'You want to go that way, huh? Since when do you make the decisions around here?'

She followed the dog down the lane.

Rounding the bend, she saw a sight that sent her into every kind of confusion. Nick was on the bridge all tall, blond and handsome. His sparkling eyes made her heartbeat race. Her knees threatened to buckle pathetically.

Ophelia, the traitor, ran up and sat beside him with a perky look of solidarity on her funny face.

'One biscuit and she's anybody's,' she said airily as if she'd expected to find him waiting.

He knocked her sideways with his captivating smile. 'I know how that feels.' He laughed.

'Why are you here?' She sighed, struggling to resist his potent sex appeal that simply wouldn't go away, despite everything. He stepped towards her only to be yanked backwards, drawing her eyes to his tether. 'What in the world? Why are you handcuffed?'

'I'm a lovelock.'

She couldn't believe her eyes. She arched a brow. 'You fall back on performance art in your spare time?'

'I plan on staying here for as long as it takes.'

'As long as what takes?' She looked down at the conspiratorial dog who gave a chipper little yelp.

'As long as it takes to make you understand that ...' He

gulped. 'That we should be together. I want to take care of you.'

'We've been over this.' She rubbed her temple absently. The promise of happiness was all around her. Her dad and Jasmine were making wedding plans, her mum's surprise romance with Mervin. But Nick was empty of love. Summoning all her inner strength, she met his gaze. 'I can take care of myself. I'm getting organized. My plans for Layla♥Art are really coming together nicely. I'm going to paint all kinds of creative spaces. And run workshops.'

'That's great. I'm happy for you.'

'So you see, you don't need to worry. I don't need taking care of.'

'I know that. It's not what I meant.'

She sent him a puzzled raised eyebrow look. 'I take it Mervin put you up to this?'

'It was more the other way round to tell you the truth.'

'So what's this all about Nick?'

He gulped, considering his reply.

'Look,' she cut in before he could speak, 'I know we have to discuss the pregnancy. But we agreed to wait till tomorrow. A night to sleep on it will give us both a chance to get our heads around things.' She took out her phone. 'I'll call Mervin, ask him to swing by and release you.' She turned away from him, beckoning Ophelia. 'Come on O.' The dog didn't budge.

'Let me be with you.'

She turned back weary and hurting. 'You've got Fran and Beth to think about.'

'Just so we're clear. I don't have feelings for Fran. What's more, I hear she's dating the father of one Beth's classmates.'

She smiled. 'I'm guessing your source is reliable.'

'Beth's wonderful, she's important to me and I'll be there for her whenever she needs me, but she and her mother have a life and they don't need me in it twenty-four seven any more now than they ever did.'

'I don't need you either.' She turned away from him, aching with the pain of the lie. He hadn't said what she needed to hear. Because he couldn't say what he didn't feel. 'I won't let you use the fact that we inadvertently made a new human being together to steamroller me into a life we don't want. You can talk until you're blue in the face you won't convince me that it's the best thing to do.'

'I want to stay here and look after you Layla. You and our baby.'

'You can't. I can't bear the thought of it.' Her head throbbed. Mustering an iota of composure, she started to walk away again. She'd die if he were to wake up one day and blame her for setting out to trap him. He might think she'd used the dodgy condom on purpose. Her mother had been accused of the same.

'I love you.' He took a step towards her before remembering that he was handcuffed to the bridge. 'I love you so much. I love you here, now, yesterday, tomorrow. I love you beyond the horizon.' She couldn't believe her ears. Her instinct was to hide. He was laying himself bare emotionally and she didn't know how to take it.

'You love me?' She repeated the words in disbelief.

'Beyond reason. That's what I came here to tell you. If you'll have me, I'll be here for you until the end of time. If that means no more movies, no press, no magazine covers, then that's fine. Whatever you want.'

'You'd give it all up for me?'

'Yes.'

'Why?'

'Because I love your village, your beach, your dog, I even love your cliff.'

'Really?'

'Yes really. I love everything about you, Layla Rivers. But most of all I love the look of concentration on your face when you paint. I could watch you forever. I love that you stand by people, and I love that you allowed me to be one of those people and that you held me close and didn't let go until I figured out what was important and what I needed to do about it.'

Overcoming the initial instinct to block out the depth of feeling she walked towards him. 'What brought this on?'

'You. I was petrified at first. I wanted nothing to do with love because I've seen the way loving too much can wreck someone. I wouldn't have wished it on my worst enemy. Now I realize that not telling you how I feel is hell. You're strong and real, and so here I am, putting it out there.'

She sparkled inside with excitement. She edged closer, and grasped his hand locking their fingers together, melting at the blaze of warmth and love in his eyes, and standing on tiptoes, brushed her cheek against his face and feathered kisses along his jawline until impatiently he took possession of her mouth in a deep, longing lingering kiss that lasted on her lips long after she'd broken away. Happily bewildered, she looked him in the eyes. 'You're incredible. And irresistible. Exactly as you are. Don't change a single thing.'

'And one other thing. I love that you're going to be the mother of our children.'

'Children!'

He placed a silencing finger on her lips. 'Let me finish.' He put his hand in his pocket and took out a bunch of keys. When she didn't react he took her hand, dropped the keys into her palm and closed her fingers around them. 'That thing I said could wait until tomorrow. It can't. I bought the farm on the cliff. For you. For us ... and our future family.'

Pure joy spread through her. He'd come back to Cornwall to buy Cliffside House and he'd done it before he knew about the pregnancy. His infectiously sexy smile was there on his face and she smiled back spontaneously, awed at the depth of his love, and delighted that she no longer had to battle the chemical fizz that had landed them in bed together in the first place.

'You're the only one that I'll ever want,' she said oh-so-softly.

Her heart skittered as he circled her waist with his free arm, holding her tight. He lowered his head and caught her lips in another hypnotizing kiss that sent her heart soaring skyward. When he stopped kissing her he looked lovingly down into her upturned face, and murmured, 'Will you marry me?'

She was wrapped around the most idyllic man, the object of a zillion women's fantasies, and he really truly wanted to be with her. She pressed a hand to his chest, felt the thundering beat of his heart beneath her palm, and said the word he'd been waiting to hear.

'Yes.'

Chapter Thirty-One

Nick had gone from believing his best hope was to fall out of love to being the happiest man alive. Being with Layla was better than brief happy madness. He'd stand a better chance of survival going over Niagara Falls in a barrel than living without her.

Every day he loved her more. Just one thing still bugged him. He'd been impatient to get married before the baby, it hadn't happened, and they still hadn't named the day. Preoccupied with her new job, the pregnancy and the house she'd been non-committal about picking out an engagement ring. So he'd taken the matter in hand. He'd sourced a beautiful antique diamond ring from a specialist jeweller, and commissioned her to rework it into a brand new ring with a retro vibe that he knew Layla would love.

The house needed updating so they lived at the cottage during the renovation. He hired Layla's dad to project manage. Ralph knew all the tradesmen and ensured everyone who worked on Cliffside went above and beyond to preserve the period character. He'd also come up with the brilliant suggestion to convert the old barn into a guest cottage.

Layla got her new venture started, honoured her initial contracts, and then put it temporarily on hold to concentrate on the interior design. They moved in a week before her due date and she was now overdue by more than a week. Nick had been making pots of raspberry leaf tea, on the advice of the lady at the store, who swore by its powers to bring on labour. He was on tenterhooks, not least because he'd planned a big moment to surprise her with the engagement ring and keeping it a secret had been getting increasingly difficult.

Nick's movie was a worldwide box office hit with work on the sequel scheduled for the fall. Being based in Cornwall wasn't a problem. He'd done a promo tour which meant he'd been away more than he'd have liked but he was always contactable. He'd never get tired of coming home to the old farm with its breathtaking views, and the brilliant sunsets, his favourite place in the world.

It was a lovely April day, unseasonably warm, perfect for sandcastles and a picnic at the beach. Layla had the jitters, tired of waiting, so Alex and Maggie, who'd been planning a visit, had come down from London.

While Maggie and Layla had a catch up in the pretty garden Nick got the picnic ready in the huge kitchen where Alex was entertaining Horatio and Phoebe.

'I'll be tackling my pre-shoot training in a few weeks' time,' Nick said, 'I've made inroads with my phobia. I've nailed the abseil.'

He'd learnt to abseil but not told Layla hoping to surprise her.

'How did you keep it secret?'

'It's been a nightmare.'

'So you're going ahead as planned?' Alex looked doubtful. 'Couldn't you postpone? Wait until after the baby?'

Nick shook his head stubbornly and closed the picnic hamper. 'It's today. I've made up my mind. I'll say I've got some important calls to make.'

'Call it off. Wouldn't it be better to stay close to the car park, just in case?'

'The cliff path's tricky but a walk across the beach won't be a problem. She's been walking Ophelia every day. The midwife told her it's good to keep moving.'

Layla squirmed in her garden chair. 'I can't get comfy.'

Maggie took a cushion and put it behind her back. Ophelia curled up in a fluffy snoring ball at their feet, making them giggle. Maggie gently put her hand on the baby bump.

'When's her highness going to grace us with her presence? How many days overdue?' The bump shifted under her hand.

'Nine.' She pulled a 'meh' face. 'I'd rather not be induced but the obstetrician has me booked in for tomorrow.'

'You'd prefer it happens naturally, but don't worry,' Maggie said, offering moral support. 'It's for the best. She knows what she's doing.'

'Jasmine says eat curry. Nick's going to cook us up a spicy feast tonight, so fingers crossed.' They each crossed the fingers of both hands in unison. 'He's been so considerate. Nothing's too much trouble. He's fantastic.' She sighed inwardly. 'I can't believe my luck.'

'Same.'

They exchanged a mischievous look.

'How are things?'

'Alex is working all hours. He's directing a touring production of *As You Like It*.'

Layla arched a brow cheekily. Maggie laughed. 'Stop it!'

'You?'

'I'm hanging with the twins, playing with ideas for my next babywear collection and I've got some TV work coming up at the end of the year, I'm presenting party looks for mums-to-be and doing a makeover for three willing victims.'

'Isn't the usual term volunteers?'

'It'll be something fab and designer-ish with loads of sparkle and stunning fabrics.'

'Ooh!' The baby kicked and Layla's enthusiasm sounded more like someone had stuck a pin in her side. 'Lucky victims,' she spluttered.

'Are you alright?'

She drew in a deep breath. 'Just a kick inside.'

'Ouch! That little one's so ready to come out.'

'She can't wait to try some of your lovely baby kit.'

'I can't wait to meet her. I bet she's got your hair. Did I mention that you look gorgeous! You're positively glowing.'

Layla had stopped dying her hair, so it had returned to its natural auburn. She'd undergone a Maggie makeover, consigned a few of her favourite pieces of clothing to the section of her wardrobe dedicated to painting, sent the rest of her mismatched gear to a charity shop and replaced the lot with new, sophisticated looks to go with the new version of herself.

'I'm planning the twins' birthday. I'd like to have the party at the beach but in case it rains I'm booking the hotel. We'll have the birthday cake there when everyone's had enough sea and sand. I'm really excited. Cassandra's coming – and Beth.'

'Drake?'

She shook her head. 'Alex invited him but he said no.

He's working on a new project. At least he and the guys are talking on a regular basis. That's something!'

Layla gave a shrug. 'From what I gather it'll be less tense without him. We could do the tea and cake at our house instead of the hotel if you like.'

'That's a fab idea. A double celebration. The twins' birthday and welcoming the new baby.'

'We're all set.' Ophelia woke up and pricked up her ears at the sound of Nick's voice. 'Listen, something's come up. I need to make a couple of urgent calls.'

'Want us to hang on?'

He helped Layla heave herself out of the garden chair and pressed a kiss to her forehead.

'You guys go ahead. I'll join you later.' He gestured to Alex. He'd installed the twins in their car seats and was waiting with the car doors open. 'The babies are good to go.' Ophelia chased her tail. 'And so's she.'

The spring sun had attracted lots of visitors to the beach.

Alex looked at Layla with concern. 'Okay to walk over to the cliff? Get away from the busy end?'

'Sure.'

He carried the stroller to the hard sand and he and Maggie settled the twins.

'Are you sure you're happy to walk?' Maggie pushed the stroller towards the picnic spot.

'Absolutely. It's boring sitting around, waiting for something to happen.'

Alex had gone back to the car for the picnic things, so Layla and Maggie wandered slowly across the smooth wet sand, and the babies fell asleep.

'Your dad's done a great job on the house.'

'Thanks. I'm proud of him.' The sun glinted on the water as they walked along the beach. Layla stooped to pick up a pebble. She rolled it between her fingers before tossing it into the sea. The dog bounded after it, splashing joyfully into the calm water. 'Dad's starting the barn conversion soon. Just now he's taking a break. He and Jasmine have their hands full with Fred.'

'Cute name.'

Layla's heart fluttered. It was the name of her grandfather, the man who'd given the lucky charm bracelet to his bride on her wedding day.

'We haven't settled on a name,' she told Maggie. 'Nick bought a dictionary. We've worked our way from A to Z.' She'd lost count of the times they had watched the changing colours of the sunset over the sea and read out possibilities. 'We only seem to know what we don't want.'

'It's a start. At least you know you're choosing for a girl. That narrows it down.'

'Fred getting a family name is nice.'

Bounding up Ophelia shook a spray of seawater all

378

around. Maggie had white jeans rolled up to her calves. Designer sunglasses perched on the bridge of her nose she looked down as the dog spattered her legs with cold water. She gave Layla an apologetic smile.

'We can take Ophelia now we've got a house. I feel bad we lumbered you with our rescue dog.'

Layla picked up a stick of driftwood and threw it into the sea not too far off. 'I don't want to fight you for her. But Nick and I love the dog. We'd miss her if she wasn't here.'

'And she'd miss the beach.'

'Plus, with Mum and Mervin, and Dad and Jasmine, there are plenty of people to mind her – no need for kennels if we go away.'

'And Alex and I have visiting rights.'

'Yep.' Ophelia dropped the stick at their feet. 'It's a good arrangement. We should stick with it.'

'Stick with it!'

They laughed at the unintentional pun.

It felt more like early summer than April. On a blanket at the base of the cliff like a beached whale, Layla questioned the sanity of having sat down.

'It might take a crane to lift me.'

'Don't be daft. Nick will be here soon. Between the three of us we'll manage,' Maggie teased, adding jokingly, 'If all else fails we'll call the coastguard and have you winched off the beach by helicopter.'

Layla drew swirly patterns in the sand with one finger. While the babies slept Alex had his nose buried in a play script, making notes in the margin. He clicked the little silver button on his pen, so deeply absorbed he didn't know he was doing it. Phoebe woke up and squeaked, quickly building to a full wail. He dropped the book and the pages fluttered in the breeze. He carried his baby daughter to the water's edge, dipping her toes in the sea, and jumping her over the gently breaking waves which sloshed lazily over the sand.

'It's not a day for the surfing crowd,' Maggie remarked.

Layla stopped swirling. 'Good. Less chance of running into Joe.'

'Are you and him okay?'

'Okay-ish,' she said, swirling again. 'Or at least, we will be with time.'

Under a parasol in his stroller, Horatio woke from his nap. He watched them with big blue eyes rimmed with fluttery dark lashes and reached out to his mum. Maggie lifted him up. He wriggled and clutched at her top. Kneeling with him propped between her knees she filled a bright red bucket with damp sand and encouraged him to pat it flat with the spade. When he was done patting, she turned it upside down and revealed a sandcastle.

'Ta-dah!'

The baby leaned forward and joyfully demolished it with his teeny hands. Maggie lifted him up so that he could stomp on the remains with his pudgy feet.

Returning from the water's edge with Phoebe, Alex dried her feet with a towel and set her down next Horatio.

'Should we start without Nick?' Layla scanned the cliff path anxiously. She opened the picnic basket and offered around the Cornish pasties.

While Alex and Maggie debated whether to eat first and then feed the twins, or vice versa, she tucked in, taking a delicious bite of crisp melt-in-the-mouth pastry.

Suddenly aware that Alex and Maggie had gone quiet, Layla followed the direction of their eyes. A hard-hatted figure had begun a cliff descent on ropes.

'How inconsiderate! Imagine landing right into the middle of a picnic! Why doesn't that lunatic go play action man someplace else?'

'So rude!' Alex said earnestly.

'Some people have no manners.'

Maggie smiled. She didn't seem too bothered.

When the abseiler was about a quarter of the way down he stopped and waved. 'He's stuck!' Shading her eyes from the sun she peered up in shock. 'Oh my gosh! It's Nick! I don't believe it. What if the rope snaps? Or he falls?' She dropped the Cornish pasty on the sand and her hand fluttered to her mouth. The dog grabbed the abandoned pasty in her teeth and ran to lie a safe way off, pleased with her find. Layla trembled uncontrollably and Maggie put a steadying arm around her. 'It's fine. Don't panic. He's been practising in secret. He wants to surprise you.'

'Why would he do something so stupid?' Layla sighed heavily and fought back tears, her heart in her mouth.

'Relax. It's okay. He thought you'd be pleased.'

'Anything could happen.'

Alex picked up Horatio. 'That isn't my brother. It's an impostor. Where's knock-kneed Uncle Nick?' He laughed, trying to reassure Layla. It fell flat and they all watched in silence as Nick edged his way down the side of the cliff. When his feet hit the sand he took off his hard hat and unfastened the rope and harness, dropping the equipment on the ground.

Phoebe went to put a handful of sand in her mouth so Maggie picked her up. 'Tell us who are you and what you've done with Nick,' she teased, brushing the sand from the baby's fingers.

With a wide grin Nick knelt down on one knee in front of Layla. Electricity sparked through her, mingled with extreme relief that he'd arrived safely. She loved him too much. His eyes glinted and he leant in to kiss her.

'You nearly gave me a heart attack. I'm impressed, though. I can't believe you just did that.'

'Everything about me has changed, and it's because of you. You're the most important person in the world to me.' He swept an arm towards the cliff. 'Without you I couldn't have done it. I wouldn't have the baby who's making her appearance tomorrow, I wouldn't have Beth in my life, I wouldn't have our beautiful home. I love you.'

She responded to his infectious smile. 'I love you too.'

'Wait. There's more.' He pulled a small box out of his pocket and opened it to reveal a sparkling ring – a glittering trio of diamonds. 'I had this engagement ring made especially for you. Let's set a date for our wedding.'

She choked back her emotions. He'd overcome his barriers, he'd chosen her, but what if she couldn't be what he needed. She felt all flummoxed, doubted he'd fully left behind the damage of his past. What if she couldn't be the right wife for Nick?

A cloud obscured the sun and a sudden strong contraction sent a spasm of pain banding around her middle and spreading out from her backbone.

'Crikey O'Reilly!'

They all laughed, the baby twins included.

'That's not the answer I was hoping for.'

'Help me up Nick. I need to go back. Now!'

'Are you ...? It's started?'

'Yes, I think so. She's on her way.'

Maggie quickly handed Phoebe to Alex and helped get

Layla up from the blanket on the ground. 'I'll call an ambulance.'

Layla breathed deeply and calmly and with the help of Nick started to walk. After only a few paces a second contraction stopped her in her tracks.

'We should get the coastguard,' Nick said.

The contraction ended. 'I'm having a baby, I'm not a sinking ship.' Holding tight to his hand she resolutely fixed on the Kandy Shack's bright sign in the distance and walked towards it.

Abandoning the picnic things Maggie and Alex bundled the babies into to the stroller and hurried along behind.

'They're sending an ambulance but it'll take at least forty-five minutes to get here. That's an hour and a half round trip. The contractions are getting closer together. I don't think you have that long.' Maggie whispered the news to Nick but Layla heard it too in a blur of breathing and walking and focusing on the sign that was slowly but surely getting nearer.

Another agonizing contraction rooted her to the spot. Nick supported her, his hand pressed to the base of her spine and she breathed through it, stoically walking on when she was ready, until the next one and the next.

'This baby's a contrary little madam,' she stammered between gritted teeth. 'She's kept us waiting and all of a sudden she's in a hurry to get here.' Maggie held her free hand and she desperately clutched it.

'Look,' Nick spoke calmly. 'We need a plan, in case the ambulance doesn't get here in time.'

Only a few feet further on Layla bent forward, debilitated by the feeling that her legs were made of lead, she couldn't move any further, and her waters broke. She sank down onto the sand. Maggie gave her a drink of water and smoothed her hair back off her face. 'It'll be okay,' she soothed, 'Nick's going to think of something.'

He felt useless, a hulking great waste of space, hit by a wave of panic he could barely control. He turned to his brother, 'Alex, give me your car keys. You're the best one to stay.'

He took off across the sand, running like he'd never run before, overwhelmed by a flood of worry and guilt. Fear speared his gut, he'd done this to her, the abseil had given her a fright, started labour. He ran on, determined to make it alright. Every particle of emotional remoteness had fallen away months ago. But a part of him had remained turned in on himself. Not anymore. He focused on Layla and what she needed from him. All he wanted was for her and the baby to be safe.

Panic on lockdown he went into overdrive. With the hospital miles away and things moving fast, driving there wasn't an option. They'd have to go home. Heart beating wildly, he stopped at the Kandy Shack and asked Shelly to call the midwife and meet them at the house. Then he sprinted to the car park and drove Alex's four-by-four to the slipway and down onto the sand. Luckily Mervin had stopped by the kiosk to see Shelly, so he directed proceedings, asking the day-trippers on the beach to move and make a safe corridor for Nick to reach Layla.

Shelly acted fast and she and the midwife from the local surgery were there when Nick pulled the car up to the front door at Cliffside. He'd made the right decision because no more than fifteen dramatic minutes later the baby's first cry stopped the world from spinning for a split second.

Epilogue

Exhausted and elated, Layla cradled their beautiful newborn daughter in her arms. Mesmerized by her baby girl, their seven-pounds-and-seven-ounces marvel with tufty auburn hair, Layla sat propped up on pillows in her king-size oasis of a bed. Happily, the impromptu home birth was problem-free. The speedy labor had left her shaken, but relieved and delighted to be holding her baby at last.

As soon as the news was out, Alex and Maggie, Ralph and Jasmine, and Mervin visited. Everyone agreed to stay to dinner, including the midwife and a local GP who'd swung by to check on Layla and the new arrival.

Shamefully it wasn't until the delicious smells of food whipped up by Alex from his brother's selection of spicy ingredients filled the air that anyone noticed the dog was missing. Alex, Ralph and Mervin offered to search the beach, insistent that Nick stay with Layla and the baby.

'Don't worry, we'll find her, she won't have gone far,' Mervin said reassuringly.

Just as the three men were about to set off there was a knock at the kitchen door and Nick opened up to find Joe with Ophelia and the discarded picnic hamper.

A cheer went up in the kitchen and the scruffy little dog looked at the room full of people as if wondering what all the fuss was about.

'I found her guarding the picnic from seagulls, although to be honest she wasn't so much protecting it as polishing it off. You won't need to feed her for a week.'

Nick laughed. 'Thanks for bringing her home.' He shook Joe by the hand.

'How's Layla?'

'Good.'

'And the baby?'

'Fantastic, a bit over-cooked, but otherwise, great. Would you like to come in? We're opening a bottle of bubbly. You're welcome to join.'

Joe smiled. 'I won't, thanks. I'm helping my parents at the restaurant tonight. Lots of last minute customers because of the good weather.' He handed over the forgotten engagement ring. 'Ophelia was also looking after this.' Moving to walk away, he turned back, 'Tell Layla I said congratulations.'

Later, when all their guests had left, Nick sat on the bed and circled his arms around Layla and the tiny bundle. Washed out but content with her newborn daughter in her arms, she inhaled the sweet baby scent, the rush of unconditional love a big contrast to the surge of inadequacy she'd felt earlier. She adored the baby's little hands and tiny fingers.

'She's a little doll.' She touched the pad of one finger to baby's soft cheek, getting to know the scrunched-up pink face. The newborn wriggled and one of her tiny baby gloves popped off. Layla patiently put it on again and carefully rocked her as she closed her eyes and fell asleep.

'I'm sorry about the abseil. I was selfish. I should have cancelled.'

She shook her head. 'The timing was a bit off. But I love that you did it. I still don't believe it.'

Nick seized the quiet moment. 'And if a wedding isn't what you want, I respect that. I won't push you again.'

She read a ton of emotion in his eyes. 'You were amazing today. I didn't panic because you were there. I trusted you to know what to do. Without your quick thinking I'd have given birth on Porthkara beach.' She pressed a kiss to his irresistible lips. 'I love you. You know how even on the greyest of days the sun is up there shining in the sky behind the clouds? Well that's what you are to me.'

Your love is the brightness in all my tomorrows.

Lightly he returned her kiss, murmuring against her smile, 'That's good to know.' He touched her chin and tilted her face to look at him. 'I want you to know you can rely on me. Always. Forever. I'm here to stay.'

'I can't describe how happy I am right now. Let's not wait any longer. How about we set a date for the wedding? Get married this summer, before you start work on the next movie?'

'You got it.' He hit her with his smile and she burst with joy as he took the ring from his pocket and slipped it onto her finger. He lowered his head to kiss the baby's crown. 'She hasn't got a name.'

'I've been thinking. How about Evie?'

Together they quietly considered the sleeping baby. Nick glanced over at the dog lying obediently just outside the bedroom door. 'What do you think O? Does she look like an Evie to you?' Ophelia gave a hushed yelp. 'I think that's a yes.'

'I chose it because my grandmother's name was Eve. The question is, do you like it?' Layla whispered.

'It's perfect. Beautiful little Evie.'

Instinctively Layla knew she'd be forever besotted with their daughter. One day she'd tell Evie about her great-grandmother, and how she'd wished for Layla to be lucky in love.

She passed the baby to Nick, loving the awe on his face, her apprehension gone.

'Hi Evie, I'm your dad. And this extraordinary woman right here, she's your mum, and I love her and you with all my heart.'

Confident that they'd be together forever, happy tears pricked behind Layla's eyes. She blinked them back. Once upon a time she'd convinced herself that Nick hadn't any love to give. She'd been wrong on that oh-so-important point. She smiled at him and moved her hand to cup his face, the brush of his stubble touched her palm and her engagement ring sparkled in the soft lamplight. Her heart skipped as she kissed him, more than anything she wanted to be his wife.

Acknowledgements

Thanks to my stellar editorial director Charlotte Ledger. Thanks also to my editors Laura McCallen and Dushi Horti. I take my hat off to the wonderful cover designer! Thank you so much!

And last but not least, thank you to publisher Kimberley Young, and all the talented people at Harper*Impulse*.